THE
DREAMS
OF A
DYING GOD

THE GODLANDERS WAR
BOOK ONE

By Aaron Pogue

The Godlanders War
The Dreams of a Dying God
The Wrath of a Shipless Pirate
The Crown of a Common King

The Dragonprince's Legacy
Taming Fire
The Dragonswarm
The Dragonprince's Heir
"Remnant" (short story)
"From Embers" (short story)

The Dragonprince's Arrows
A Darkness in the East

Ghost Targets
Surveillance
Expectation
Restraint
Camouflage

THE
DREAMS
OF A
DYING GOD

THE GODLANDERS WAR
BOOK ONE

AARON POGUE

47NORTH

Text copyright © 2014 Aaron Pogue
Originally published as OBERON'S DREAMS by 47North, May 2013
All rights reserved.

Published by 47North, Seattle

www.apub.com

Amazon, the Amazon logo, and 47North are trademarks of Amazon.com, Inc., or its affiliates.

ISBN-13: 9781477817803
ISBN-10: 1477817808

Cover design by Kerrie Roberston
Illustrated by Chris McGrath

Library of Congress Control Number: 2013949807

Printed in the United States of America

For Daniel, who saw what I was missing.

(**1**)

In the high desert south of Jepta, where the sand and sheiks alike wore blinding white, the man at the edge of the market crowd stood out like a signal fire. He bore the fine, sharp features and the haughty, bored expression of a lord, but even dressed in silk he had the manner of a rogue. He wore only loose black pants and a bright-red sash and the plain thong sandals of a sailor.

On his hip he wore a cutlass, not the heavy scimitars and long, curved knives native to this sun-seared land. And in his hand he held a velvet bag, straining with its weight in thick-edged coins. It was his outlandish dress that drew servants and slaves from all across the camp to gawk, but the bag of gold drew at least as much attention. This was, after all, a place for doing business.

At the very center of the crowd, a dozen hulking guards defined the edges of a circle occupied by nearly naked men in chains. Through all the civilized lands of Hurope, slave trade was forbidden, but no king among the Godlanders could reach this far into the high desert. Today two hundred souls would find new masters, and tomorrow this place would be nothing but dunes.

And of course there were more than a few among the white-robed men who served as agents of the Godlanders. Some few noblemen even came from the gentler lands up north to make their own transactions. But one and all, they came in careful disguise.

Now their precautions only magnified the strangeness of the man at the edge of the crowd. Though no one looked his way, everyone's curiosity was fixed on him. Fair as a Godlander nobleman, tan as a lowborn dockworker, and entirely out of place among this crowd.

Who was he? He held far more interest to the crowd than the broken slaves upon the block. In whispered rumors he was called the pirate king, and whether here to buy or sell, everyone watched to see what he intended.

He intended nothing more than to start rumors. Ethan Blake was only here as a distraction.

✦

Far across the camp, a man in even stranger costume stole between the tents, this one dressed in black from head to toe, with a heavy cloak despite the cruel sun. Captain Corin of the black flag *Diavahl* moved like a shadow on the sands, gliding among the low, tan tents until he found the one he wanted. It was the largest in the sprawling market camp. The man in black looked both directions, then lifted the tent's flap and slipped inside.

Corin blinked against the sudden darkness. The air inside the tent was thick and foul with the stench of cruel captivity and noisy with the moans and misery of those still waiting to be sold. The captain pressed his lips tight and hoped he could find what he needed here.

Before Corin's eyes could adjust to the gloom, a heavy hand crashed down on his shoulder and spun him in half a circle. He stared wide-eyed into the close, dark face of an armed guard. It was a face stitched with scars and missing more than a handful of teeth from its evil grin. "You are not the first who's tried to gain an advantage with a little stealth, my friend."

Corin grunted, abandoning a futile struggle. Instead, he flashed a disarming smile and shrugged. "You can hardly fault me for trying."

"It is a breach of the Agreement of the Sands." The voice like gravel showed no hint of understanding.

Corin paled. "And what…what's the punishment for that?"

"You must leave this place. We will trade with you no more."

Corin sniffed in cold disdain. "From what I've seen, I do not wish to trade with you anyway. I'll gladly leave—"

The guard's grip never lessened on his shoulder. "There is more, my friend. I say you will leave this place, and you will leave it three pounds lighter than you arrived. Gold or silver will suffice."

"Three *pounds* of silver?"

The gap-toothed grin flashed again. "From time to time, there have been those who could not pay the fines."

"And did you show them mercy?"

"We found a compromise." The guard made a slashing chop with the edge of his left hand, stopping just above his own right elbow. "Three pounds." He made another chopping motion, this time striking just below the right knee. "Three pounds. We compromise."

Corin stared. After a moment, he smiled weakly. "Silver. I…I can pay in silver."

"You would be surprised how many can."

"But all my coin is with my camel."

"I will come along," the guard said amiably. "I do not mind the effort."

Corin moved as if to leave, and at last the guard released his shoulder. But Corin hesitated, one hand on the tent's flap, then threw a last look back over his shoulder.

His eyes were finally adjusted, and in a glance he saw what he had come for. Iryana. She knelt in a corner, all alone. Even the other slaves would not go near her. Her dark skin still showed the bruises from her mistreatment at the slavers' hands, and all the filth could not conceal the stain of blood.

But she was undiminished, staring straight at Corin with eyes bright and harsh against the gloom. There was no pleading in them, no forgiveness or accusation, not even hope. There was only an unyielding, unspoken demand. *Rescue me.*

Corin rolled his eyes, then turned back to the guard. "Listen…may I ask your name?"

"I am called Razeen."

"Of course you are. Razeen, the agreement *is* already broken. If I must pay three pounds of silver, will you at least allow me the transgression I am paying for?"

"You have already stayed here far too long."

"So moments more will barely count at all. I *might* yet find another pound of silver…"

The guard glared for a long moment, then he grunted. "Two more."

Corin nodded right away. Razeen nodded back and tapped Corin's shoulder. "Five pounds, then. One way or another."

Razeen returned to his place just inside the tent and stood watching his new benefactor. Corin licked his lips and turned away, pretending to survey the whole crowd of waiting slaves. At last he made a show of noticing the girl alone. He cocked his head in curiosity, then drifted her direction. The unfortunates he passed did not cry out to him. They shrank away, trembling, and he was grateful for that. He had no wish to meet their eyes.

He couldn't have met their eyes. Iryana held his gaze. Her eyes were dark and commanding. Corin stopped, standing over her, and spoke under his breath in the civilized language of his homeland.

"I warned you not to run away."

She shrugged one shoulder like a queen, despite her chains, and answered in imperfect Ithalian, "I am a prisoner either way."

Corin looked around. "I kept you better than this."

"A slave is a slave. At least this way I will earn someone some silver."

"We would have found far more than silver at Jezeeli."

"You are a fool for thinking it. Jezeeli is a place of tragic loss. It is not a treasure trove."

Corin grinned. "Care to prove me wrong?"

"You do not have wealth enough to win me from this place!"

He shrugged. "I know a trick or two."

"You cannot beat these men with tricks. They only answer to violence and gold."

Corin turned in place, feigning one last measuring look over the slaves there, but the guard Razeen beckoned impatiently with one hand and made a vicious chop with the other. Corin's time was spent.

"I've paid in gold enough to learn my tricks," Corin said, almost offhand. "And more than a little violence. I think I can handle a few slavers."

Iryana laughed in dark contempt, but Corin wasn't listening. He was counting time, waiting for his cue.

In the distance, someone screamed.

The guard spun, concerned, and Corin acted fast. He knelt by Iryana, hands searching for the locks that bound her. He found them open, dangling from the loose ends of her shackles. Iryana raised her hands, showing off, and said, "You are not the only one with clever tricks."

He grinned. "That's why I came for you. Now close your eyes."

"What? Why?"

Instead of answering, he swung his heavy cloak around them both, dragging her head beneath it. Then he stabbed his free arm up, scattering a cloud of silvery dust that hung suspended in the air. The powder glowed with a brilliant light, soft and clean and beautiful as it drifted out to fill the wide tent.

Then it exploded with a roar like thunder and a searing burst painful even in the shadow of his cloak. Corin didn't wait. He caught the woman's wrist in one hand and drew a dagger in the other.

Two quick slashes carved an exit in the tent's fabric, and Corin and the girl emerged in sunlight nearly as painful as the silver flare. The shouts and screams that had been Corin's cue still rang within the camp, but for the moment they were distant, near the auction block.

Corin turned the other way and three quick steps brought him to the tent's edge. A guard he'd noticed earlier was gone, drawn by rumors of Ethan Blake or by the uproar Corin's first mate had caused in the center of the camp, so Corin sheathed his dagger and turned his attention to escape.

But Iryana stopped. She planted her heels and hauled back against him with more strength than a girl her size should have possessed.

Corin spun on her. "Are you mad? We must run!"

"*You* must run," she said. "I may still find a kinder master on the block."

Corin licked his lips, weighing his arguments while precious time slipped by. Then, ten paces back, Razeen dove through the exit Corin had made. Slaves dragged behind him, clinging to the big man's legs in utter desperation, but he barely seemed to notice.

His attention was all on Corin and the girl. While one hand still rubbed at his blinded eyes, Razeen stabbed the other after the fugitives and cried, "Thieves! Enchanters at the tent of trade! Get after them! Kill them all!"

Corin met Iryana's eyes and shrugged. "It's up to you." Then he turned and ran.

(2)

Corin glanced back once as he passed the edge of camp. Iryana chased him, but after her came guards responding to Razeen's cry. All along the camp's edge, they came boiling from the lanes between tents like ants from a spoiled hill. Corin pounded across the sand, his black cloak flapping after him.

The girl came alongside him, running hard despite bare feet and bruises. Corin tossed her a grin. "You came after me!"

She growled, "You left me little choice, but it barely matters. They are already catching up, and the desert is their home."

"I know," he said. "Just run."

They ran. They topped a dune with less than thirty paces' lead on the closest pursuers. But there below, just beyond a rough outcrop of stone, waited two saddled camels.

At Corin's side, Iryana gave a startled cry of relief, but a moment later she groaned. "We won't have time. The guards are too close. There are too many!"

Corin threw a glance back, risking a spill down the sandy slope. He looked just in time to see the line of white-robed warriors top the dune behind them.

"Looks like just the right number to me," he said. "But where in Ephitel's wretched name is Blake?"

She caught Corin's sleeve as he turned back to the camels. "Is this him?"

Where she pointed, another figure was just now cresting a smaller dune to their left. It was the man who'd drawn so much attention at the auction block. Now the bright-red sash clung to his sweat-slicked torso, but despite the splash of blood on his bare skin and the complement of angry sheiks pounding along behind him, he was grinning.

"Blake," Corin said, equal parts relieved and irritated.

"They'll cut us off!" Iryana screamed. She stopped, still ten paces from the camels, and looked around frantically. To their right, the sands climbed into a sheer, nearly concave dune. "We're trapped!"

Corin said nothing, though she was clearly right. Still, he coaxed her into motion again, almost dragging her down to the camels. She struggled so much that the tardy Blake was able to reach the beasts one step ahead of them.

Blake paused as they arrived, one hand on the reins, and narrowed his eyes at Iryana.

"You brought her out?"

Corin busied himself handing her up to a seat on his own camel, showing no regard for the angry mobs rushing down on them from two directions. "I couldn't let them sell her off."

"You *should* have let them sell her off!" Blake shouted, scrambling into his saddle. "All you needed was a word! And after all, she is the one who ran."

"These slavers are not gentle men."

Blake spat. "Neither are we. Gods on high, Corin! All you needed was a word."

Corin stood unmoving, holding his first mate's gaze as the first of their pursuers arrived. They were the sheiks who'd followed Blake from the auction block, a smaller crowd. But orders rang among them, barked in the strange language of the sands, and they fanned out into a loose circle surrounding the fugitives.

A moment later the second force arrived, all those who'd come swarming from the camp behind Corin and Iryana. There must have been at least a hundred, every one among them armed. Most of them fell into ranks outside the ring of sheiks already watching, but a handful of soldiers from the second force pressed through to the center.

Razeen moved at their head. He stopped just outside arm's length from Corin and surveyed the camels with some appreciation, but his expression turned sour when it touched on Blake and dark indeed on Iryana.

Still, he feigned a gap-toothed smile for Corin. "As I told you, friend, we will collect the weight that's owed. You're not the first who's tried to run."

Corin sighed and stepped forward. His eyes traced the edges of the heavy swords among these accusers. Seven here. Another twenty in the ring of sheiks, but hundreds more arrayed beyond them. Soldiers filled the sandy slopes.

Corin showed a lopsided smile. "How many try?"

"Thirty-seven in my time. Five or ten a year, I'd guess. And none has made it. Ever."

Corin reached toward his belt, but Razeen's curved blade cut through the air and stopped just short of his throat.

With exaggerated care, Corin completed his gesture. He drew the dagger from his belt and dropped it in the sand. Corin met the big guard's eyes. "You seem overcautious."

"I have seen your tricks."

"Of course," Corin said. "But have you seen my pirate crew?"

Razeen blinked, confused. He glanced at Ethan Blake, but Corin shook his head.

"That's just one man, however impressive his disdain."

Razeen frowned at Blake, then raised his eyes to the ring of surrounding sheiks, to the larger force that had followed him from the camp, and finally up to the tops of the dunes.

"Too far," Corin whispered.

Then on the slopes above them, one hundred and forty men threw off their linen wraps. Beneath they wore the loose, light trousers of sailors and the red silk sash that Blake had made so popular. Daggers and Ithalian short swords gleamed in the desert sun, but not as brightly as Corin's grin.

Razeen cried, "How?"

Corin shrugged. "You brought them to me. Blake, take the sheiks' swords."

"We should kill them now," Blake said as he slid from his saddle.

"Ephitel bless your murderous heart," Corin said. "But we do not want a blood feud with these slavers. Tie them up."

"This is no joke—"

"And this is not a council," Corin snapped. "You have my order. Tie them up and leave them here, then bring the men to camp."

"Bring?"

Corin grinned. "I'm borrowing your camel. See you at the cliffside."

The captain swung up into the high saddle and nodded to the great sea of his men outside the frail circle of slavers. He threw a mocking salute to Razeen, avoided Blake's glare, and grabbed Iryana's reins. Then he led her from the watching crowd, between the dunes, and off toward the sunset.

They went a while in silence, but Iryana made no effort to escape. She came easily along, her strange, dark eyes cutting into the back of Corin's neck. At last, almost irritated, he asked, "What's on your mind?"

"A time is coming soon when you will wish that man were dead."

Corin glanced back and shrugged. "He is just a slaver's guard. And I will leave these sands behind—"

"I do not mean Razeen," she said softly. "I mean the man you left in charge."

"Blake? Ha! He is no threat."

"He hates you."

"With all his black little heart," Corin said.

"You know this, and still you leave him so much power?"

Corin shared a secret smile. "He alone among all my crew is wholly and utterly predictable."

"Even though he hates you?"

"*Because* he hates me…and still he follows me. That should tell you much about his ambitions. But perhaps your people are not so complicated."

She favored him with a smirk. "Or we are not so simple."

Corin laughed, bright and clear. "Oh, there is nothing simple about me. As for Blake…aye, I'll give you that. But I know the shape of his schemes."

She reined up hard and rounded on Corin, her dark eyes flashing. "You do not know as many secrets as you claim, and I know more than you'd believe. I can see the treachery draped across that man like Aeshmir silks, and it drips with the blood of clever men."

"I am not without my bloody rags," Corin said.

"You are clean as sand-polished bone against his stain. You are shifting shades and interwoven tones, but there is a beauty and a harmony in your madness. He is just one shade and just one tone."

"Iryana—"

"No." She spoke over him. "Hear my words and understand. He drips with dark ambition, and you stand in his way."

Corin licked his lips and forced another smile. "I hear you," he said, with unaccustomed gravity. "And I tell you true, I know full well the treachery that reigns over that man's heart. I will not underestimate him."

She tore her gaze away, but not before he saw the sadness in her eyes. "There is not treachery enough within your heart to truly understand a man like him."

"Oh, Iryana." He took her fingertips in his hands and waited until she turned to him again. Then he grinned at her with a new confidence. "Soothe your pretty heart. I am bad enough to handle Ethan Blake."

She smiled through a sheen of tears, and Corin reached up to brush away her hair. "Gods' blood, I'm downright wicked. Now come! Let's desecrate a tomb."

(**3**)

The pirates' camp was not too far from the spot where the slavers had made their temporary market. It huddled in the precious shade of a deep, narrow chasm wind-carved from the sandstone cliffs. Jagged walls soared high above a path barely wide enough for a cart. The path rose gradually as it went, twisting for more than a mile before it reached another stretch of trackless desert.

At the canyon's nearer mouth stood makeshift tents and wooden wagons and heavy water barrels crafted of lumber from far-off places. Everything within this camp was out of place among the shifting sands, but none more so than the shiny bronze cannons mounted on two carts, both aimed back toward the open dunes. They were the surest reason Corin feared no retribution.

But Corin's thought was not on them now. He didn't even slow as he led Iryana past the cannons and through the silent camp.

"Your tents are empty," Iryana said.

"I did not want a fight."

"It would have been easier to hide behind your cannons. But you brought every sword at your command to the slavers' market?"

"If there's one thing we do well, it is ambush. The unsuspecting make such easy prey."

She considered him in silence just long enough to make him wonder at her thoughts. Then she smiled and said, "You needed me."

He shrugged, not meeting her eyes. "I came for you."

"Did you find it, then?"

Corin nodded, his eyes fixed on the towering cliff wall to their left. Iryana's gaze raced on ahead, searching not the high walls, but the uneven, twisting footpath. What she sought was some way up the slope, but she spotted it soon enough. The pirate crew had cleared a pit from the valley's sandy floor. Corin heard her gasp. "Godlanders should not come here!" she said. "This place remembers what you've done."

"This place is only sand and stone," Corin said. "And, with any luck, some relics worth a huge amount of gold."

"Your people care for nothing else."

Corin glanced at her. He shrugged. "My crew, at least. They have not enjoyed the hospitality of your sands. But when the door is opened—"

She shook her head frantically. "This is no place for you. The shadows remember your people's sins. The fires will consume you, the soot will choke your lungs, and you will leave here empty-handed."

"All except the last, perhaps."

"This is no joke! You are always laughing, but Jezeeli is a place of grief. It is a memory of loss, and nothing more."

Corin held her gaze for a moment. "I mean no disrespect to you or yours, but this is my life's work. It is my destiny to find the lost city."

She snorted. "You have been searching for three years."

"Three long years!"

"Using a map you stole."

"Stealing is my *other* life's work. You must admit I do it well."

She shook her head. "I owe you my liberty. I'll grant you that. And you were not a cruel captor even when you dragged me from my own people's tents. But I will not assist you in this plot."

"I do need you, Iryana. You said it before, and you were right. My men tire of the burning sands, and if I don't show them some reward soon, I'll have far more to fear than just Ethan Blake's ambition. I'll be the first captain to face a mutiny a hundred miles from the sea."

"Then leave! Take them to the sea and steal Godlander treasures as you've always done. Forget this place."

"I can't," Corin said. "Perhaps a month ago, but now we have spent too long on this adventure. We *must* uncover the lost city."

"Why? Why is it so important to steal a memory better left forgotten?"

"Because I am not the only one who's searching. Rich men, powerful men, and tyrants all are searching for this place. I will not let them have the glory."

"You mean the gold?"

"I mean the glory."

She sniffed in open disdain. "Is your name not grand enough for you?"

"I care little for my name, but theirs is far too grand. They already own the histories of my nation. I would prefer to rob them of the chance of robbing yours."

Iryana shrugged. "You bear a strange kind of generosity. You'll rob this memory to prevent other men from doing so. You rescue me from a slaver's block so that I can be your slave."

Corin suppressed his first response and shrugged instead. "Wicked as I am, I make a better steward of precious things than the men whom I oppose. But if you chafe so much at my authority, I set you free. Turn and run. Now. If I end in chains, you will not much enjoy the hospitality of the ones who take my place."

"I have known little enough of hospitality in my time," she said. "I will find my own way free."

"Please," he said, serious at last. "Don't underestimate what they could do."

She cocked her head and stared at him with a crooked smile. "I just said these things to you."

"But I am their captain."

"And I am just a slave. Why do you care so much for my destiny?"

"I learned to sail from a man who'd fled his chains," Corin said. "But more than that, I grew up in the streets of rich Ithale. I have seen the sins of my people. I come from a land that would make slaves of all men, and that has borne in me a certain sympathy for those who suffer."

"Such nobility from a thief!"

"It isn't hard. The only ones with anything to steal are those who own the chains."

Iryana narrowed her eyes. "On the sea, perhaps. But here? All you take from here will be the memories of these wretched tribes."

"As I said before, I'm only here to challenge those who will come after."

"It isn't easy to believe. A thousand years your people have not disturbed this place. Perhaps you learned some secret, but why should I suspect there would be others?"

"I could offer you their names. I found the map that led me here on some nobleman's spoiled son. I learned the secrets of this place in the library at Rikkeborh. Trust my word, the Godlanders were coming to this place. I merely won the race."

"So many answers," she said. "And never hesitation."

"It is the one thing I cannot afford."

She shook her head and met his eyes. "Then tell me this: What will you do if I refuse?"

"I'll ask again."

She laughed, but there was bitterness in it. "Ethan Blake would have me beaten."

"Ethan Blake would slit your throat," Corin said. "He has no love for slaves at all."

"Then he would leave here empty-handed. There is no way to enter Jezeeli without my aid, so—"

Corin shook his head, cutting her off. Then, without saying a word, he extended one arm back the way they'd come, pointing at the huge bronze cannons.

Iryana gasped. "He wouldn't dare."

"He would," Corin said, a touch of sadness in his voice. "And I would, too, to keep that treasure out of the hands of some greedy lord."

"You would fire on the forgotten city?"

"I would blast a way through solid stone and pray it didn't do too much damage to the treasure buried on the other side."

"It is not a treasure hoard. It is a sacred place."

"Then let me in. Open the way for me, show me a chamber full of sadness and regret, and we will leave this place forever. Refuse, and you can see how much destructive power those things hold."

Corin watched a tear spill down her dusky cheek, but in the end she nodded.

"Good." He breathed a sigh and took her arm. "I'm glad to hear it's settled. Because unless I miss my guess, the boys are back."

Corin turned again, looking past the cannons this time. The horizon beyond the valley's mouth was now a rolling cloud of dust, and beneath that backdrop marched an army of weary pirates. Ethan Blake came along at their head, and he looked angry.

Corin shook his head. "And I do *not* want Blake to have to use the cannon."

"Beware that man," Iryana whispered.

"Get to your tent."

"I thought you needed me."

Corin glanced her way. She looked prepared to go to battle. Her jaw was clenched, her hands in fists, and there was murder in her eyes. Corin sighed.

"Wait for me at your tent," he said. "I'll need you soon enough. But there is still some work to do."

She hesitated, still intent on arguing, but Corin turned away to watch Blake's approach. Still she lingered for a moment, but then she surrendered with a huff and Corin felt a small relief as he heard her footsteps receding across the sand.

He'd risked too much, rescuing her. And he had won no great victory in compelling her to open the gate for him. But she'd become entangled in this plot, and she was his responsibility. He couldn't leave her to the traders, and he certainly couldn't leave her to Blake's care. Even if it had to be against her wishes, he'd see her safely on the other side of this affair, and likely with a fortune to pass on to her granddaughters. All he had left to do was end this strange adventure.

But as Corin watched the furious approach of his first mate, he remembered Iryana's warnings concerning the man. Blake was pompous, reckless, and ruthless. Corin had no love for his first mate, but there were those among his crew—among any pirate crew, even Old Grim's—who spoke no other language than violence. It had been useful to keep Ethan Blake around to manage those.

But like a gale-force wind, Blake's power could prove difficult to harness. The only respect Corin had ever won from the man had come from shows of power. Perhaps taking the camel had been a step too far, but the card had been played. Corin didn't dare back down. Not against so cutthroat an opponent. The only way forward was to raise the ante. The captain met his first mate's glare, unconcerned, and when Blake finally stormed to a stop before him, Corin frowned. "You look tired."

"I am tired, *Captain*. All the men are tired." He glanced over his shoulder. "How long will you make us toil in this senseless pursuit?"

Corin kept his gaze locked with Blake's, but he raised his voice. "Not much longer. Not at all. But right now, you all have important work to do!"

Corin's deckhands obeyed the order, murmuring their assent as they flowed past Corin and Blake toward the pit they'd carved from the valley's floor.

"Strange reward for victors returning from battle," Blake said.

"It was not *meant* to be a battle," Corin said. "Just a minor skirmish. How much blood was spilled?"

"Not enough. Not near enough. You should have let us kill them all. And then, after depriving us that natural right, after miles of trek across the open desert, you send us all straight back to our labor?"

"We all want to be finished with this business, Blake. We are so close. There may be grumbling—and rightly so—but they are good hands."

"If you're so anxious to be done, why waste a day of work to steal one rebellious slave back from the sheiks?"

"I have told you before, we need her magic—"

"There is no magic among these people and plenty in the cannons."

Corin shook his head. "Some tasks require a more delicate hand."

Blake sighed and shook his head. "Those are not the right tasks for pirates. Everything about this venture is wrong. We should return to the ships. I'm not the only one saying it."

Corin nodded toward the men. "They will serve me for a while yet. Sand or sea, they're all hard workers."

"They're ready to be out of here," Blake snapped back. "I am, too, if it comes to that."

Corin didn't meet his eyes. "Are you sure of that, Blake? Are you in such a hurry to get back to the ship?" The first mate was already nodding, but Corin went on. "Back to *my* ship?"

That stopped him. The mouth worked, but Blake made no words. A cruel smile tugged at Corin's lips, but after a moment he relented and climbed to his feet. "You'll have your own command soon enough." He clapped his first mate on the back. "That's why you followed me a hundred miles from the shore, right?"

"I followed you because you're my captain," Blake said hurriedly.

Corin's mouth twitched with the same dark smile. "Of course."

He shaded his eyes and looked across the narrow valley to the far wall, where his men worked industriously at the base of the sun-seared cliffs. The huge carved figures of men and gods looked down on them, patiently watching while a hundred lawless sailors dug a path through years of rubble. There had to be a door beneath it all. There had to be.

Just then he heard the shout. He saw the excited face of a messenger hurrying their way, and a smile split his face.

"Iryana!" he called toward the girl's tent. "I need you now!" As soon as he heard her grumbling approach, he clapped his first mate on the back. "Now! Let's see if we can find enough gold so you won't have to tell those lies anymore."

(**4**)

Across the narrow valley floor, a towering cliff face glowed almost golden in the desert sun. The soft stone was carved with nearly human figures that towered hundreds of paces high. Iryana grumbled disapproval as she caught up with Corin beneath the timeworn faces' demanding gazes.

The air felt hot as a blacksmith's forge, but Corin did his best to ignore it as he hurried ahead of his first mate across the narrow valley. There a path had been dug into the settled sand and stone of the valley's floor, and Corin followed the path down until the loose walls of excavated earth loomed on either side.

Then suddenly the wall on his right opened out onto a wide pit, taller than a man and nearly forty paces across as it crawled along the base of the huge cliffs. The air might have been cooler here, trapped in a little box of shade, but it was crowded with the stink of men at work.

Corin saw Blake's lip curl at the smell. The pirate captain shook his head. An end of their arduous journey, and the man could still object to the stench. Corin sighed and fixed his eyes on the sandstone doors now revealed at the far end of the excavation. Thrice as tall as a man, they curled in a wide, pointed arch that looked more like an ironwork gate than a door into a mountainside.

That thought dragged his eyes back left, along the wide strip of rock his men had needlessly unearthed. The same pattern marked the stone all the way down and plunged behind the soft earth embankment to the left—not a gateway here, but a barred wall, a huge iron gate etched in solid stone. And it was not the crude work of ancients, as it should have been. It looked light and delicate, almost living, like the finest masterwork outside one of the great houses in rich Ithale. Corin chewed his lip as he considered it. So many mysteries, even after all these years of searching. Excitement burned within him at the thought of all the answers he might find behind these timeworn cliffs.

At his side, Blake was evaluating the stonework, too. "Huh," he said. His sharp chin stabbed toward one of the carved figures high above the uncovered gateway. "So this is truly your Oberon after all?"

For just a moment, Corin clenched his jaw to still a sarcastic response. He took a long, slow breath, then forced a smile. "So it would seem."

Blake shook his head. "I thought the slave girl was only humoring you. I've certainly never heard of him or seen his likeness."

Iryana shook her head. "The Godlanders have truly forgotten Oberon?"

Blake shrugged. "Little worth remembering. Stooped and old. He looks a fool to me."

Friendly, Corin thought. *Not foolish. Friendly.* There was no room for the distinction in the first mate's head, but Corin had learned his trade at the feet of Old Grim. There was no sailor on the sea more vicious, more brutal, more feared than dark Old

Grim. But to his friends, there was no one more friendly, more measured, more insightful.

The face that both men considered now was barely more than a shadow on the stone, ten paces wide and fifty paces up a sheer cliff. But they had been here for weeks now, living beneath the unblinking eyes of those faded faces, and now they were all familiar.

There were others with their own features. Hundreds, probably, stretching far to the left and right. This was near the center of the range, if not the precise center, and there to the left, where the excavation had begun, was another towering figure, his feet carved in and eroded away some short distance above the delicate tracery of the long-buried gate.

That figure did look familiar. Carved in crude lines far more fitting to their age and worn thin by the sleeting sand that blew on the sun-scorched wind, still, it was recognizable. Familiar. It was the towering, powerful figure of the mighty Ephitel, tyrant god of all Ithale. Corin didn't like to look at him.

"It just seemed so unlikely," Blake said. Corin caught the motion as his first mate glanced sideways at him. "This far from the world. Buried under a century of sand—"

Corin cut in quietly. "Ten centuries, at least."

Blake shrugged in disinterest. "The treasure at the heart of stars, you said."

"The power," Corin corrected again.

Blake ignored him, eyes aglow as he stared at the image of a god. "The wealth that made the nations of our world."

"Understanding," Corin said. "Or it might have been 'magic.' The translation is difficult."

"The knowing," whispered Iryana. "There is magic in knowing."

Still the first mate went on, unheeding. "Such a treasure, so long lost. It seemed a child's story, until you showed us these faces in the middle of nowhere. And then to claim this sad old elder was the guardian of it all."

Corin pressed his lips together in frustration for a moment. "You'd be amazed what two hard years of serious study might reveal."

Blake looked over at him for the first time. After a moment he laughed and shook his head. "I didn't really believe a word of it. All this time...I was certain you were mad."

The corners of Corin's mouth quirked up, but there was no softness in his eyes. "But the pay was so good."

Blake nodded. "For that much royal silver, the men would have built you a castle from this miserable sand."

"And yet, in the end, I was not such a fool after all." Corin turned on his heel and started across the excavated pit. His men were gathered in a half circle around it, watching with quiet interest as their captain and first mate led the exotic local toward the stone-carved gateway. Corin saw nervous glances skitter toward the door from time to time before snapping back to him. He frowned.

"There will be fortunes after all," Blake said, oblivious to the nervousness among the crew.

Corin noticed a spring in the first mate's shiny-buckled step. But he wasted no time on Blake's wretched priorities. He fixed his attention on the doors, the gateway carved in stone. It was certainly a portal. Not just a decorative carving, but a passage into the mountain's interior. The legends had been clear on that, but it was apparent here, too.

Corin's men had worked with shovels and pickaxes, crude tools, but as they'd cleared the dirt away from this wall, they'd revealed perfect, deep-cut lines that defined every edge of the gateway. A great knot of scrollwork at the heart of it contained a perfect keyhole. And between the impression of wrought-iron bars, Corin could see a broad paved path lined on both sides with rich shops and houses.

And yet...he blinked, and it was gone. There was no street. There was no city. There were not even any bars, but the impression of iron bars given by the marks on the stone. Still, it felt so real. The gates were nothing more than a carving in sandstone, but it seemed he might just reach out to the clasp and pull them wide open.

He closed his eyes for a moment, caught a deep breath, then shrugged and stepped forward. His right hand stretched toward the impression of a huge iron ring on the southern gate. But just before he might've bruised his knuckles on sandstone, Blake darted forward fast as a viper and dropped a hand on Corin's outstretched arm.

The first mate was surprisingly strong for a nobleman's son. Corin didn't fight the grip. He turned an ice-hard gaze on Blake and raised one eyebrow in question. "Is there a problem?"

Blake licked his lips. "We need to talk."

Corin spotted the feverish fire in his first mate's eyes and dropped his arm. *Now* Blake made his move? It would have been better done on the water. A mutiny this far from sea made no sense at all. But then, if Blake was to have any hope at all, it had to happen before Corin delivered the reward for all this effort. Corin sighed. "Now is not the time for this, Blake."

"That is no longer yours to decide." The first mate shifted his position, squaring up before Corin, and the captain saw the flash of spirit in his first mate's eyes.

Corin shook his head. "No, no, no. This is too soon. You're like a spoiled little child."

Blake's brows crashed together and the fires roared hotter. "Be careful how you speak to me. We're a long way from the waves that know your name."

Corin cast a sarcastic glance over the first mate's shoulder at his loyal crew, but he saw only frightened interest. They were not at all surprised. "All of you?" he asked, disappointment dragging at his tone. "Not one of you insisted on seeing the treasure before you betrayed me?" He met Blake's eyes and shook his head slowly.

"Three years you've searched," Blake sneered. "Three years you've studied ancient tomes. You would not have led us here for nothing. But it will cost you everything. Pirates were never meant to be scholars." He stared at the carved stone gates, then around at the walls of sand. "We weren't meant to be explorers and nomads."

Corin sighed and shook his head. "It is no job for clever little lords. You are wrong on every other point. I've been studying more than old books. I study men, Blake, and this attempt is no surprise at all."

Blake's grin was a twist of contempt. "So smooth of tongue, but you will not bluff your way through this. And this is not just an attempt. The men are all with me."

The loose circle around Corin shuffled uncertainly, but they did not withdraw. They avoided Corin's gaze, but they did not back down. He sighed. "All of you? All of you will follow this foppish—"

"Enough," Blake said softly. Corin felt the cool edge of Blake's cutlass burn against his collarbone. He never caught the motion, never heard a sound, but it was there. Fool or not, the man was deadly with that blade.

Iryana cried out, but Corin silenced her with a gesture. Blake's eyes began to drift in that direction, and Corin had no desire to let him drag her into this drama. Corin wanted Blake to forget the girl, so he rounded on his first mate, regardless of the nasty gash it left along his collar. With all the haughty disdain he could muster, he asked, "What can you offer them that I cannot?"

"I am a pirate, where you are not. I will let them be pirates, where you have not." He looked hungrily at the exposed wall. "We will enjoy this wealth you have led us to, but we will enjoy it on our terms. Your mad obsession has worn out every hand."

"And all that effort has—"

"No!" The slightest pressure from Blake dug the sword's tip against bone, and Corin had to suppress a groan.

"Enough!" Blake snapped again. "Drop your sword."

Corin forced a cold smile. "I have not drawn my sword."

"Drop it now! Someone come and tie his hands."

Corin raised his eyebrows in a mask of bored surprise. "Yes? They are all with you, aren't they?" Corin sniffed. "So who will come and take my sword?"

No one moved. They had seen him kill from worse positions than this.

Blake spat at them, "Will you really play the cowards now? Your cards are shown. The treasure is right here!"

"Ah, but there is more to life than treasure," Corin said. Blood ran hot and sticky down Corin's breastbone, and every tiny twitch of Blake's hand grated sharp steel against Corin's nerves. He fought to keep his voice calm and level. "You never knew Old Grim, did you, Blake?"

"Slave-son trash," Blake spat. "The seas are better off without him. Even pirates need some honor."

Despite the pain, Corin had to suppress a grin at that. He saw the looks of surprise and doubt pass among the men. Most of them knew Old Grim, and those who didn't still knew his name.

Corin nodded to Charlie Claire. "There are rules, aren't there, Charlie?" He met the nervous eyes of Sleepy Jim. Corin extended his empty arms. "You want to clap me in chains, Jimmy?"

David Taker started forward, and even that was a surprise. But he was one of those vicious men who spoke Blake's cruel language. Corin pretended he hadn't noticed. He turned lazily to Blake. "You should have waited until the gold was in their hands. A little solid sparkle can overcome reason, but lacking that, these boys know right from wrong."

Blake slashed his cutlass wildly at nothing, venting his fury as he rounded on the watching men. "What is wrong with you all? Every man among you said we should—"

"Oh, well, *said*." Corin waved dismissively. "It's easy enough to say, Blake, but acting on it is something else."

He took a step after the first mate, showing his back to some of the men, and they crowded closer—not to grab him from behind, but to see the show. Corin couldn't quite suppress the smile this time. "As I said, you should have been studying, too. Human nature need not be a mystery."

"You're cowards, all!" Blake frothed.

Corin shook his head. "But you are the mutinous dog."

The sword flashed back to Corin. It hung a hair's breadth from the skin of his throat, and it wavered erratically now. "Don't you dare insult me, sir!"

"I am no sir," Corin said. "And you are now a dog. You might have been a captain, but your gambit has failed. Now drop your sword, and go with whatever honor you have left."

"Oh, no!" Blake's voice was manic. "No. Let them quail at their chance. But I can cut you down right here! You're unarmed. Call me a dog one more time—"

"We are all dogs," Corin said, deliberately, infuriatingly calm. It drew just the response he wanted.

Blake's sword flashed back, readied for one brutal slash, and in that moment the air hissed with the sound of all the other blades being drawn. The first mate's eyes went wide as nearly every pirate in the crew drew arms against him.

But Corin still stood unarmed. He smiled pityingly and shook his head. "It was a bold bid, and it could have worked if you had just waited half an hour. But now, you are a dog. Jim... put him on a leash."

Sleepy Jim took up a loop of rope he hadn't even touched at Blake's earlier order. Now the deckhand stomped toward the first mate, and Charlie Claire came forward with sword drawn to back him up. Corin didn't look right at David Taker, but from the corner of his eye he saw the brutal deckhand slinking back toward the circle's edge. That man might find himself forgotten when next the *Diavahl* set sail.

No one else spoke up for Ethan Blake. Corin waited just long enough to see the disbelieving defeat take hold in Blake's eyes, then he turned his back. He looked to the carved stone wall, not to the slave girl still waiting nearby, but he spoke to her. "Iryana, it is time to open the way."

She came to his side, gripping his arm with surprising intensity. "Have you not seen proof of my wisdom? I warned you against Blake, and I warn you now against desecrating this sacred place. Take your men and go."

Corin gave her a smile. "Aye, you warned me of Blake, and you see how he has been muzzled?"

"I see you soaked with blood."

The gash at his collarbone still ached, but it was just a flesh wound. Drying blood lay sticky on his shirt, but his spirit soared.

The winds were with him now. "You see me victorious. But it is a fragile thing unless I give the men their gold. Open up the way."

She shook her head. "You would lose more than your life. I will not give it to you."

"There are still the cannons."

"Use them if you must," she said, tears in her eyes. "Then let the retribution fall on you. But I will not be the one who gave you entry to that place. I will not have your blood upon my hands."

Corin held her gaze, unblinking, hoping she would yet relent. But there was iron in her core. At last he shook his head and said, "I should have known. Clever as you are, you must bow to your superstition. It's in your blood."

"Call it ancient wisdom. You pirates own the claim to superstition. I have seen how they jump at shadows." Instead of answering, Corin drew a small wrapped bundle of silk from a pouch on his belt. He spilled out of it a tarnished tin ring and a thin copper hoop. Iryana hissed in shock, and Corin smiled at that. He held the jewelry out toward her. "How is this for ancient wisdom?"

"I cannot be bought with such cheap baubles," she said, but her voice trembled.

He laughed at that. He hung the hoop from his earlobe and slipped the ring on his right hand. "Am I doing it right?" he asked. The astonishment in her wide eyes was answer enough.

Corin didn't know if this would work, but he knew the motions anyway and time was short. He turned, raising both arms to the walls, and cried out to the stone, "*Iftah! Ya! Simsim!*"

Iryana grunted as though someone had punched her in the stomach, but otherwise silence poured across the excavated pit, smothering as a Feland fog. No one moved. And then, with the grinding whisper of heavy iron hinges, the carved stone sank back into the cliff face. It revealed a deep shadow, a yawning cavern just behind the cliff's facade.

"Behold," Iryana whispered. "The gateway to Jezeeli."

(5)

A whisper passed among the men and then a wild cheer. Corin did not move. He only stared into the darkness, disbelief battling with the wild exhilaration clawing at the back of his breastbone.

"We've done it," he breathed at last, inaudible beneath the noise. And now the thrill of victory won through. Now he grinned and turned to Blake again.

"You silly little pup, with your fancy waistcoats. You might have gained more wealth than all your family's houses could contain, but this little spot of toil was too much to ask of you."

Corin turned and met the eyes of all his men. "I have asked much of all among you. I have dragged you from the sea and spent you on this wild hunt. Perhaps...perhaps your first mate heard you grumbling. I will not fault a man among you for complaining. But only one of you raised arms against me."

He touched a hand to the drying blood at his collarbone, then pressed his palm against his black shirt, still wet to the navel. He showed the bright-red palm to the men, then crossed the little distance to the place where Blake stood, now disarmed, his hands roughly bound.

Corin pressed his palm flat against the man's bare chest, leaving the crimson stain of his accusation.

"Blake will have nothing more from us. He risked everything on this gamble, so we will give him nothing." Corin stared down at him for a moment, then nodded. "Nothing. No punishment for what he's done, but no share of this great treasure. No horse from our pickets. No water from our stores. No place among our tents. Let him find his own way from this place."

Corin ran a look around the circle and saw admiring approval. It was a good pirate punishment. Even in this bleak desert, a man might be marooned.

He hid his smile and turned his attention to the passageway. "Torches!" he cried. "Bring me torches. Let us see what we have won." He headed for the archway.

"Stop!" cried Iryana. She sounded frantic. "By Oberon's name, Corin, do not trespass here!"

Corin spared a sad smile for the miserable native. "You do not have to come." He raised his voice. "You have served us well, Iryana. Take a camel and anything you can carry, and return to your people's tents."

"There is no treasure for you here," she screamed. "I swear it. Not for Godlanders. There is only the record of your sins."

Corin hesitated a moment, then went to her. He stood over her for a moment, holding her eyes, then bent his head to speak softly near her ear. "You must get out of here. If Blake had accomplished what he intended...I could not have saved you. For all their useful traits, these are not good men."

"And you ask me to leave you to their mercy?"

Corin shrugged. "I am not a good man, either. But I would not like to see you come to harm. Take the offer I have given you, and get far from this place." He stepped back, still holding her eyes. She didn't move. She didn't blink.

"Please," Corin whispered. "Take a camel and go."

Behind him, Dave Taker raised his voice. "Captain? Is there a problem with the girl?"

Corin ground his teeth and turned away. "Not at all. She has served us well. Now…let us see this treasure. Who has my torches?"

"There is some light already," called Charlie Claire, staring past the doorway. He sounded nervous, and Corin nearly chastised him for the very superstition Iryana had accused them of, but then Corin saw it, too. The glow was thin and gray, an eerie twilight, but it was enough to see by. Corin forced himself not to look back at Iryana. He rested one hand on the hilt at his belt and strode into the mountain.

The entrance was a tunnel, the same size and shape as the scrollwork gate, but roughly hacked from living stone. It went five paces deep then opened up to left and right. The ceiling soared away above, too, so Corin felt himself on the edge of one huge, open chamber. The feeble light didn't show him much, but the vastness of the place was a taste in the air, an echo in the ear.

The floor was not a cave's rough floor, but cobbled stone. The rock wall was irregular and jagged like a natural cavern's, but it did not seem a real part of this place. It was the boundary. But within the cavern, there seemed an unreal space, like something out of dream. Like the heat-haze hallucination Corin had seen before.

He stepped forward onto the cobblestones and a new shape loomed out of the darkness. A tall, square block ahead on his right. Another step made it clearer, even in the gloom: a three-story building, looking for all the world like a fancy shop off

Prince's Way in Ithale's capital. He saw the shadow of another beyond it, and just perhaps another across the wide street.

He stopped in the deep and echoing silence, straining his ear, but the only sound of life in this whole place was the nervous rustle of his bravest followers shuffling in behind him. They hung back, but Charlie Claire came up behind Corin. He carried a torch that flickered against the darkness, and still it took him a moment to recognize what he was seeing. At last the sailor gasped.

"By all the gods!"

A frightened whisper fluttered among the rest of the crew. Corin turned his back on the row of storefronts dancing in the torchlight.

Charlie's eyes strained wide. "What is this place?"

"We've found the dead god's tomb."

Charlie shook his head. "This is no tomb. This is a city! Those are shops. That's the sign of a money changer, but it never swung in a summer breeze. Not here. Who made this place?"

"A race long dead," Corin said, loud enough for all to hear. "I have been studying Jezeeli, and no civilized tongue has spoken its name for more than a thousand years. We are safe."

"You never said it was a city!" Charlie cried.

I never believed it was, Corin thought, but he kept that to himself. He let his eyes dance with mischief. "I asked much of you. Blake was not wrong on that count. We have all toiled toward this day, and this last secret I saved as your reward."

He stepped aside so they could see right up the wide boulevard. "A whole forgotten city, yours to plunder! This is fitting work for a pirate, no?"

A dozen voices answered, "Aye!"

Corin grinned back at them. "Fetch Blake in here. Let him see what he will miss!" It took only a moment, and every man among the crew came back with him, until they crowded the little plaza at the foot of the road.

The first mate's gaze was hard as steel, flashing fury not yet touched with despair. Corin only grinned more deeply. Despair would come.

"My men," he cried, "this place is yours! Despoil it of its riches!"

They cheered at that. They surged forward, leaving only Corin and Blake as they charged up the way, pouring through open doors and into all the shops. The farther they carried their torches, the farther the place seemed to stretch. It felt endless.

"Gods' blood," Corin breathed. "Even I had not imagined a place such as this."

"You do not deserve this reward," Blake growled.

"Oh, it is mine by right. You whined at what I asked of you, but I've spent more effort than the crew combined to find this place."

Blake sneered. "It will still be in vain."

"Your mutiny is dead. Be glad you're not and hold your tongue."

The first mate smiled, showing far too many teeth for a man in bonds. "I'm not alone. My father's men will find me here, and they will take what you have found."

"Your father's—" Corin began, but he stopped himself short. "You always struck me as a nobleman's son, playing at being a pirate."

"An infiltrator," Blake said. "A planted spy, for the glory of the Vestossi name."

"Of course you're a Vestossi," Corin said. "There's nowhere in the world I can escape Ephitel's wretched protégés. But why would I leave you alive to tell them?"

"Because you're weak. You are a scoundrel when you should be a gentleman, and you are soft when you should be hard."

"I am a pirate," Corin interrupted, growing bored.

"You are like no pirate I have known."

"No." Corin grinned as his men began emerging from the shops, their arms laden with spoils. "No, I am far, far richer. I'll take one day's head start, then let your father try to find me."

Charlie approached first, coming from the money changer's shop on the closest corner. Corin saw no sparkle among the bundles in his arms, and he recognized confusion on the sailor's face. Five paces brought him close enough for Corin to see what he carried.

"Books?" Corin asked.

Charlie nodded, still looking baffled. "The place was full of them. They're in no language I have ever seen."

Blake sneered. "Now you can read?"

The sailor answered quietly. "I know the shapes of letters, Blake, and these are not the letters of men."

Corin plucked a book from the bundle in Charlie's arms. It was bound in supple leather and stitched with fine silk thread. Rich, soft paper seemed untouched by time, and the symbols on the pages were indeed quite alien. They bore some similarity in look to the scrollwork on the stone-carved gates.

"This is your treasure?" Blake asked. "Books?"

"There is value in old books," Corin said, distracted. "But look at their condition."

"And these as well?" Blake asked, nodding past Charlie to the other returning looters. Sleepy Jim was next, from the shop across the street, and he carried books, too. Corin frowned. Clever Karr had books, too, and David Taker. They dumped them at Corin's feet, expressions demanding explanations, and every man among the crew, no matter where he'd gone, brought back books.

"Perhaps this was the bookbinders' lane," Corin tried, but the expressions on their faces denied it as clearly as the money changer's sign. Corin wet his lips. "We should search farther in—"

"We tried the other avenues," Dave Taker said. "I looked through four dozen different doors, and everywhere was only books."

"There must have been a strongbox somewhere, a shelf of silver—"

"Books," David said. "Just books in every room. Go see yourself. This place...this place is wrong."

"We never should have come here," Blake said softly. To Corin's horror, even Jim nodded along.

"There is good money in old books," Corin repeated. "Don't let the traitor fool you. This book alone"—he waved the one he held—"might fetch a hundred pistoles in silver at the universities." He waved to the pile spilled at his feet. "Just here, we have a fortune! If there are more—"

"You haven't seen the rooms," Dave answered. Too much white showed in his eyes. His voice cracked. "The slave did warn us, Captain! You heard what she said. We never should have come."

Corin stormed up to him. He managed by sheer rage to loom over the taller man. "Would you join Blake in bonds, you gutless dog?"

The man did not back down. "I would leave this place. That's all I know. We never should have come."

Too many of them nodded now. Acid boiled in Corin's stomach—anger and fear in equal parts. He'd come too far to lose this now.

"You heartless cowards! I've seen you face the despot's grays. I've seen you board a ship full of gladiators. I've seen you cut down enemies and lords. Would you quail now for fear of books?"

None of them would meet his eyes but Blake, who grinned with the thrill of victory. "You brought us to this desert hunting gold. Pirates in the desert!" He spat his disapproval. "A little solid sparkle can overcome reason, but lacking that, these boys know right from wrong."

"Still your tongue or I'll still it for you," Corin snapped.

Blake's smile twitched. He jabbed his chin toward David Taker. "Cut me free."

Corin caught Taker's eyes before the man could move. "Show me. Show me these terrifying libraries."

Taker nodded once, mute, then turned on his heel. Corin jerked his head toward the treacherous first mate and raised his voice to the other men. "Bring him along. Bring everyone along." Corin looked at the book in his hand, the pile at his feet, and slowly shook his head. Then he stomped off after his guide.

He followed up the boulevard in the flickering gloom of their torches. As they passed the money changer's shop, he glanced in. Books were everywhere, stacked in neat piles of varying heights. He caught only a glimpse of it, but he saw the same through the next open door, and the next. David Taker passed half a dozen shops before stopping at a door that hadn't yet been opened. He stepped easily aside, ceding Corin the opportunity to try this one.

Corin's hand closed on the dusty brass knob, but he hesitated. His whole crew waited in the street behind him, more than a hundred deadly men, and all of them afraid. Corin could feel Blake's hateful gaze, his mocking grin. The pirate captain turned the knob. He pushed the door open to a slow, grinding creak, and torchlight danced into a long-abandoned room.

It showed him books. Not on shelves or tables, not neatly sorted for storage or sale, but stacked in tottering piles. Corin entered the room, moving as though in a dream, and his eyes roved over the stacks.

There were hundreds of books. Thousands. Not a stick of furniture, not a strongbox standing open, not so much as a discarded boot. Just books. They were all identical in shape and binding, and the air was rich with the scent of ancient paper. Corin turned in a slow circle. He saw an open doorway beyond the piles, and the room it revealed was full of books.

A dark stair climbed up to another floor, and even the steps held little piles of books. Corin backed slowly out the open door and into the boulevard. His eyes traveled up the building's facade to the dirty windows of a second floor. Knowing what to look for, even through the gloom he could see the squared edges of more books piled high. His gaze went on up to a third floor. A fourth.

And there to the right was another building like this one. They stretched half a mile to the first intersection, and beyond that were more. Across the street were more. It was a sprawling city, hidden from the world of men, robbed of life and wealth but completely filled with books.

(**6**)

Brows drawn, Corin turned until he found David Taker still waiting by the door. "How far did you search?"

"Three blocks, north and west and south. I sent Hocks the other way, and he just came back to announce more of the same. Some places that look more like houses. One he swears was a smithy, but books where the forge should have been. Books for an anvil."

"As...as I said—" Corin licked his lips and cleared his throat. He raised the book still in his hand. "This book alone is worth more than its weight in gold. And we have thousands here." He glanced down the way and tried not to shudder. "Hundreds of thousands."

David Taker took a long step closer. "Why, Corin? Why books? This is not what you expected. What is this place?"

"It is a tomb," Blake cried out. "Every one of you can see it. It is a tomb, and these books are the sleeping dead. Didn't the slave girl tell us that? The dead remember!"

"That's nonsense," Corin said. "It's a safe, dry place. This is a cultural treasure. Think of it more as a temple—"

"And we should anger these gods?"

Fury flared in Corin's breast, fed by fear, but he quelled an urge to snap at the first mate. Blake was playing to the men's anxiety. Corin had lost control of the situation. He took a slow, deep breath and surveyed his crew.

"These are secrets," he said at last. "This place is a treasure trove of secrets, and pirates thrive on secrets. This is a fortune—"

"It's a grave!" Blake cried, and Charlie Claire groaned in wild fear.

"You have seen your share of graves," Corin tried.

David Taker answered under his breath. "Never from inside."

"You led us here," Blake accused. "You led us here, you ignored the slave girl's warning, and now we will leave this place empty-handed if the desert's fires don't consume us first."

"You wretched dog!" Corin snarled, but Blake dismissed him with a shake of his head. Even with his wrists bound before him, the man could play a lord.

He ran an imperious gaze over Corin's crew. "You heard what the slave girl said. Corin brought her because she knew this place. It holds the record of our sins, she said."

A tremor of superstitious fear shook the pirates.

Blake nodded. "Our only sin is disturbing this sacred place. And that is on your captain's head. Repent it now, with me, and let him be the one who burns."

"No one is going to burn," Corin said. "If you want to leave this place, we'll leave. Grab an armload of books, everyone, and we'll leave a kingdom's worth of relics here to rot."

"Sacrilege," Blake cried, justified. "We are pirates, aye, but are we grave robbers? Here?" He shuddered theatrically and shook his head.

One glance showed Corin how much ground he'd lost. How? How had Blake won their hearts? He'd played to their fears. It would be easy enough for Corin to play along—to leave the books undisturbed and come back alone in the future. But he would have no future. Fear gripped the crew right now, but it would evaporate beneath the desert sun, and only gold would tame them then.

He knew all those things in the space of one angry grumble, and he answered with an unaccustomed show of emotion. He threw the book down on the dusty street. He stomped it underfoot. "Shall we leave empty-handed, then? That is what he recommends!"

"I recommend we refrain from robbing graves," Blake answered, all cool calm.

"This is no grave!" Corin cried. "This is a town. You see with your own eyes. These are stock houses full of goods, all of it ours for the taking."

"Dusty parchment and faded leather," Blake sneered. "No more than I'd expect to find in a forgotten catacomb."

Corin sniffed. "I'll swear it is as good as gold. Sleepy Jim! You remember when we robbed the scholar's ship?"

He nodded. "Aye, aye, we ransomed the boy for three hundred crowns."

Corin spread his arms. "And then we ransomed him his books for three hundred more."

That drew another murmur from the men. Enough of them recalled that little coup. Corin stooped to grab the book. He made a show of dusting off the print his boot had left, then folded back the cover and riffled through the pages with a silk-soft whisper that seemed to hang in the air.

Hope and greed alike shone in the pirates' eyes. Corin smiled. "You hear that? An ancient artifact in such condition. You know enough to guess how much it's worth."

"It's sacrilege," the first mate screamed again, but he was frantic now.

Corin turned to him. "Sacrilege? What sacrilege? It is a book well made." He riffled the pages again. Again they whispered to the cavern's heart, speaking of opulence and opportunity.

Corin smiled straight at Blake. "Don't you hear that? They want to be read. The true sacrilege is leaving them buried."

Blake opened his mouth to object again, but Corin silenced him with the barest rustle of paper. Smooth and soft as a lover's whisper, it spoke in every ear. Corin smiled his victory. He snapped the book shut with a clap like thunder. "Gentlemen!" he cried, ready to order them to the pillage.

But the whisper still hung in the air. The pages were still trapped, but a breathy voice spoke from nowhere. "Vennngeance."

Corin's blood went cold. Every face arrayed before him turned pale. They all had heard it, too. An echoed whisper, "Revenge." And louder, "Revenge!" And now more whispers overlapping. "Revenge! Revenge! Revenge!"

Every eye was on the black-clad captain, but he had no words at all. He felt the book within his hands, small and ordinary, but all around him spectral whispers screamed throughout the tomb.

Blake recovered first. "Burn the books!" He bellowed the command with a nobleman's arrogant authority, and the common souls of Corin's crewmen obeyed him in their fear. Oil-soaked torches flew at every open door.

Corin screamed in rage. "No, you fools!"

A thousand whispers answered him. "You fools! You fools! You fools!"

He ignored the whispers now. He'd given years to find this place. He dove to catch the nearest torch as it flew, but it tumbled past his grasp, rolled on the stone floor inside the nearest shop, and fire flickered up the stack of books. His effort mattered little anyway. Another dozen torches found other open doors, and all around them books as dry as tinder caught the flame.

He ran toward an open door, then fell away as fire blossomed in the neat, tall piles. The next shop wasn't burning yet, and he reached desperately for the books atop one stack. Someone behind him grabbed his shoulder, but Corin shook free.

"Run, Captain! We must flee!" Sleepy Jim caught at him again, and Corin allowed himself to be dragged from the building just as flames began to lick the outer wall.

Fire, red like blood, washed down the lane. Corin blinked against the acrid smoke and stared at all the storefronts now ablaze. All the books. All the treasures in this place on fire.

He held a fortune in his arms, but there were kingdoms to be had! And Blake had set it all on fire to win himself a boat. Blake! Where had the wretched man gone? Corin spun, straining his watering eyes against the smoke to find the first mate.

But Blake was just where Corin had known he had to be. He stood beyond the fire's reach, twenty paces from the storefronts' end, where Jim and all the rest had dumped their books. All the other men had fled the cavern, but Blake and big Dave Taker stood over the tiny hoard and stared at Corin and Sleepy Jim.

Blake's wrists were bound tight, but Dave Taker held a knife in his right hand. In his left he held a blazing torch. Corin broke into a sprint, but even as he moved, Dave Taker slashed the first mate's bonds.

Corin raced toward them, fire raging on his heels. "Protect those books!" Corin screamed. "They're all we have left now. Don't let him burn those books!"

Dave raised his eyes to Corin once again, uncomprehending, but Blake understood the stakes. His only hope among these men was to destroy the captain. He shook his bindings free, ripped the torch from Dave's hand, and plunged its flames into the pile.

"Revenge!" the whispers screamed.

Corin skidded to a stop next to the growing fire. He kicked desperately at the books, trying to scatter them, but Blake struck him a vicious backhand blow that sent the captain reeling. "See how he serves the ghosts?"

"The gold!" Corin shouted. The forge-hot blaze began to roar behind him, and Corin bent to grab one untouched tome. "You dogs, save something!"

But while he was bent, Blake brought an elbow slamming down against the back of Corin's neck. The captain sprawled, and before he could fight back, Blake planted a polished boot between his shoulders and stepped down.

Sleepy Jim shoved a hand hard against the first mate's chest, but it wasn't enough to dislodge him. "What are you doing?"

Blake held his voice level. "Corin awakened something evil here. A price must be paid."

Before Jim could have answered, a thousand ghostly voices clamored over each other. "A price must be paid!"

Corin struggled, but Blake stamped down harder and drove all the air from the captain's lungs. The air burned hot as an oven, and sweat shone on every face, but Blake seemed unconcerned with the fire. His attention was wholly on Sleepy Jim, who alone seemed prepared to stand up for the captain.

Dave Taker loomed close behind Blake, his eyes sometimes darting to the dancing flames, sometimes darting to the exit. Blake only held Jim's nervous gaze, his eyes as hard as steel. Seconds burned away like coals inside the roaring blaze, and then at last Sleepy Jim lowered his eyes in shame. He stepped past the united mutineers and fled the burning cavern.

Blake turned a grin to Dave Taker. "Back to the ships, and we'll be proper pirates once again!"

Corin struggled weakly, still woozy from the blows, but the motion caught Dave Taker's eye. "And what of him?"

"He is far too clever to leave alive." Blake's fingers traced the hilt of his cutlass, but he shook his head. "It's not my way to kill a helpless man. Pick him up."

He moved his boot, and Dave hauled Corin to his feet. The captain spat a mouthful of blood. "What have you done? You've burned it all."

Blake shrugged. "There are books enough in my father's library."

"Your father! He was searching for this place. How could you destroy it?"

"I've learned to like the pirate's life. All I needed was a solid crew. And now you've given me one."

"They will not follow you!"

"They will when they see your great project has left us empty-handed."

"Because you set our treasure to the torch!"

Blake waved that away. "What is one treasure to a lifetime of command?"

Corin strained to meet Dave Taker's eyes. "And what of you, who've heard that confession? You'll stand with him?"

Blake's smile glowed in red reflection. "I've named him my first mate."

Corin fought Dave Taker's grip, but the huge man would not relent. "That's it? That's all he had to offer?"

Behind him, Dave moved his grizzled mouth up close to the captain's ear. "It's more'n you," he growled. "You've passed me over twice. I'd let you burn for no reward at all."

Corin thrashed and struggled, but he couldn't break free. Before him, Blake began to back away, moving slowly to the exit's mouth. He raised his voice so it would echo through the tunnel, to the frightened crew that must have been waiting at the other end.

"A price must be paid," he shouted. "Let Corin answer for his crimes to those he's wronged. But we have played no part in it, so we will wash our hands of him. We'll give him nothing."

Corin sagged in Taker's grasp. Blake grinned and carried on. "Nothing! No punishment for what he's done, but no share of this great treasure. No horse from our pickets. No water from our stores. No place among our tents. Let him find his own way from this place."

Then he nodded to Dave Taker, and as casually as if he were tying knots, the big man shattered Corin's ankle with one vicious kick. Corin tried to run, blind now to everything but pain and fear, but Dave caught him easily, one hand at his shoulder and one at his knee. The big man swung around in a tight circle and then let go, and Corin flew a dozen paces through the air.

The hateful flames reached out to him, still begging for revenge, and Corin disappeared within the fire.

(7)

Corin hung in a moment suspended above the hungry flames. Within that moment, he felt no pain—not the fire's blistering heat, not the stab of broken bones, not even the old fatigue of too many days' hard work under an unforgiving sun. Within that moment, even through the choking smoke and creeping darkness, he could see the cavern with extraordinary clarity.

He saw the shops ablaze and saw the fire spreading. For a moment he could see the city all spread out, even larger than he had imagined. It sprawled for miles over rolling hills and gently curled around a little lake. There was a palace all of silver, marble, and gold. There were avenues and parks. There were grand cathedrals and twisting towers. And from this edge, the fires could take it all.

Then time returned. Corin landed hard. His head hit paving stones and a light brighter even than the raging fire flashed behind his eyes. He gasped for breath and coughed at the thick, unpleasant air.

He rolled three times and landed staring up. Light and heat and sound. He heard the growling crackle of the flames. But there were other sounds within the noise. Corin imagined he could hear the rattle of a cart on brick-paved streets, the clatter of a thousand striding boots, the greedy cries of merchants and shouts of little arguments and fights.

Corin took another measured breath and winced at the bruises on his ribs and the agony around his broken ankle. He sucked in air, and it was sour in his mouth—not with the acrid sear of choking smoke, but with the smell of sweat and men and animals packed too close together.

He blinked three times against the light, then stared up at a bright-blue sky. A summer sun sat low and hot, wreathed with tiny wisps of woolly clouds. A four-wheeled cart rolled by, scant inches from his right hand, then a boot stamped down by his left shoulder. He bent his neck and saw a street alive with busy shoppers who crowded along the storefronts and now gathered around Corin.

He struggled up onto an elbow as questions rang inside his head. *What in Ephitel's wretched name is happening? Where am I?*

He looked up to find a stern-faced woman standing over him. She wore outlandish pants, the gray of ash and creased along a seam, and above them she wore a blouse of brilliant white. And above that, she wore an irritated scowl. "Find somewhere else to spill your sick, you worthless drunk, or I will bring the guards."

Those last words cut through all the strangeness, all the impossibility, and moved Corin to motion. He raised his shoulders, and even that much exertion hurt. He groaned and reached to press a painful rib, then scooted back and heaved himself upright. It jostled his ankle, and he almost screamed.

That much of reality remained. The fire was gone. The cavern was gone. But broken bones were a familiar agony to a boy who'd learned to survive in Aepoli's shady alleys, and Dave Taker's vicious blow had left Corin crippled even in this...this dream? This waking madness? What was this place? Corin considered what he'd seen in the crowd around him. The busy street felt so familiar, but the clothes were strange—too bright, too clean, too neat of hem, even for the lords on Prince's Way. What would a proud Vestossi pay for a single bolt of that strange cloth?

And the men were strange. They moved about their ordinary business just like ordinary folk, but nearly every one of them stood a full head taller than the people of Ithale. They wore a thousand shades of skin, but every one among them had the same basic build. Tall and thin, high cheekbones and narrow faces, flowing hair left loose. And men and women, old and young, on busy errands or at an idle stroll, these lords and ladies all moved with the easy, rolling grace of seafarers and soldiers.

Here and there among them, rare as the south wind, he spotted ordinary folks. They looked small and awkward in the crowd, and their tanned skin and dirty clothes named them all farmers, sailors, or servants. Every sign of wealth belonged to those elegant creatures, larger and sleeker and prettier than ordinary men, who so densely packed the streets. For just a moment, Corin recalled the ancient carvings on the sandstone cliffs, of Oberon and Ephitel and dozens more like them. This city was crowded with lords and ladies who looked like living gods.

Another wave of pain bent Corin double, his gut a knot of stabbing cramps. A groan escaped between his teeth, and then the angry woman was kneeling over him. She thumbed back his eyelids, staring close, then pressed a finger to his throat. She tried to help him up, but the agony in his ankle drew another cry, and she let go. Her eyes narrowed, and for a moment she just stared, then she rose again like a mainmast sail and grabbed two strong men from the curious crowd.

"Get him in my shop. Right now. And you. Fetch me Jeff from Snakestaff Lane. No, shoulders and knees! And stabilize his neck. Move it! Now!"

Corin saw the sign above the money changer's shop as he was carried through the door. It was the same sign he had seen in an enormous, deserted cavern. Was this Jezeeli, then? In another time? Another world? There was no room left in him to be surprised. He recognized the room beyond when they carried him in, though it was mostly devoid of books now.

A heavy mesh of polished steel divided the room in two, and in the cage it made were four small vaults. Shelves above them held stacks of heavy paper trimmed in gold and green. The floor held leather bags in piles, their sides worn with faded lines that traced the rounded edges of coins. Minted gold and silver stood in neat little stacks atop the vaults.

The money changer had a desk outside the cage, hastily abandoned as she'd gone to check on Corin in the street. Its blotter held one of the expensive sheets of paper, with scrollwork on the edges and a detailed embossed seal. Those embellishments did more than decorate the page; they made the devil's work of forgery.

Rare was the document that demanded such an expensive medium. This sheet looked remarkably like a gentleman's credit note, and even those were often satisfied with just a waxen seal. But all the vaults in all Ithale could not have honored the sum the woman had been draping in calligraphy. No king could have requested such a note.

But the gentleman himself was in the room, leaning lazily against the wall while he waited for the money changer's return. The gentleman was tall—taller even than the lords and ladies who packed the streets, and more heavily built. His eyes were bright and sharp, a cutting blue like that traitor Ethan Blake's, and possessed of the same easy arrogance. His jaw was lean and strong, his shoulders broad, and there was something in his stance that screamed of violence restrained. But only just.

And on his hip he wore a sword so fine some kings would have gone to war to own it. His left hand rested on its guard, his thumb idly sliding the blade up and down against the scabbard's throat. It filled the room with a constant steely hiss.

The weapon was a massive thing, with a blade wider than Corin's spread hand, with silver on the scabbard, gold and gems upon the guard, but the grip was honest steel just like the blade. Sliding from the sheath, it sang of blood and shadows and the death of nations. The man who owned that blade might well demand the outrageous sum on the unfinished credit note. But then, the man who owned that sword would not need gold.

The man who owned that sword showed an inconvenienced frown as he watched the porters bringing Corin through the shop, and he turned it full upon the money changer as she came behind them. *She* was one of those rare few of normal build, though she used her voice to make up the lack in height. Still sour, she chivied the conscripted porters up the stairs.

Then, behind them, she turned with profuse apologies to the waiting gentleman. "Some nameless drunk, my lord, forgive his sins. But he'd done himself some violence somehow, so I fetched a leech to look him over. Shouldn't think they'll disturb us further—"

The gentleman sniffed sharp disapproval. "You bring a leech to tend a drunk in off the street? His bill will come to more than the blackguard's worth. My guards can take him off your hands—"

"No need to trouble them, my lord. I have a friend."

Then Corin lost the rest of the exchange as he was carried up the stairs. They took him to a little sitting room and stretched him on a couch beneath a window. One man pushed aside the sash to crack the window. Still baffled by this place, Corin expected billowing smoke or the dreary silence of the cavern tomb. Instead he heard birdsong and a busy market street, and he felt cool air against his face.

The other of the men had busied himself at a cabinet on one wall, and now he brought a heavy glass with a splash of amber whiskey. He pressed it in the pirate's hands, then ducked his head and followed the other porter from the room.

For a moment Corin floated on the gentle waters of exhausted bafflement. The breeze was pleasant on his face, the noisy hum a kind of lullaby, and even before he tasted it, the spicy vapor off the brandy glass glowed warm and soft inside his head. He released a pent-up sigh and sent some tension with it, sinking down into the soft cushions. He sighed again and sipped the whiskey and closed his eyes.

This couldn't be a dream. No dream could ever hurt as much as this. His ankle was a throbbing agony. It felt as swollen as a banquet goose and heavy as an anchor. He would be crippled no matter what the leech attempted—too many little bones, too many joints—but at least they might do something for the pain. Even the bone saw would hurt less than this, and gods knew he wouldn't be the first to sail the seas with missing limbs.

He stopped at that and something like panic finally broke through his shock. Home. He had to find a way back home. Whatever this place was—and it seemed real enough—he'd left behind a girl who needed his protection, and a traitor who needed his revenge.

(8)

But what was this place? By every indication, this was the same Jezeeli he had found. Moved somehow by mystic arts or madness, this was the place he'd found behind the cliffs. He knew the shop. He knew the street. But it was not a tomb. It was alive and in the open, apparently as rich and powerful as it had been in the legends.

How many legends had he read? All of them with different names for the city—he'd found Gesoelig and Gesaelich, Jesalich and Jazil—and different locations all around the Meddgerad Sea, but all of them had spoken of its wealth and grandeur. All of them had spoken of the king, mighty Oberon, who'd conquered hells and made the gods his loyal vassals. They'd spoken of forgotten magic and powers lost to man, of scholars who held secret understandings of the dreams behind the stars.

But they had all been stories. They'd painted jeweled Jezeeli as the city of the gods, but not…not a real place. Not a sister city to Aerome in Ithale. Not full of heavy-handed shopkeepers and curious bystanders and spoiled gentlemen. Even as he thought it, Corin remembered the gentleman downstairs. He remembered the sword. Now *there* was a piece of legend. There was something out of story. It cried to Corin's thieving soul and overwhelmed everything else.

The man who owned that sword had power. A man like that could open doors. If this place was anything like Aerome, a man who wore such an extravagant display would also have a wizard to his name, and a wizard might send Corin home. Corin had seen the cold disgust in the man's eyes, but he could overcome it. He could steer a man as easily as a ship. It was never hard to learn the prevailing winds. Corin had learned much just in the brief exchange downstairs, and he could guess a volume more, but every hint he captured would aid him more.

So he braced himself against the pain he knew would come and pulled himself upright enough to catch the windowsill. He slid the thin pane shut to block the pleasant breeze and, with it, all the noise. Silence settled on the sitting room, but blood pounded in the pirate's ears. Fire like a living coal burned in his foot. He breathed in frantic little gasps and fought it down.

He pushed away the pain and tried to focus. There were voices down below. Corin heard the personalities before he heard the words. Their cadences rose up the narrow stairway like the rise and fall of little waves against the hull. The lady's voice was carefully polite, but Corin heard the brittle edge of her disdain. The gentleman gave orders in everything he said. He was loud and resolute and unyielding.

But however Corin strained his ears, he could not make out the words. Even when an argument raised both their voices. The pirate dashed off his expensive whiskey, braced himself against the pain, and lowered himself to the floor. He dragged himself toward the stairs and down, stifling groans every inch of the way. But he found strength as he came closer and finally understood the words.

The gentleman shouted in anger. "Well, blast it, girl! I've told you twice—"

The money changer interrupted with a pretense of patience in her voice. "Tell me again, but it will make no difference. Oberon himself made that decree."

"And with good reason, but you cannot believe he meant it to apply to me."

She sighed so loudly Corin heard it in the sitting room. "The law is law, my lord. It's not for me to choose how it's applied."

"It's not," the gentleman boomed condescendingly. "That's why you're not in charge. That's why I am."

"My lord—" she tried to object, but he spoke over her.

"I am Oberon's right hand," he said. "I am the lord protector and prince of Hurope. If I request a writ of provender—"

"It's not the note itself! It's the goods you want."

"I am the lord protector! What else would I demand?"

"My lord," she persisted, "I would not challenge your intent, but law is law. All you need is Oberon's approval."

"I have it! I have it in my titles and my name!"

"But not on paper," she said soothingly. "Forgive me, lord, but paper is my world."

"You would thwart me for a scrap of parchment?"

"You would stoop so low as to ask one of me?" she answered. "A writ of provender by my hand is worth what it is worth *because* I follow law."

"And I would pay what it is worth, but you insist—"

"I insist for both our sakes," she interrupted smoothly. "For your safety as much as mine."

"Only because you support these foolish games! I grow tired of your rules, outlander. And yes, I know who writes these rules for Oberon."

The money changer lowered her voice until Corin could barely catch the words. "These rules make the world."

"You're wrong. The magic of my people makes the world. Your rules only constrain it. If we are to play by such rules, we should be gods above the manling crowd. Not slaves to paperwork." With a casual gesture he struck the pile of carefully prepared forms from her hands. "If you earn my ire, outlander, Oberon himself would not protect you."

He raised his hand as if to strike her and, unthinking, Corin took half a step to intervene. His ankle buckled at the barest weight, and he collapsed into the room. He caught himself on hands and knees, grinding his teeth to stop the screams of agony. When he could breathe again, he found them both staring down at him.

The gentleman arched an eyebrow. "Your drunk is listening in doorways." His hand fell to the hilt of that magnificent sword.

The money changer darted between them and spoke breathlessly. "I'm sure he means no harm."

Corin struggled up to lean against a wall. "No. I just…I just want to go home."

The gentleman sneered. "And where do you call home? I do not recognize your fashions."

"Another time," Corin said. "Another place. Some kind… some kind of magic."

The money changer turned to him, eyes wide and worried. "Hush. Be still. Your whiskey's talking."

"No," the gentleman said. "No, I would like to hear what he has to say."

She turned to him. "My lord, he isn't well. He's had a nasty fall."

"Even so—"

Before he could say more, the bell above the outer door announced the physician's arrival. The gentleman looked that way and then harrumphed.

"I should have known you'd summon another like you. Tend to your manling gutter trash. I will be back with the scraps of paper you'll respect."

The shopkeeper didn't answer, and neither did the new arrival. The bell jangled once again, the door slammed shut, and Corin let himself collapse upon the floor.

Who was this man? Oberon's right hand? The prince of all Hurope? Corin shook his head. The Godlands had no prince. They never had. Or, rather, they had dozens. Maybe hundreds. If this man held a fraction of the power he claimed, he'd be as powerful as any lord alive.

And Corin would play him like a lute. The nature of the man was utterly transparent. This prince had arrogance enough to drown a whale; he was a bully well accustomed to his privilege. Just another posturing Ethan Blake.

But Blake had won. The thought caught Corin broadside, but he shook his head. Blake had been even more a fool than Corin had believed. And when the darkness had cried out, Corin's crew had let him down. They'd answered stupid confidence instead of reason. It wasn't Blake who'd won, but Corin's crew who'd failed him.

He'd learned a lesson there. That was the key. He knew Ethan Blake, and he knew this prince. Down to the core. All Corin needed now was an audience. With ten minutes' time, he'd be a trusted confidant. With half an hour, he'd have some way back home. The man had mentioned the magic of his people, hadn't he?

Corin rolled onto his side as a shadow fell over him. The figure looming there was unimpressive. Not one of the lords and ladies so common on the street, but...plain. An average height and build for any Godlander, but dressed in fine, strange clothes like the shopkeeper.

Was that what the gentleman had meant by "outlander"? Corin had thought of the graceful townsfolk as alien, something like the legendary elves from the Isle of Mists. But perhaps they were the natives here. Perhaps Corin's own people had come from somewhere off.

Or perhaps these outlanders were something else altogether. In size and shape, this new arrival might have fit in on the streets of Aerome, but his clothes were strange. His tunic and trousers alike were made of some flat, untextured blue, and over all he wore a long white coat. His shoes were strange, as was the bracelet on his wrist. He lingered for a moment in the door, then glanced back behind him to the money changer.

"He isn't one of ours?"

"I sure don't think so."

"Then what's he doing here?"

Corin called out, surly, "He's wasting away while you ignore him."

The new outlander turned back to Corin. He knelt beside him at the bottom of the stairs, all the while watching Corin like he was some wild beast. Resting on his heels, elbows on his knees, he showed Corin a big, bright smile.

"How you doin'? My name's Jeff."

Corin waited for more. When the stranger didn't offer it, Corin frowned. "I have never known a name like Jeff. Although… there was a Geoffrey Kirkwood at the university…"

Jeff laughed. "Just Jeff. Plain old Jeff. And you are?"

"Corin. Corin Hugh. Captain of the *Diavahl*."

"Yeah. And Jeff is weird." Still chuckling, Jeff slipped a knapsack off his shoulder and tore it open, rummaging within its contents until he brought out a broad white box, an extraordinary pen, and a small book. He flipped through to a blank page and scratched at the page with his pen. Then he glanced up at Corin again.

"Can you read, by any chance?"

"Not a lot."

"Uh-huh. Where are you from?"

He said it casually, but Corin spotted the tension in his wrist and across his shoulders, the pinched lines around his eyes. Still...he could think of no good reason to lie. "Born in Aepoli. Sailor these last nine years."

"Nine! You're lying! You don't look a day past eighteen."

Corin didn't answer.

The money changer stepped up close behind him and mumbled something in his ear. Jeff whistled softly and scratched something else in his book. "One more question, then I'll see you right. Got it? Good. What year is this?"

Behind him, the money changer gasped. Jeff threw an irritated look over his shoulder, and that gave Corin half a heartbeat to think. What year? Was that the secret to this place? Had he stepped out of time?

Again, he couldn't guess what would make a useful lie, so he reluctantly settled for the truth. "It's the ninth of Ippolito."

The outlanders both looked puzzled.

Corin bit his lip. "It's...I believe the twenty-third of Francis. And something in the thousands south of the Meddgerad, but they don't count by kings."

The money changer frowned. "You do?"

Jeff said, "How many thousands? Two? Or ten?"

Corin shook his head. "One. One thousand, two hundred and...eight? Eighty? I don't know. I only heard it once."

Jeff leaned back. "Twelve hundred years. We're already past that now, so they must be counting from some other date."

"Gesoelig's founding?" the money changer guessed.

"No. That wouldn't give the northern nations time to adopt a new time scheme."

"Then what?" the lady asked.

"I don't know," Jeff said. "I suspect it hasn't happened yet."

Corin said, "Perhaps it's me." A stab of pain spoiled the joke, and he doubled over clutching at his calf.

Jeff spat a curse and ripped open the low white box. "Close your eyes," he said. "I'll have you better in a moment. Just…close your eyes. You'll be glad you did."

Corin had seen chirurgeons at work before. He quickly complied. He tried not to hear the rustle of strange instruments as Jeff set about his work.

Jeff asked, "What's he doing on the floor?"

He clearly meant the question for the money changer, but Corin was glad of the distraction. Eyes still closed, he answered. "There was a man here threatening the lady."

"Threatening?" Jeff asked, alarmed.

"I'll tell you later," the money changer answered. "Just get this one taken care of."

Corin shook his head. "No. I need to know more about that man."

Something sharp and hot lanced into his ankle, but it wasn't yet the bone saw. It lasted for a moment and then relented. Corin fell back, gasping. After that moment of liquid fire, the background agony of his broken ankle seemed to be relenting. He caught a dozen panting breaths and pursued his questions.

"Please," he gasped. "I need information."

"What do you want to know?" the money changer asked.

"Who is he? What is he in this town? Where can I find him?"

"Don't go looking," Jeff warned. "He isn't nice at all."

"But he does like to give speeches," Corin said through gritted teeth.

Jeff laughed at that. "They all do. Something in their... hardwired in their souls, I guess. God bless 'em."

The money changer grumbled some frustration then answered Corin seriously. "That was the prince and lord protector, though I suspect you might have heard that."

Corin shook his head. "I...wasn't listening. Too much pain."

"Of course," she said. "He oversees our defenses and our police forces. Our watch, I mean. He doesn't have much patience for strangers."

"Oh, I think I can win him over." Eyes still shut tight, Corin smiled. He felt light. The pain had dwindled till he barely noticed it. "A man like that...he always needs a helping hand."

Just then, Jeff caught his calf in a sure grip. Corin tensed despite himself. This would not be fun. He fought to take slow, calming breaths while a tight pressure clamped around his lower calf. Next would come the saw blade. Or did they use a knife to cut away the muscle first? He clenched his teeth and waited for the searing pain.

It didn't come. Jeff clapped his hands together once and gave a sound of satisfaction. "That's broken bad," he said. "I can't do much for it here, but at least the pain is gone. You'll want to keep it elevated and stay off it for at least two weeks. It's mostly set, but if you'll come with me to my office, we'll get it cast."

"Set? Cast?"

Corin snapped his eyes open to meet Jeff's gaze, and the leech looked startled. Nervous.

The money changer barked a laugh. "You never even try."

"There's not much room for role-playing in modern medicine," Jeff shot back.

Corin looked from one to the other. Then he glanced down at his foot. There'd been no saw. There'd been no amputation. Instead, he wore some kind of boot. It seemed stiff as steel plate, but light as leather. It gripped tight around his calf, but below that, his whole foot was numb.

He looked at Jeff. "What did you do?"

Jeff threw a miserable glance at the money changer, then almost whispered, "Just a local anesthetic."

Corin frowned. "A what?"

"Druid magic," the money changer said. "All of this is druid magic."

Corin's brows shot up. "Oh! Oh, you are druids?"

"Yep," she said. "Right off the ship. We meddle in things man was never meant to understand."

Jeff said, "That's hardly fair."

She shook her head. "It's how it has to be."

Corin looked back and forth between them, mystified. At last he shook his head. All this was beyond him, but he had a question far more pressing. He said, "The prince."

"No. Forget him," the money changer said.

"I don't believe I can. What is his name?"

Jeff answered, though the money changer tried to stop him. He didn't seem at all concerned. He shrugged and said, "That's Ephitel. Ignore him."

Ephitel. He *had* looked a bit familiar. But Corin hadn't thought to compare him to the ancient marble friezes or the etchings carved in stone. But aye, the resemblance was there.

So *that* was Ephitel. The tyrant god of all Ithale.

Corin closed his eyes and groaned.

(9)

Of all the gods in all the world, why did it have to be Ephitel? But of course it was. That arrogant bravado. That sneering swagger. It was the hallmark of the whole Vestossi clan, and they'd been Ephitel's anointed throughout Ithale for years.

How many years? The druid's question struck Corin again. How many thousands? What was this place? *When* was this place?

Corin caught Jeff's sleeve. "Who are you, druid?"

"I think that hardly matters," Jeff said. "The real question is who are you?"

Corin pointed toward the door. "That was really Ephitel? *The* Ephitel? I'd heard stories he once served Oberon, but…"

Jeff frowned. "What do you mean, *once*?"

The money changer stomped her foot. "Don't you say another word! Jeff, we are so far outside the strictures—"

Perhaps the druids' magic could send him home. Or perhaps Oberon's. Strange as these creatures were, Corin needed their aid. He raised his voice before the money changer could stop him. "Ephitel is chief among the gods. Where I come from. He's a scurvy dog, but he runs things."

The money changer rolled her eyes and collapsed into a wide armchair. "See? That's the kind of thing we should *not* have heard."

Jeff rounded on her. "Are you mad? Do you have any idea what this could mean?" Back to Corin. "How can Ephitel be chief? What about Oberon?"

Corin's mouth fell open. He'd heard more than a touch of affection every time they'd mentioned Oberon. After a moment Corin snapped his mouth shut. They didn't know. After a moment more, he looked away. "Oberon's…gone. Forgotten. Just a legend."

Jeff turned to the money changer. "Emily—"

"Aemilia!" she snapped. "My name here is Aemilia."

"This is not the time for that. Do you understand what he's saying?"

"No!" She threw herself to her feet to confront the leech. "I don't understand a word of it, and neither do you. You're pretending. You're guessing. And you're about to do something rash based on *no* understanding of the strange magic in this place. That's why we *have* the strictures."

"Em—"

"No. No. No. We are *not* supposed to talk of these things at all."

Jeff rolled his eyes. "Only in front of the sons and daughters."

"Well, what is he?" she asked, stabbing a finger at Corin.

"I don't know what he is! This is unprecedented."

"And why don't you take that as a warning?"

Before they could argue more—before Aemilia could chase Jeff away—Corin chimed in. "I'm a Godlander. That is all. Born and raised in Aepoli. I'm nothing strange."

Both the druids stared at him for a moment. Aemilia threw her hands up in disgust.

Jeff smiled. "There is no such place. What is a Godlander?"

Aemilia hissed at him. "You need to shut up. Now."

Corin tried his best smile on her. "Are you so determined to keep me here on your couch?"

She blushed. "I never suggested—"

"And I would never impose on your hospitality," Corin said, climbing awkwardly to his feet. Aemilia was no use to him, but Jeff seemed more than ready to talk. Corin held out a hand. "This gentleman said something about his office?"

"No. You're not going with him."

Jeff stiffened. "He's my patient, Emily."

"He's dangerous, and you know it. He's out-of-bounds for both of us. We must send him to the palace."

Jeff rolled his eyes. "Oh, come on! You heard what he said. If Ephitel gets his hands on this guy..."

Corin did not like the sound of that. "Please, my lady. I am lost and afraid and most grievously injured. Entrust me to your companion's care. I'll see no harm comes of it."

She shook her head, firm, and Corin flashed a look of abject defeat. He let his shoulders stoop and turned away. Over his shoulder, he said, "I understand. I'll go. Thank you for your aid."

Aemilia only grunted. Corin took a tender step toward the door, showing his limp. Then on his second step, as his weight settled on the damaged ankle, he collapsed, clutching theatrically at the strange boot. "Stormy seas! That hurts!"

"You see?" Jeff whined. "He needs my care."

She only rolled her eyes and dragged Corin back to his feet. "You can play a role almost as well as one of us, but I can see what you're after, and you won't get it from Jeff. He'll pretend because he's *nosy*, but once he's shot you full of penicillin, he's exhausted his usefulness."

Jeff tried to object, but she rounded on him. "What do you know about time travel? What do you know about geography and politics?"

Corin shook his head. "If he knows anything at all, it's more than I."

"No," she said. "I will not allow it. I'll give you both to Ephitel myself before I'll let you have that conversation."

Jeff bristled. "You wouldn't." He did not sound sure.

Aemilia did. "This is not a game, Jeff! If we break the strictures, we'll only make this world into…into the one we left behind."

Jeff held her eyes for a long time without answering. Then he looked away, ashamed.

Corin was not ready to surrender. "Your dedication does you great honor," he said. "Send the leech away and hear my story yourself—"

"Ha. No. I will *not* defy Oberon's law just to satisfy my curiosity."

"But if you show such care, perhaps we can find *something* safe to discuss, and you can help me find a way—"

She shook her head. "I already know too much. The strictures are clear. You're an anomaly, and that makes you a threat."

"But you are the druids. You should understand me more than anyone—forced to the edges, forgotten by the world, powerless and…and hated for your knowledge."

Silence settled over the room. Jeff and Aemilia exchanged worried glances.

"What is so strange?" Corin asked.

"We're not powerless and hated," Jeff said. "We're somewhat secret, but we're not outcasts. We're Oberon's favored people."

"Ah." Corin shrugged. "I'm sorry. That will not last."

Another grave silence fell. At last Jeff said quietly, "This is serious, Emily."

She sighed. She looked very tired. "I know."

Corin took half a step toward her. "Then you will help me?"

"No."

Corin caught her eye. "Then who? In all this strange world, who?"

"Dana!" Jeff cried, eyes wide. "I mean, Delaen."

"Delaen?" Aemilia shouted. "Are you mad?"

"It was your suggestion," Jeff said. "Quantum temporal theory and sociological development are her core qualifiers! How's that for time travel and politics?"

Aemilia stopped herself short of arguing. She shut her mouth and brushed past both men to stand looking out the window on the bustling city. Corin watched her draw a heavy breath. Without turning, she asked, "What do you know of Gesoelig, stranger?"

Corin licked his lips. Honesty served him here. "Even the name is nearly forgotten. I know only what I could find in ancient books. Hints and rumors."

Jeff looked sick. "Emily—"

"I know." She caught another slow breath then nodded. "I'll take him to Delaen."

"I can," Jeff volunteered, but Aemilia shook her head.

"No. You've broken too many things already, Jeff. And I care about Delaen."

"Who is Delaen?" Corin asked. "Will she speak with me?"

"More than speak," Jeff said, eyes bright. "She'll understand. She specializes in things like this."

"Careful, Jeff," Aemilia said. "There's no such thing as 'things like this.' That's the definition of an anomaly."

He frowned at her back. "You're taking this too seriously."

"You're not taking it seriously enough," she said. "I swear to you, if you say another word about it—ever—I'm handing you over to Oberon personally."

Jeff took a step back as though she'd hit him. "Emily—"

"Aemilia," she said. "Remember that. And you'd better start calling yourself Geoffrey, or you're going to get sent back anyway."

He swallowed hard. "You really think so?"

"This is not a game," she repeated.

Corin could not guess what "sent back" might mean, but it held some promise for his future. Feeling lighter, he took a step toward her. "Have some compassion. Please. He only wanted to help me."

"He could have ruined everything," she said. She finally turned back from the window, and there were tears in her eyes. "You could have ruined everything. Or even me. I should have left you in the street for Ephitel's goons."

"My only desire is to go home," Corin said.

Aemilia smiled, though the bitterness in her eyes ran deep. "Funny. Mine's the opposite."

She chased Jeff back to his shop, slinging admonishments all the way to the outer door lest he mention this to anyone. Then she summoned a courier and sent him off with two messages, but still she would not take Corin to see this Delaen. She encouraged him to rest his injured foot while she attended to important business, and he could hardly object to that. He gave her an hour, and just as he stirred himself to protest, she came bustling back.

She brought a change of clothes for Corin—long pants and a cotton shirt and a leather coat that barely reached down to his belt. He refused the coat, insisting on the same black cloak he'd worn since leaving Aepoli, and she relented soon enough. That one had a cowl deep enough to hide his face, and she tugged it into place before she let him leave the shop.

She locked the door tight behind her, and despite her commanding manner, she swept her gaze up and down the street like an amateur cutpurse. She kept one hand almost possessively on Corin's sleeve, dragging him through the crowd, but she moved down the city streets in frantic little bursts, like a mouse crossing a scullery floor.

In one of these strange pauses, while Aemilia scanned the face of every elegant local on the bustling thoroughfare, Corin stifled a yawn. "What can you tell me about books?"

She shook her head.

"I only ask because the Jezeeli I found—"

"No!" she snapped. "Tell me nothing of Jezeeli. Tell me nothing! Save it for Delaen."

"Why are you so afraid?"

"You do not belong here!'

Corin smiled. "You don't have to tell me. But I have no intention of harming you."

"Your intention matters little. Your *existence* here could ruin everything I've spent my life on. And, agh, even saying that runs counter to the strictures."

"The strictures?" Corin asked. "Oberon's law? Is he so terrible as that?"

Her lips pressed to a thin line. After a moment she said, "No. He is not terrible. And I will say no more."

"But—"

"No. You, too, will say no more. Hold your tongue until I deliver you to Delaen, or I will hand you to Ephitel's guards."

She nodded across the busy street to a small knot of soldiers swaggering easily through the milling crowds. Everyone made way for them, careful not to catch the soldiers' eyes or brush too close to their apparent path.

The Vestossis had guards like that, on the streets of Aerome and Meloen and Aepoli. They earned that careful respect through the frequent application of casual and unanswerable violence. The Vestossis' guards had taught Corin some of his earliest lessons in villainy.

A thought struck Corin and he turned to Aemilia. "Why was Ephitel in your shop?"

"I told you—"

"Not to speak of my world," Corin said. "But you can tell me of yours, if only to pass the time on our journey."

"We will not be long," she said. Corin watched her eyes while she watched the knot of strolling guards. When at last Ephitel's soldiers turned a corner and slipped from sight, she began to move again.

There was a clue to her erratic movements, but it was not the whole story. Twice more she stopped short to avoid crossing paths with the uniformed guards, but other times...

It took Corin longer than it should have to understand, but in time it was the memory of home that showed him. Back in Aepoli, the brutal city guards had not been the worst of the Vestossis' agents. That honor belonged to the investigators.

Surely this golden city had not sunk so low? But even as he thought it, Corin caught Aemilia watching one. Just a face in the crowd. Not a uniformed soldier. Not a grand, imposing figure. Just a forgettable face, just plain clothes, just an easy gait. But his eyes were dark and sharp and always moving. Like a rat's. Like a spy's. What kind of lord chose to spy on his own people?

His Majesty Ippolito Vestossi, for one. And Lord Protector Ephitel. Corin shook his head. Nowhere in the world—nowhere in *time*—was far enough for him to escape those wretched tyrants.

"If you had told me you feared Ephitel's investigators, I might have saved you some time," Corin said. Before Aemilia could respond, he caught her wrist and dragged *her* into the flow of the crowd. Jeff's druid magic served him well. Corin felt no pain in his injured ankle, though the boot turned strangely on the cobblestones.

"What are you doing?" she yelped behind him. "If you draw their notice—"

He shook his head without slowing. "I know these men. They have a knack for spotting nervous eyes. Be bold, and they'll ignore you."

"This is a risky ploy."

Corin flashed her a smile. "It is the only ploy I know. Come. Show me the way."

She went more quickly then, acting on his advice, and some of the tension began to ease from her posture. In time, she even answered Corin's question. "Food."

He raised his eyebrows. "What?"

"The lord protector wanted a writ of provender for excess rations."

"Oh." Corin went several paces, weighing that, then said, "That does not seem so strange."

"The lord protector thought so, too. But I know more than he suspected. He asked the same writ of me last month, and two months ago, and five months before that."

Corin frowned. "That still—"

"He never executed them," she said. "I would know. And now he has asked them of other scribes as well. We do talk among ourselves. In the last month, he has collected more than a dozen of them, and he came to me for another."

"Perhaps—"

"Every one has been an order for excess rations. If he has kept them all, he has enough to feed an army for years."

"An army like the Guard?"

She shook her head, definite. "An army such as Gesoelig has never seen. We have our regiments, but Oberon does not maintain a standing force."

Corin licked his lips. "You suspect he intends an uprising?"

"What? No. What would he have to gain from fighting Oberon? Oberon has laid low every pretender this corner of shadow can raise against him. Even Ephitel would not dare."

"But in my time—"

She raised a hand, cutting him off. "Tell me nothing of your world, stranger. But Ephitel need not rise up against Oberon to betray him. And us."

Corin frowned, considering everything he knew of the tyrant god. And what would that god do with a standing army? "You mean war? He intends to start a conflict?"

"Yes. Conquest. There are lands rich enough out there to make another kingdom. Another power."

"There are other kings than Oberon?"

She frowned for a long moment. "No. Not yet. There are city-states and tribes. There are manling nations growing. There will be kings in time, but Delaen advised against establishing them outright."

Corin frowned. "What? Who is this Delaen?"

"You will meet her soon enough. And…how many strictures am I breaking? You have a talent, stranger. You are a compelling listener."

Corin grinned at her. "I'm compelling in more ways than you could imagine."

She shook her head, irritated, but a blush touched her cheeks.

After a moment had passed, Corin said, "You suspect Ephitel intends to carve a nation from among the city-states?"

Aemilia frowned at him instead of answering. Her eyes darted again, searching the crowd for the blank-faced investigators. Corin was keeping careful track of the three in his field of view. None was close enough to overhear.

"I would expect him to choose a city somewhere near the center of the Meddgerad's northern coast," Corin said. "Those are the places we call—"

"No!" Aemilia shouted, pressing her palms hard over her ears and drawing far more attention from the investigators than Corin's calm voice could have done. "You must tell me nothing of your world!"

"I won't! I won't!" Corin pulled her arms down and dragged her through the crowd, around a corner, and up another cross street just to escape the piercing eyes that had watched them.

He stopped on another busy street to let Aemilia catch her balance and her breath. He couldn't quite suppress a chuckle. "You aren't very careful, for a secret agent."

"I am *not* a secret agent," she said. "If anything, I am an auditor. The druids were not meant to hide in shadows, but Ephitel—" She stopped herself short and fixed Corin with a vicious glare. "Why can't you hold your tongue?"

"You have my apologies," Corin said shortly. "It will not be a problem again. Just lead me to this Delaen, and I will trouble you no more."

Aemilia huffed once and rolled her eyes. Then she pushed away from the wall. "Very well. Come. It is not far now."

(**10**)

Moving faster now, she led him up a broad boulevard and into a sprawling plaza. Paving stones of marble gleamed, bright and clear, and the storefronts facing the plaza displayed luxuriant wares. At the heart of the plaza stood a fountain larger than a house, carved with the figures of these lords and ladies, intermingled with woodland beasts and all manner of strange creatures.

This seemed the perfect place for a conclave of the king's favored people. Corin marked three buildings among the opulent shops, any one of which might have served as a council hall. Any one of them would have deserved a plaza all its own in Aepoli.

Aemilia sped ahead of him, slipping through the crowd and clinging to the edges of the plaza. She moved along the storefronts to her right, away from all the halls Corin had noticed. He frowned, fighting to catch up with her despite the crowd, and asked, "What is this place?"

"The Piazza Primavera," she said, distracted. "One of the busiest in the city, which serves us well. Do you see any investigators?"

"What?"

"You have displayed a knack for spotting them. Is anybody watching us?"

Corin frowned. "I see no one."

"Good!" She grabbed his hand and dragged him off the plaza into a dark, close alley between two of the towering mansions. Corin gawked. At the very edge of opulence, this dismal alley looked too much like the rough streets where he'd grown up. It was no place for Aemilia's silk slippers or gem-strewn hair. She paid no mind to the muck but strode purposely ahead to a rough plank door set in a dirty wall. She knocked three times, then crossed her arms over her chest and stood with toe tapping until the door cracked open. A voice within called, "Who's there?"

"It's me," Aemilia said smoothly. "And I've brought…a problem."

"You always do," the other answered, but the door swung open and the man standing sentry beckoned them urgently. "Get in here, then. Quick. Before you're seen."

"I know the risk as well as you," Aemilia hissed, but she wasted no time dragging Corin in behind her.

The sentry slammed the door behind them. The rasp of the solid bolt rang loudly in the tiny anteroom, a closet scarcely three paces square lit only by the seep of light around uneven doorframes. Corin reached immediately for the handle of the opposite door, anxious to escape this confined space, but the sentry interposed himself and slapped the pirate's hand aside.

"Who is this you've brought us, Aemilia?"

She ignored the question, but she made no move to force into the inner room. Instead, she answered with a quiet calm, "Who else is here?"

"Dale and Kaleoth, Tian and Kris and Maredon. Umm…"

"Delaen?"

"Oh! Yeah, she's here."

"Good. Jeff should be here soon, unless I miss my guess. Call them down to council."

"Do we have enough—"

"I don't care about a quorum, Julian. This is bigger than our rules. This man is out of time."

For the first time, the sentry turned to Corin and looked him up and down. Julian was a portly fellow, tall and broad and deep, with a thick brown beard and merry cheeks beneath suspicious eyes.

"Out of time? It's not our role to thwart Ephitel's justice."

"You misunderstand me," Aemilia said. "We need to see *Delaen*." She laid a heavy emphasis upon the name of the druids' expert in time travel, and Julian gasped in sudden understanding.

He turned to Corin again, eyes wide. "From what time?"

"This is no conversation for dark thresholds," Aemilia snapped. "Call them all to council, and bring Delaen to me."

At last the sentry stepped aside. He shoved the door wide and bustled through, leaving enough room for Corin to breathe freely for the first time since they'd entered. The open door bathed Aemilia in the twisting copper torchlight from the room beyond.

Smoke washed into the room, too—hearth smoke and pipe smoke intermingled—and with it the aromas of a much-turned stew and stale beer. Raucous voices and the clatter from the other room spoke just as plainly, proclaiming this place to Corin with a deep familiarity.

"A shady tavern?" he asked. "I thought you were Oberon's chosen people! I thought we were going to your council hall, but you brought me to a bolt-hole."

She gave him a measuring look, up and down. "Forgive me. I expected you would find the setting comfortably familiar."

"Familiarity is not my concern. You're hiding. There is a fear in the air that does not much match the little you've told me of these people."

She rolled her eyes. "You didn't see how Ephitel treated me, then?"

"I thought he hated *you*. Are all your people outcast?"

"Not outcast. Not in the public eyes. But very much endangered. I knew this before you ever spoke forbidden lore, even if Jeff can't see it. Ephitel believes we are a threat."

"But you said Oberon—"

"Oberon wears the crown, but Ephitel holds the sword and aims the bow. And we believe he hopes to wear the crown as well."

"I have made fine friends in this strange place. You are enemies of Ephitel."

"And you as well," she said.

"Hardly enemies. Where I come from, he is a distant and terrible figure with far better ways to spend his time. He does not know my name."

"And yet the way you recognized his secret police, the way you moved within the crowd...you seem comfortable enough defying authority. Why are you so angry that we must do the same?"

Corin shook his head. "It isn't anger. It's disappointment. I'd hoped you would be powerful enough to help me."

"Hold to that hope. We are likely your best chance within this place. You would do well to submit yourself to our guidance—"

"*Your* guidance? Ephitel has taken an interest in me, and you suggest some other slinking rats might somehow aid me."

"Hidden things are not powerless things, and rats are known to hold their own against superior foes."

Corin sighed. "For that alone you think I should help you?"

"No." She turned her back on him and headed to the common room. "I think you should pray that *we* help you."

He watched her go and wished he had convinced her to let him go with Jeff. That one would not have been afraid to talk. That one would have told him what he needed to know, and right now, what he needed to know was how to get home. He had no wish at all to get tangled up in the affairs of this strange city, when he had pressing affairs of his own in the desert south of Jepta.

He frowned into the smoky light of the common room. Perhaps these druids were his only hope, but they made dangerous accomplices. He licked his lips, thinking.

What manner of fool would he have to be, to stand in defiance of a god? He *knew* what Ephitel was to become. He knew the sort of men Ephitel favored, and the lord protector would surely have such followers in this place as well—men like Ethan Blake and the vicious Ippolito Vestossi. Corin had survived this long by hiding from such men, not by standing up against them.

He nodded once and turned away, fumbling for the bolt on the outer door. He would disappear among the natives, let Ephitel forget about him, then find his way back to Jeff once things were settled. But just as his hand found the latch, an old woman's voice stopped him. "You are not much welcome here."

She sounded kind, but not strong. Without turning, Corin hazarded a guess. "Delaen?"

She chuckled. "And I am meant to be the wise one."

"I've no wish to stretch my welcome thin," Corin said, sliding the bolt on the door.

"Do not misunderstand me," she said. "We've no ill will toward you, but you bode bad things for a world we've learned to love. Oberon suggested we watch out for you."

"He knew that I would come here?"

"Not...as such. But if what I've heard is true, you defy the rules of this place. Yet somehow Oberon seemed to believe it would come to pass."

"That clarifies some things Aemilia let slip."

Delaen considered him in silence for a moment. "You do not seem much rattled by your situation. Did Aemilia truly answer all your questions? Or was it Jeff?"

"She would not speak, and she would not let him speak. As for me...I'm never much rattled by my situation."

"You have no questions, then?"

Corin's head buzzed with them, but he hadn't half as much information as he would need to guess which ones were relevant. He settled for bravado instead.

"Just one. Who are all these lovely lords and ladies?"

"Ha! That is an interesting question, indeed. But I will give you answers before I ask my own. It is only fair. So know this: the people of Gesoelig are the kinfolk of its founder and the maker of this world, King Oberon. You might know them as fae or fairies or perhaps as elves—"

"Elves and fairies," Corin said, shaking his head. "I am in a storybook."

"Not...not in any real sense, no. Yet still you do not seem shaken."

He gave a shrug. "I'm a pirate and a wanderer. I spend all my time in unknown waters, and I usually come out richer for it."

"Fascinating. You may be just the man we need."

Corin turned to her, irritated. "What purpose could you have for me?"

"We need your aid against Ephitel."

"Of course! You are at war with him, after all. And here I am trapped in a fairy tale. So what does that make me? Am I to be another Aeraculanon, bound by prophecy to kill a god?"

"You against a god? I have no reason to believe you could win."

"Then what am I to do? Why am I here?"

"Perhaps to warn us what will come."

Corin shook his head. "I can tell you less than nothing. My world does not remember this place. I searched for it for years before I even learned Oberon's name."

"That is a warning in itself," Delaen said. "And perhaps *that* is why you're here. To take a memory away. To remember us to your people."

"This is a favor I would gladly give," Corin said, stepping closer to her. "Send me home."

"I'm sorry, but there is nothing in all the druid lore that could accomplish that."

"Then why did Aemilia bring me here?"

"To hand you off to me, I think. She is not a woman afraid of a challenge, but you are...well, outside her scope."

"She wanted to call a council."

"Yes. She would. But there will be little benefit for you in that exchange. They will all want to see you—a man outside time—but none of them can aid you."

"Then what am I to do? How can I take a memory away if no one has the power to send me back?"

She smiled at him, showing strangely perfect teeth for a woman so old. "I never said there's no one. Go to the one who brought you here. He can make it happen."

"Ethan Blake? He's still back there. Likely halfway to my ship by now, with..." The thought crept up on him, but now it laid him low. His throat constricted, and his stomach sank. "...with Iryana in his power." Those words came out a whisper.

Delaen took two steps closer and rested a hand on Corin's shoulder. "I do not mean Ethan Blake. I mean Oberon. He brought you here, whatever his reason, and if you will aid me in one simple task, he can send you home."

"I have no part in your troubles here." Corin's voice sounded far away, even to his own ears.

"But you have troubles of your own. Who is this Ethan Blake?"

"A man I underestimated."

She nodded. "A traitor?"

"Aye. After Ephitel's own heart."

"And who is Iryana?"

For a moment, Corin couldn't answer. He cleared his throat and shook his head. "A girl. A slave I bought at market. I had a use for her."

"And Blake stole her away? Blake put her life in danger?"

"Worse."

"Then you are wrong in every way. This world—every leaf, every life, every last decision—this world is built from Oberon's dreams. He made this place and brought us here, and his dreams are bright and good."

"I have my daydreams, too, but the world I know—the world outside this city—I could not call it bright and good."

Delaen stepped closer, eyes wide and flashing with passion. "And I would prefer not to see this world become the one you know. If Oberon loses his dominion, if Ephitel and his cronies seize control of this world, it will become a dark and wretched thing."

Corin sighed. "I cannot fight Ephitel."

"Of course," she said. "No more than I could. But your needs and mine are in perfect alignment."

"How so?"

"The only way you can get home is by the magic of the king."

"Oberon?"

"Indeed. You must go to him and plead your case, and he will send you home."

Corin nodded. "And your need?"

"I need you to tell the king what you have learned. Tell him Ephitel becomes a threat."

"You can tell him that," Corin said. "Aemilia has evidence—"

"Alas, we can't. He will no longer listen to his druids, but you...you will capture his attention. Before you leave, do this one thing for me. Warn him that a dark rebellion's brewing. Warn him that Ephitel is fielding an army."

Corin licked his lips, searching for the catch. He couldn't find one. "That's all you ask? You want me to give him your report before I go?"

"That's all. And pray he listens."

Corin took her frail hand in both of his and looked into her eyes. "In that case, you have my word. Although I'm not very good at praying."

She offered him a friendly smile. "Then go."

"Go? Now? But isn't there a council?"

She hesitated, then shook her head. "No. This is no time for council. Aemilia tells me that you drew Ephitel's attention. Already rumors run thick in the streets that Aemilia has angered him, and he asks for information concerning you."

"But if he's moving now, there's hardly time. Come with me—"

"He moves against the druids, not against the city. Everything we know is that he's hoarded certificates for rations, but it will take him time to make use of such things, to build an army out of writs of provender. We still have weeks or months, but Oberon must act *before* that army's raised."

The thought of provender set Corin's stomach growling. He stretched up on his toes, looking toward the smoky common room. "Must I go *right* now? Isn't there some stew?"

Delaen laughed. "The king will see you fed, but tarry not before you reach his throne. There is no time left to waste."

Corin frowned. "But Aemilia—"

"Is not cut out for grand adventure. It is her only flaw."

The pirate licked his lips. "Can the druids give me nothing?"

The old woman arched an eyebrow. "I have given you direction, boy. What more could you ask?"

Before he could find a cutting answer, she nodded to the door. For a long moment he stood unmoving, defiant, but then he hung his head and went out into the alley.

The door slammed shut behind him, and he heard the bolt slide home. He was on his own.

(**11**)

Corin hovered near the tavern door for some time, hoping Aemilia might come looking for him. He reached up more than once to knock, to demand something more in aid or explanation, but both times he restrained himself. At last, with a weary sigh, he turned his back and started down the narrow alley.

Ephitel an elf? It was almost too much to imagine. The god of all Ithale—fiercest and most powerful of all the gods—and in this place, he was barely more than a man. A man of high position, true…and every bit as treacherous as the Vestossi snakes who ruled beneath his patronage. But not yet the tyrant he would become. Was there really a chance to stop him?

Corin shook his head. Would that matter? Would it affect his own time? Could he save his world from Ephitel's treachery? If he did…if Ephitel never came to power, would that mean there were no Vestossis? Would there be no Ethan Blake to betray him?

These were some of the questions he had stopped himself from asking Delaen, and still he did not regret that choice. It didn't matter. Corin had no plans to save the world. All he wanted was to get back home, to set right the things that had gone wrong. But first, he had to navigate this strange place.

Corin hesitated when he reached the alley's mouth. Despite the late hour, the city streets still bustled. This place was so much like Aepoli. Lurking in the shadows, watching unsuspecting souls flow by, Corin felt a shock of memory—of a boyhood ten years in his past and perhaps a thousand in his future. How often had he waited just like this, terrified, hungry, and alone? There had always been grand plans. And insufficient resources. And enemies he couldn't hope to defeat.

His weary sigh became a lazy grin and, favoring his hobbled leg, he pushed out into the busy throng and headed for the palace. That was the real key: recognizing the challenge. Everything about this place had seemed impossible and strange, and for a moment he had foundered. But now he had his ship aright and sails full. Now he was home.

Corin's booted foot found an uneven paving stone and tripped him hard against a lovely elven lady wrapped in purple satin. Corin caught her just short of falling, and she gasped in affronted shock.

Her eyes grew wide to see a simple man—a manling, Ephitel had called him—clinging to her robes. "You...you..."

Corin summoned a blush and brushed at the delicate cloak where he had gripped it. He offered her a wealth of most sincere apologies, then slipped away into the crowd.

And now he had a purse.

Habits from his childhood came surging back, light and easy as a summer breeze, and before he'd crossed the wide Piazza Primavera, he had claimed a silver chain, two jeweled cuffs, and a beggar's writ in Aemilia's own hand. He'd always been a nimble touch, and these petty burglaries gave him some hope that he could truly navigate this strange society of gods.

His growling hunger somewhat dimmed that thrill of victory, but the purse now on his belt offered him an answer. He watched the signs above the street until he saw a likely looking inn, then paused outside the door to scan the common room for any sign of Ephitel's men. Seeing none, he raised his chin and strode into the room. This was not his part of town, not the sort of tavern he preferred, but he didn't know the city well enough to find a sufficiently shady tavern. Still, with stolen diamonds on his tattered cuffs and silver at his throat, he looked near enough a nobleman, especially when he dropped his purse atop the bar with an expensive clatter.

A barman bustled up to greet him, and Corin met the man with an impatient sigh. "Wine. And bread. And something rich and warm." He sniffed the air. "Is that quail?"

"Duck, milord," the barman said.

Corin winced. "Oh, very well. A plate of that. And sausage if you have some."

The barman frowned, and when he spoke his voice was all affront. "We do make a fine duck, milord. Better far than sausage. Or…are you from the north?"

Corin hid his smile, but it was good to know some things had not changed so much. "I am, and dearly missing the food of my sweet Dehtzlan. But more than that, I thirst for information. What can you tell me of the politics at court?"

"I would prefer to tell you nothing."

Corin showed him a worried frown. "Have things truly grown so bad?"

"I am not a powerful man, milord, and I have no one to protect me. Ask me for wine or rooms, but do not speak to me of court."

"Very well. And you have rooms to rent?"

"One or two, upstairs."

"Just one," Corin said, snatching up his purse. "And see it's clean. I'll take my meal down here while that's arranged."

"I assure you, all our rooms are clean—"

Corin cut him off. "Even so! I am rich in standards and poor in patience. See it done." He turned away and took two steps toward a corner table before calling back with easy authority, "And don't forget the wine!"

Corin fell into a chair with his back to the wall. No news to a stranger, eh? That didn't entirely confirm the druids' suspicions, but it proved they were not alone in their paranoia. Corin would have preferred hard information over such scanty confirmation, but at least he had finally succeeded in procuring food. The duck smelled fat and seasoned, and any wine at all could satisfy Corin's palate. Best of all, the request for a room suggested settling at dawn, so he could likely get away without paying a livre for the lordly meal.

Feeling mighty pleased, the pirate laced his fingers together behind his head, rocked back in his chair, and looked right into the eyes of the purple-robed lady whose purse he'd snatched. Corin's mind raced as she surveyed the room. How could she have caught him? He'd been careful. And how could she have followed his weaving path through the crowded plaza? But surely she hadn't stumbled into the same inn. What would be the chances? She gave a little squeak as soon as their eyes met, and in a flash she came to loom over his table.

For the first time, Corin noticed how bloodshot her eyes were. Harried. The corners were lined with old worry, and her stunning red hair showed here and there the fragile gray of much misfortune. She was not old; everything about her spoke of springtime youth, but it was one much muted by malingering frost.

Pity flushed warm and sudden in the pirate's cruel heart, and right behind it burned a pang of guilt, but he suppressed them both as he rolled smoothly to his feet. He bent in a smooth bow, securing the purloined purse more perfectly beneath his cloak, then offered her a smile.

"Good even to a lovely lady. May I serve you in some way?"

Her troubled eyes narrowed. "You sneaking, thieving wretch!"

He didn't let himself scan the room again for guards. He held her eyes and frowned in mock confusion. "Have we met, milady?"

She jabbed a finger at his face, threatening. "You accosted me in the Piazza Primavera."

A couple at a nearby table turned in shock, and some gentlemen two tables over started to their feet, but Corin made a soothing gesture and met the lady with a surprised recognition. "Gods' blood, that *was* you, wasn't it? What fortune brings you across my path again? If you've come to demand a more intimate and… prolonged apology for our earlier encounter, I'll be delighted to comply."

"You will truly pretend you don't know why I'm here?"

Corin shrugged. "I have always been a lucky man. Today need be no different."

She held her glare for a heartbeat longer than Corin had expected her to, but still, it broke. Uncertainty creased her pretty brow, and once again the pirate had to hide a smile. These nobles were predictable.

He swept a hand toward the table. "Sit with me a while, and we shall clear the matter up. Some wine is on the way, and the barman won't complain to bring another glass."

No sooner had he spoken than the barman proved it true, delivering the open bottle and two glasses, then deftly departing before he could become involved. Corin poured a glass of dark-red wine and passed it to the lady. "To chance encounters and friendly fortunes?"

She cocked her head, outrage and indignation broken up and scattered by Corin's self-assurance. Her hand was still extended, hanging between them in a forgotten accusation. "But...you..."

Corin pressed the glass into her hand and drew a chair for her to sit. "But I would be your friend. Whatever misunderstanding there is between us, I have every confidence we can settle it."

"You...you stole my purse," she stammered, sinking down.

The gentlemen two tables over sank back down in their own chairs. The couple nearest shook their heads and pretended not to listen. Corin took his seat across from the lady and pretended shock. "Are things so bad in Oberon's own city? Are there thieves upon the streets?"

"You mean apart from you?"

Corin spread his hands. "I am no thief, my lady. If you dropped your purse in our encounter, I'm sure we'll find it on the road. Or perhaps a friendly guard will have it for you."

The lady stared at him for a moment, then she snorted in laughter. "Where have you come from?"

"Up north," Corin said, holding to his lie. "This is my first visit to Oberon's shining city. I did not expect a threat of thieves."

She chewed her lip for a moment, considering him. "Is there anywhere so far away that you could be so blind? Or do the king's lieutenants truly spread their lies that well?"

"I don't understand."

She leaned forward, elbows on the table. "Gesoelig is no shining city, farmer. The king has lost his grip, and those who seize control have little care for the people on the streets."

"Ephitel," Corin said. "He would make slaves of us all."

"And not just the manling crowd," she said. "But his fellow elves as well! Can you imagine?"

Corin blinked at the lady, but quickly concealed his shock. "Who will stand against him?"

"Against Ephitel? Are you mad? None would stand against him. He is the lord protector."

"I know a druid who defied him just this afternoon."

"Ha! And she'll be dead by sunset, or buried in cold chains. He shows swift justice in this city."

Corin licked his lips. "I notice you said *she*. Do you know the druid in question?"

The lady paled. She tried to hide her chagrin behind a long gulp from her wineglass, but Corin caught it. He leaned back. "How much do you know?"

She shrugged. "Rumor travels fast these days."

"But not *that* fast, I think. How much do you know?"

The lady set aside her glass and met Corin's eyes with a frank expression. "If anyone would stand against Ephitel, it would be the druids. They could not hope to win, but they are foolish in their way. And loyal as a dog to Oberon."

"And Ephitel knows this? He watches them?"

"Everyone knows," she said. "And everyone watches."

Everyone watches, Corin thought. That had been the way of it in Aepoli. The best way to avoid the investigators' attention was to help focus it on someone else.

The pirate shook his head. "Aye. Everyone watches. Especially those who hope to gain some favor."

The lady swallowed hard, ready to offer some objection, but Corin waved it away. "The university at Rikkeborh could not promise a better education in betrayal than the one I've gained since yesterday. And I was not naive before. I recognize a trap when it is closing around me, and you are hardly subtle. You recognized me on the street. I should have known it then. How much did Ephitel pay you to catch me? How did you lure me to bump you in the first place?"

She sucked a deep breath, ready to deny it all, but a heartbeat later she deflated. "I didn't. That was chance," she said. "And he has paid me nothing, yet. But there's an offer on the druids, and you've been added to that list at a double portion. As soon as I recognized you, I thought…I thought if I could lead you to an investigator…"

Corin shook his head. "And what's your trade, when you are not a sneaking traitor?"

She looked down at her hands. "I was a courtier once."

"Ah," he said. "Your trade was being rich and pretty." She gave him a tight smile, and he shrugged a false apology. "And now?"

"I've nothing. Ephitel's forces seized my father's lands. I thought if I impressed him—"

"He would not have served you well," Corin said. "He does play favorites, but only with those he respects or fears. You would be lucky if he even paid the promised bounty."

With eyes narrowed, she said, "You seem to know him well, for such a stranger to the city."

Corin sighed. "I have seen the world he made." Curiosity flared in her eyes, but he waved away the question. Instead, he dipped a hand inside his cloak and tossed her purse down on the table. "Here's your coin. You're too pathetic to deceive."

"Wait!" she said, frowning. "You really stole my purse?"

He chuckled. "And I'm giving it back. Now I've paid you better than Ephitel ever would."

"I could still turn you in," she said with a glance over her shoulder.

"You could. But you'd be better served by far to let me go."

"How so?"

"My goal is to reach Oberon on his throne. I hope to open his eyes to what is happening. Perhaps no one is brave enough to challenge Ephitel, but Oberon could end this all."

The lady shrank away, eyes wider still. "You would see the king?"

"I will."

"And you think he might help you?"

"I think he might help us all."

Her jaw worked soundlessly. Corin waited patiently for her outburst. She could call him mad, and he could scarce deny it. Instead, she threw herself across the table, clasping both hands in the fabric of his shirt. "Take me! Please. Take me back to court. I have to see the king."

"You were prepared to betray me."

"That was before I knew you. But you…you give me hope for a chance to set things right."

Corin hesitated, and something hot and desperate flared in her eyes. "I beg it of you. You will not regret me. I know the court. I know people there. I know my way around the palace."

"I'd planned to go alone, to avoid notice."

"Ah!" she cried, springing to her feet and feverish with victory. "You see? Already you prove my worth. No one goes alone at court, least of all a manling. You will draw far less attention with a lady at your side."

Corin rubbed his chin, considering. "But there are those who know you."

"Only friends! If any of them still hold a place. But I was never powerful enough to have an enemy."

After another heavy pause, Corin sighed. "I must admit, you could be useful."

She caught his hand in both of hers, looking thrilled. "You mean it? You will take me?"

"I think I must."

"Then come!" She dragged him to his feet and away from the table.

"Not *now*," Corin said, struggling against her surprising strength. "I mean to have a meal first."

"Then we will find you one," she said. "But not here. Come on. We have to leave."

Eyes narrowing, Corin asked, "Why? Exactly why?"

With a blush upon her cheeks, the lady shrugged. "I wasn't sure I could subdue you on my own."

"So you summoned some guards here?"

She looked away. "Nearly so."

"How near?"

She met his eyes. "Ephitel himself. He should be here soon."

(12)

As if in answer to his name, two of Ephitel's guards slammed open the tavern's door and burst through. Corin cursed and shook off the woman's hand. He spun around, hiding his face from the men at the door, and stared down at the table while his mind raced.

Before Corin could fabricate a plan, Ephitel's voice rang out from the direction of the doorway. "Ho! Tavernkeeper!"

The lady shrank against him, breathless. "What do we do?" Corin almost thought she sounded excited.

"We make a desperate plan and hope for the best," he said. He snatched up his glass and swallowed the rest of his wine at a gulp, then reached instinctively into his cloak for a purse that wasn't there.

Instead, his hand closed on the washed-leather bag that had served him so well when he'd rescued Iryana. He threw one quick glance over his shoulder, surveying the room, and saw the tavern's owner emerge from the kitchens, wiping his hands anxiously as he headed toward Ephitel and the guards.

Time was short, and the circumstances were imperfect, but he saw no other way out. A pinch of the dwarven starburst powder had served him in the slaves' tent, but this common room was not as dark, and his opponents were better prepared.

He cursed softly to himself and dropped the whole bag on the table. After a moment's consideration, he turned it upside down, careful that none should spill, and ripped away the braided cord that tied it closed. Now it was little more than a leather cloth gathered over a pile of dust more valuable than a prince's ransom.

The lady bounced upon her toes, anxious to be away. "Really? At a time like this, you pay your bill?"

"Something like it," Corin said. He darted to the nearest table and grabbed the sleeve of the lord seated there, shaking his attention away from Ephitel.

"Please," Corin panted, "please, for the love of Oberon, do *not* let Ephitel see what's on that table!"

Then Corin grabbed the lady's hand again and, without a backward glance, dragged her hastily toward the kitchen. His clothes were well suited to skulking through the gloom, and once the lady stopped protesting, her dark-purple cloak served just as well.

The noisy arrival of the guards had caused some commotion, and as the patrons farthest from the door stretched up on their toes to gain a clearer view, they made a screen for Corin and the lady to slip behind. They went together through a narrow door and right into the sear and clatter of a busy kitchen.

A servant's entrance in the back wall stood open on a narrow alley. Corin grinned and started that way, but he'd barely gone a pace before the lady said, "He'll have guards on that escape."

Corin snatched a pair of heavy knives from a nearby counter, eyed them critically, then tossed one aside in favor of a corer. "Of course he will," Corin said. "But likely only one or two. I can handle one or two guards in a narrow alley."

"Do you mean manling guards or Gesoelig's elves?"

The question stopped Corin in his tracks. He turned to her. "Are they much better?"

She rolled her eyes. "Better than a manling? Yes. Stronger. Faster. Smarter."

"Then arrogant and self-assured," Corin said. "I'll take them by surprise."

"Not Ephitel's men. Careless men do not last long in his command."

Corin rolled his eyes and sighed. "Then let me think." He scanned the room, meeting the curious eyes of a scullery maid and the glare of a cook too outraged to find his voice. Corin offered him a nod, then peeked back out into the common room.

Ephitel and his two guards had found Corin's abandoned table. The tavern's owner was standing behind them, talking frantically, but Ephitel focused entirely on the other patron Corin had spoken to. The ugly little lord was telling everything. At a gesture toward the kitchen, Ephitel nodded and sent the two guards rushing that way.

Corin waited still, just long enough to see Ephitel's eyes dart toward the overturned bag, then Corin grabbed the lady's arm and ran for the back door. He ripped the door open and shouted out into the alley, "Help! Help! He's in the kitchens, dressed up like a cook!"

Then he stepped behind the open door a moment before a uniformed guard came charging in, with another on his heels. Corin dropped the coring knife, caught up a heavy pan from the counter there, and dealt the second soldier a vicious blow to the back of the head. The leading soldier turned at the disturbance, but Corin caught him on the upswing and dropped him senseless.

The lady was still standing where he'd left her, her jaw hanging open. Corin shook his head. "And you said they were smart."

The door to the common room flew wide, one of Ephitel's guards looming nearly large enough to block the gap. Corin glanced over the man's shoulder, then cursed and dove toward the alley door, dragging the lady behind him. He closed his eyes and flung his cloak over his face, but even so—even in the alleyway outside the kitchen—the flare of light and sound stabbed through his head and sent him sprawling.

The effect would have been worse within the kitchen. The guards would be no more threat than those that Corin had assaulted. And in the common room itself, Ephitel would be as good as blind and deaf for hours, if not days. Corin grinned despite the pounding in his head. He blinked to dissipate the purple haze across his vision, then swallowed hard when at last he could see.

A contingent of the Guard was waiting in the alley. Not one or two, but more than a dozen. Some were armed with swords and some with bows. Far more men than Corin could have felled with a stolen pan. But every one had been staring at the open doorway. Now they lay upon the ground or crouched in pain, clawing at their eyes and putting up pitiable wails.

A dozen in the back. How many more out front? It seemed an awful lot to capture one informant. But then…how much did Ephitel know? The druids had expected Corin, had recognized him from something Oberon had said. Could the king have shared the same predictions with his once-trusted lord protector? Could Ephitel know from their short encounter how much a threat Corin truly was?

The lady's groans dragged Corin from his thoughts. She'd had her back to the blast, chasing Corin out into the street, so she was not as badly stricken as the ambushers had been. Still, she stumbled after Corin, eyes strained wide but obviously unseeing.

Corin pulled her close to tell her, "It will pass."

"I'm blind!" she cried.

"You're not blind. It will pass."

"I am! And deaf as well!"

"You'll end up dead or Ephitel's prisoner if you don't shut up. Stay close to me. The powder's effects are not permanent."

When she did not cry out again, Corin nodded and led her down the alley at a trot. There was at least another contingent of the lord protector's guards stationed on the street, but most of them were worse off than the ones he'd left in the alley, and the rest were caught up in a crowd of curious onlookers attracted by the commotion.

Corin and the lady bumped and shoved their way against the current, then finally broke free of the press and settled into the flow of traffic two blocks over. They mixed in with the crowd, moving ever away from the tavern. When Corin judged he had at least two miles behind him and no suspicious eyes watching, he pulled the lady into the shadow of a doorway.

For some time he simply leaned against the stone wall, exhausted, while the lady caught her breath. Then he asked her, "How's your hearing?"

"I hear the sound of bells," she said. "But I am not deaf."

"And your sight?"

"I couldn't stalk a fox by moonlight, but I don't think that's required."

"Not at all," Corin said. "And whatever remains will pass soon enough."

"That is not what troubles me," she said.

"Then what?"

"I did not know there were manling sorcerers. It is a fearsome thought."

Corin chuckled. "I'm no sorcerer. I'm just a man with useful friends."

The lady's eyes narrowed. "What manner of friends? I've never seen the druids do anything like that."

"Not the druids. A dwarf from Aerome."

"Oh, dwarves," she said, dismissive, but a moment later her eyes went wide. "A dwarf! Was that black powder?"

"Not black powder, or everyone in that tavern would be dead. But something like it, yes. Something far more expensive."

The lady wasn't really listening. She tapped a finger to her chin, then shook her head. "Friends with the dwarves. No wonder Ephitel is so interested in you."

"What?"

"The prince has sought for years to get his hands on a good supply of black powder. If he heard of a mere manling who had found a way—"

"I grow tired of that name."

She shrugged. "It is the way of things."

"Still, that cannot be the reason behind Ephitel's interest," Corin said. "I haven't used that powder before in this…place."

"Something about you caught his interest! He is offering a large reward for your head."

"He brought half a regiment to arrest me."

"And *now* he knows about your alliance with the dwarves."

"I don't have an alliance with the dwarves! I stole a leather pouch from a wizard's study."

"Oh." She brightened. "Good."

"Good?"

She shrugged. "It means you will still take me to the king. If you could have offered Ephitel black powder, he'd have bought your loyalty."

"You overestimate his generosity and overlook the larger problem."

"Which is?"

"He's hunting for me now. Our only hope of thwarting him lies in the palace, and I suspect there are more than a few of Ephitel's guards between here and there."

"Thousands," the lady said. "Those who aren't on the streets are stationed—"

"In the palace?" Corin didn't even wait for her nod. "Then I'm out of ideas. We'll have to leave."

A melancholy silence settled over the two of them. Corin peeked out from their nook, searching up and down the street for any sign of Ephitel's guards, then shrank back into the shadows.

The lady was staring at him. "Leave?"

"It's our only chance. We'll slip out of town, find some quiet country place to hide until—"

"Country?" Her voice was shrill. "I'm not leaving the city!"

"Would you prefer to fall into Ephitel's hands?"

"No, but—"

"Then we have to run," Corin said. "It's part of the game when you're playing against powerful enemies. If we give him time to forget about us, it'll give me a chance to learn more about the situation. Make some connections. If I had half the resources here that I commanded back home—"

"What resources?"

The lady's question brought Corin back to himself. He shook his head. "Useful friends, again. I was well connected back home."

Her eyes narrowed. "Connected to what?"

"The city's darker element. There are those who trade in secrets—"

"Oh, thieves," she said, in the same way she'd dismissed the thought of dwarves before. "You'll certainly find more of them here than you would hiding in some manling farmer's barn."

"Yes, but only if I'm at liberty," Corin said. "This is delicate work. It takes time."

"Not really. Just meet with the Nimble Fingers. They call themselves thieves."

This time it was Corin's turn to stare. His mouth worked for a moment before he found his words. "Nimble Fingers? Jezeeli has a Nimble Fingers?"

The lady frowned. "Are there others? I thought it was Avery's own idea."

"Avery? Avery of Jesalich?" He blinked. "I never made the connection."

"What connection? You're a bit obsessed with connections."

"Avery of Jesalich is a legend. He founded the Nimble Fingers."

"He's a bore," the lady said. "But if that's the sort of folk you want to spend your time with—and more importantly, if that will keep me out of the country—I'll be happy to introduce you to him."

"You know Avery of Jesalich?"

"Gesoelig," she said. "And yes. He's my brother."

(13)

Corin found himself in another furtive dash through streets a bit less crowded now that night had fallen. The lady led this time, picking a path with easy familiarity but little care for stealth. At the third turn, Corin had to catch her waist and drag her back behind a wall while half a dozen guards passed on patrol. Instead of thanks, she grunted her indignation, and set off again a moment later.

Corin struggled to believe this reckless girl could be related to the legendary Avery. Founder of the Nimble Fingers. According to their lore, Avery had robbed kings and pickpocketed the gods. Corin nearly missed a step as the words struck him. Gods walked these streets, after all. It could very well be true.

But Avery had built a network of thieves and fences that spanned the world. He'd laid out the rules that governed life outside the gods' law, and those rules had governed Corin's world until the day he took to sea.

Every city in the world had some shady tavern where the Nimble Fingers met, but Corin had not expected one in this time and place. It seemed too practical a thing for this strange city. Too real. Even Aepoli's small Nimble Fingers had far more to offer Corin than the druids could, and now he went to meet the very founders of the organization. To meet Avery himself!

Corin had to contain his excitement as the lady led him out into a courtyard very much like the Piazza Primavera. This time his eyes slid past the gaudy meeting halls and sought the shady alleyway that might lead to the tavern.

But the lady led him straight to the doors of the gaudiest of meeting halls. Black silk banners adorned the carved marble facade, and manling servants dressed in rich black livery lined the wide marble stairs. Corin glanced nervously over his shoulder as he followed her up the stairs, then ducked his head respectfully—and concealed his face in the process—as he passed the private guards stationed outside the doors.

He needn't have bothered. More guards stood at attention just inside, looking sharp in their tailored uniforms. Corin caught the lady's elbow and hissed, "Are you mad? What is this place?"

At the same time, a fresh-faced young lord came bustling up the hall toward them, his eyes locked on the lady. "Are you mad, Maurelle?" he called. "What are you doing here?"

The lady raised her chin and fixed the newcomer with an icy glare. "I am not, *Parkyr*! I've brought someone to speak with Avery."

"But...you haven't even heard?"

"Heard what?"

"Avery is gone. Ephitel's men just came for him."

Corin laughed. "That won't last long."

The lord and lady both turned to Corin, confusion clear in their expressions. Parkyr asked, "Maurelle...who is this manling?"

"He's the one Ephitel wants," she said. "He bumped into me on the street."

"*This* is the one Ephitel wants?" The fancy lord gave a sniff. "I thought he would be taller."

"Whatever size I am, I am a threat to Ephitel's treachery," Corin said. "But I have need of your organization. How many do you have?"

"How many what?"

"Nimble Fingers!"

Parkyr spun on Maurelle. "He knows about that?"

"I do, and you have nothing to fear. How many are there in your organization?"

"Well…we've only just started. So there's…well, Avery and me."

The lady rolled her eyes. "Yes, but you're connected, right? You know the criminal element?"

"We *will*…in time."

Corin stared, stunned. "You are the Nimble Fingers. You and Avery."

Parkyr shrugged. "Just me now. Won't be much of a club."

"A club?" Corin raised his eyes to consider the hall. The foyer opened down onto a sprawling room furnished with high-backed chairs and low, heavy tables. A barman dressed in livery waited at his station against the far wall, and here and there around the room were servants—manling servants—dressed in uniform and waiting patiently.

Everyone was dressed in black.

"The Nimble Fingers was a club," Corin said, awestruck.

Parkyr sighed. "It could have been glorious, but without Avery—"

"You speak of him as though he's lost," Corin said, with less confidence than he'd felt before. "But he's Avery of Jesalich—"

"Gesoelig," Maurelle corrected.

Corin ignored her. "Don't you expect him to escape?"

"From Ephitel's men? Are *you* mad now?"

"Perhaps I am," Corin said. He rubbed his forehead, thinking. Avery of Jesalich was more than some nobleman's son. Even if the Nimble Fingers had truly started like this, it *became* one of the world's most powerful political forces, and it did that under the guidance of Avery of Jesalich.

Corin needed Avery. His only way home seemed to pass through the palace, and if he hoped to slip past Ephitel's guards, he needed help. If anyone could help him, it would be the Avery of legend.

Corin turned to Parkyr. "Where are they taking him?"

"The palace, probably."

"Of course. How long have they been gone?"

"Moments. I'm surprised you didn't see them on the plaza."

"Then we can catch them?"

"Catch them?" Parkyr asked, his voice rising. "You're lucky they didn't catch you."

"Even so, I can't allow them to keep Avery. I need him."

"It doesn't matter. Ephitel has him. You can't defy Ephitel."

"I have been defying him for years." Corin frowned. "Why didn't we see them on the plaza?"

"We did," the lady said. "They rode right past us, but I never imagined they had Avery with them."

"Rode?" Corin's heart sank. He'd seen no soldiers on horseback. "They took him in a wagon?"

"A coach," Maurelle said. "The blue one with—"

"Curtains drawn," Corin said. "I should have spotted that. And they were moving fast. Parkyr, please tell me you know the back roads through this city. Can we catch them?"

"Not on back roads," Parkyr said. "But on the main streets—"

Corin shook his head. "That won't do. I can't afford to show my face."

"Then we draw our curtains, too," Parkyr said. "What's good for the goose, eh?"

Corin turned slowly back to Parkyr. "You have a coach?"

"Just a little hansom my father bought me, but it should carry us all."

"Then show the way!" Corin snapped. "Gods' blood, we have to hurry!"

Parkyr disappeared to speak some brief word with his servants, then returned a moment later to lead Corin and Maurelle back to the stables. Impatient, Corin darted on ahead and entered the stable just as the driver finished hitching two gorgeous horses into their harness. The beasts were worth a fortune, and though the carriage was a small one, it looked sleek and fast and worth just a fraction less. Maurelle and Parkyr paid them all no mind. They swept swiftly past the patient driver and settled fussily into facing seats.

Corin climbed in just behind them. Three times he'd ridden in carriages, in all his years. Twice it had been in chains, and never in a coach as fine as this. The pirate settled on a black silk cushion, feeling more out of place than he had at any time yet in this strange city. Outside a whip cracked, and the carriage slipped into motion.

The chink of dishes caught Corin's attention, and he turned to find Parkyr offering him a china cup, brimful of gently steaming tea. Maurelle sipped at one of her own.

Corin shook his head. "You can't be serious."

Parkyr frowned. "Is something wrong?"

"We do not have tea on a jailbreak!"

Maurelle barked a laugh. "I told you!"

The gentleman's face fell, and he shrugged wretchedly. "I didn't know. I'll throw it out."

Corin snatched the cup from his hand with a deftness usually reserved for richer treasures. "I will overlook this instance. Do you have anything to eat?"

"Sh—should I?"

"In this instance, yes."

Parkyr groaned. "Maurelle made me leave the scones."

"Of course she did," Corin said. He gave a groan and took a long gulp of the hot tea. "Perhaps this isn't such a sin."

Parkyr's face lit up. "You see? The thieves' life doesn't have to be a base one. I've always said as much."

"But you do try to be a thief?" Corin asked.

"Oh, yes! Two hours every Sunday, and whenever I can get away."

"Ah." Corin licked his lips. "And—and Avery?"

"Almost as often."

Corin hid his disappointment. He set aside his teacup and met Parkyr's eyes. "What talents have you learned?"

"I've been working on picking locks!"

"That is a worthwhile start. What manner of locks?"

Instead of answering, Parkyr rummaged in an inner pocket of his coat and produced a small bundle in a washed-leather bag. The bag bore a craftsman's seal and boldly proclaimed, "Beginner's Set." Below that, in block letters, "Opens any lock."

"Any lock at all," Parkyr said.

Corin sighed. He peeked inside the bag, hoping for some work of elven genius, but the contents were precisely the sort of crude, stylized toys so often peddled to the bored sons of noblemen.

Corin closed the bag again, bouncing it in his hands. "Have you tried them against manacle locks, by any chance?"

Parkyr shook his head. "So far...it is mostly conversation."

Conversation. This was not the Nimble Fingers Corin had hoped for. "I understand. Can you fight at all?"

"Not well."

"No. No, why would you?"

Before Parkyr could try to answer, Corin shook his head. "It barely matters. I will find a way." He reached once more toward his cup, but just then the carriage slammed to a hard stop, spilling what was left of the tea across the floor.

"Oh, dear!" Parkyr cried. "Driver! What's happening?"

Corin didn't wait for an answer. He spun to the nearest window, twitched aside the curtain, and recognized an angry mob as soon as he saw it. Parkyr's coach had traveled perhaps a couple of miles from the Nimble Fingers hall. The palace shone like silver moonlight, nearer now than Corin had seen it yet.

But the streets and plazas between here and there were packed with angry men and women. Torches raised in anger lit the night, and the shouts and jeers of the crowd made a hornet's-nest buzz.

Parkyr's coach could not have gained another pace, so densely was the plaza packed. To Corin's delight, theirs was not the only carriage trapped by the press of angry men and women.

"We may be in luck," Corin said over his shoulder. "Is that the jailer's coach?"

Maurelle pressed in close beside him. She smelled of nervous sweat, but her voice thrilled with excitement. "That's him! See, at the window? That's Avery!"

"Fortune has delivered us an opportunity," Corin said. His gaze touched on Parkyr. "And one we dearly needed, I should say. Parkyr, speak with the driver. Find some place clear of the crowd to wait for me, that we may leave quickly when I return."

"When *we* return," Maurelle corrected.

Corin shook his head. "No. Stay with Parkyr. It's far safer—"

"And this is my brother," Maurelle said. "In the hands of my family's enemy. I want to help."

Corin could find no easy answer to that, and time was short. Resigned, he turned to Parkyr. "And you as well?"

The young lord paled. "Me? I...uh...I'd planned to help from in the carriage."

"Good," Corin said. "A noble sacrifice. We will make you proud. Maurelle, are you ready?"

"Not in the least! What is our plan?"

The buzz outside the carriage was rising toward a roar now, and the jostle of the crowd set the light cab rocking like a boat upon the swell. Corin shrugged and answered the lady's question: "We get Avery and we get out of here." A rock smashed against the outer wall with a bang that made Maurelle and Parkyr both jump.

Corin grimaced. "And we do it fast."

(14)

Corin raised his cloak before him almost like a shield as he cracked the coach's door, but no more stones seemed to be aimed in their direction. He gripped Maurelle's trembling hand and led her swiftly down from the carriage and into the press of the angry crowd. She'd scarcely left the coach's step when the driver cracked his whip and bulled a way out of the mob.

In a strange way, moving through an angry riot proved easier than navigating the normal throng that packed this city's streets. The crowd's attention was all focused in the same direction Corin wished to travel, but no one in the crowd seemed particularly anxious to rush to the front. Agitated as they were, they all seemed perfectly content to let someone else run on ahead.

As he went, Corin tried to gauge the source of the crowd's ire. The shouts and jeers were more noise than rhetoric, but Corin felt a flash of hope when he heard more than one angry objection aimed at Ephitel's name. The prince's fierce investigators usually kept close enough watch to prevent the organization of a mob like this. How had this one come to pass?

As quickly as he thought the question, Corin found an answer. A flash of gray hair within the youthful crowd caught his attention. The woman quickly turned away, but Corin recognized Jeff's form two paces away from her, conspicuously silent and sharp eyes watching. They stood at the very heart of the riot. Perhaps directing it. A little help from the druids at last!

Corin had scarcely turned toward them before Delaen shook her head in a definite no. Jeff raised his hand to shoo Corin toward the jailers' carriage. A *little* help, anyway. Corin cursed and dragged Maurelle on.

"What *is* the plan?" she asked. "We can't just charge up and open the door!"

Half a dozen soldiers had emerged from the trapped carriage, and now they stood in a loose circle around it, keeping the angry crowd at bay with bared blades and blows from their heavy truncheons. Some of them looked angry, some regretful, but every one of them seemed ready to do violence to protect their charge.

"Only six," Corin mused. "When he brought a regiment to the tavern. He must not have expected us here."

"There would be more within the carriage."

Corin shook his head. "There's scarcely room for more. But who would sit inside a box with such a threat outside? I think they'd much prefer the room to swing a sword."

"Even so, we cannot conquer six of them."

"Three," Corin said, circling toward his right. "See? We'll let the carriage block the view of those on the other side, so now we only need to worry—"

"Three is as bad as a regiment!" she snapped. "You cannot hope to best three of Ephitel's men in combat."

"Not by myself."

She laughed. "I will not serve you any better than Parkyr there."

"I don't need you to," Corin said calmly.

"Then what—"

"Charge up and open the door," Corin said. Before she could object, he raised his arm high and pointed to the guard standing near the carriage's front axle. That one had a blade already wet with blood. Corin made the gesture big and glanced over his shoulder to see if the druids were watching. Jeff gave a little nod.

Corin turned back to Maurelle. "In a moment, that guard is going to fall."

"How?"

"With some help from the people of Jezeeli, I think." He raised his arm again, pointing to the guard right by the carriage door. This one, too, was using his saber against the crowd, but he had managed with threats what the first had done through pain. "Then that one will fall," Corin said. "As soon as he goes down, run to the door."

Maurelle watched the third soldier swing his truncheon and drop a man senseless. She whimpered. "What about that one?"

"Leave him to me," Corin said. "Just get inside the coach."

Maurelle clenched and unclenched her fists and stood bouncing on her toes, nervous but excited. He squeezed her shoulder and asked, "Are you ready?"

She nodded.

Corin turned his head, making sure the druids could see his profile clearly. Then Corin nodded once. "It should be any moment now."

His eyes fixed on the forward guard, and he hoped for a well-thrown stone. A coordinated push might work as well, but there was greater risk of bloodshed. He watched, waiting, and even as intensely as he stared, he almost missed the strike. Not a stone, not a forward charge, but a tiny dart that glinted glass and steel. Corin had never seen the like. The delicate thing zipped through the air and buried itself in the soldier's neck. A heartbeat later, the guard collapsed.

Maurelle saw him fall. She gave a nervous whimper, but as soon as the second guard fell, she darted forward. Rushing through the startled crowd, she leaped the fallen guard and locked her grip on the carriage door. Her charge drew the third guard's attention.

She saw him coming and she cowered, raising one thin arm to protect her face, but she held her ground, even when the soldier raised his club. Corin felt a flash of pride at that. Then he threw himself upon the guard and caught him from behind.

Corin's right arm locked around the soldier's throat, and with his left he dealt a vicious blow to the soldier's temple. The soldier fell. Panting hard, Corin met the lady's eyes, then nodded to the coach's door. She pulled it open.

Avery of Jesalich sat inside. Alone. Corin breathed his gratitude to fortune, then shoved Maurelle ahead into the cab. He slammed the door behind him and turned to meet his idol.

He dreaded the thought, but Corin had half expected Avery to prove another simpering dandy like Parkyr. To Corin's relief, Avery—even in chains—looked more like a general than some spoiled prince. He held himself erect, tense as a coiled spring, and his dark eyes flashed with a heartfelt passion. He directed it all at Maurelle. "What are you doing here?"

Corin answered for her. "We've come to take you away from Ephitel."

Avery turned his disdain toward Corin. "I do not know you."

"No," Corin said. "But I'm an admirer of your body of work."

"I'm no admirer of yours," Avery said. "How dare you bring my sister into this mess?"

"Excuse me," Maurelle snapped, "but I brought *myself.*"

He rolled his eyes at her. "Well! Then you are more a fool than I thought."

"I'm here to rescue *you!*"

"And I am only a prisoner because Ephitel wanted to catch *you*," Avery said. "Now you've delivered yourself into his hands."

Corin threw a glance at each of them. At a time like this they bantered. He tried to hurry them on. "Not quite. Err...on all counts. Ephitel does not want her, he wants me. And we still have a chance to escape."

"*I* want my sister clear of this," Avery snapped. "And I don't want you anywhere near her. Right now, I consider you far more a threat to her than Ephitel's jailers."

"Avery...I need your help. I know what you are capable of, and I need your skills."

The elven thief turned up his nose. "My skills are not for hire."

For a moment Corin said nothing. He merely held Avery's hostile gaze. Then he looked away. "Well, it is your good fortune that mine are."

He produced the shoddy lockpicks borrowed from Parkyr. They were barely better than a toy, but the heavy manacles used a crude lock and Corin's talents were sufficient to the task. He hesitated one twist shy of slipping the lock, and asked quietly, "Will you trade your services for your freedom? Or will you leave your sister in my hands?"

Avery bristled. "You, sir, are no gentleman."

"Not even a little bit."

"What do you need?"

"To see the king."

"That is not such a difficult thing."

"But Ephitel wants me dead."

Avery frowned. "Ah. I see. And you need me..."

"To help me find a way inside. Or to connect me with the kind of men who can."

"That is *why* I made the Nimble Fingers."

Corin gave him a count of seven heartbeats, then asked, "Well? What will it be?"

"It will not be easy."

"I fought an angry mob and three of Ephitel's jailers just to get this far."

"I suppose you did." Avery gave a heavy sigh. "Very well. I accede." He jerked his wrists, which yanked at the chain and made the lock jump in Corin's hand. The lock twisted against the picks still in place and opened with a *click*.

Avery rubbed his wrists as the chains fell away. He nodded to the far corner of the coach. "Should we take her?"

Corin turned, confused, and for the first time he noticed the prone figure on the coach's floor. Aemilia lay unconscious, draped in chains of her own.

Corin said. "She's a druid, and we can't let Ephitel have her. Do you think you can carry her?"

Before Avery could answer, the door behind Corin flew open. Corin fell away from it, twisting to see, and recognized the soldier he'd assaulted outside the carriage. An ugly purple bruise already showed on the jailer's left temple, but his eyes were sharp and clear. He drew back the heavy truncheon to attack.

Corin had no time to make a plan, no room to maneuver, but Avery uncoiled like a snake, snapping out a kick that passed just by Corin's nose and connected hard with the soldier's jaw. The soldier reeled away, stumbled two paces, then collapsed.

Beyond him, the druid Jeff stood with his arm extended, a strange little weapon like a miniature crossbow in his hand, the glass-and-steel dart not yet fired. Delaen waited by his left shoulder, guiding a pair of strong stallions on leather leads. She hissed something in his ear, and Jeff hurriedly concealed the weapon. Then he rushed toward the carriage door. Beyond them, the crowd was draining from the courtyard.

Corin nodded to Jeff as he approached. "They have Aemilia. She's unconscious."

Corin scooped her up, with some help from Avery, and passed her across the cab and down into the druid's waiting arms. So close by, Corin caught Jeff's expression clearly. It was apology and regret, though it lasted just a moment. Jeff tore his gaze away, heaved Aemilia's limp form up in front of his saddle, and scrambled up.

Corin tried to follow after him, but Jeff quickly spun away. Corin shouted, "Wait! We have a coach!" but the druids didn't meet his eyes. They didn't wait. They galloped hard across the emptying plaza and disappeared down a dark alley.

Corin was left standing alone, surrounded by the fallen forms of guards and the rioters those guards had felled. While Avery and Maurelle came down behind him, Corin shook his head. "So. That's why the druids helped."

"And that," Avery said, pointing past Corin's shoulder, "is why the crowd is thinning."

Corin had already spotted it. Ephitel rode into the plaza, shining like a star in silver-chased armor. More than a hundred mounted soldiers rode behind him, fanning out as they entered the plaza until they filled the far edge from end to end.

Avery darted to the rear of the carriage to look past it, back toward the Nimble Fingers' hall, but Corin didn't bother moving. "The other way is blocked, too," Avery called.

"Of course it is," Corin said.

"We'll never get this carriage moving fast enough to escape the cavaliers."

Corin shook his head. "Not a chance."

"So how did you plan to escape?"

"In Parkyr's coach."

Avery heaved a disappointed sigh. "You're going to need another plan."

"I've just devised one," Corin said, while Ephitel spurred his line forward at a walk. The prince had eyes like a hawk's, sharp even behind his visor, and they never drifted from Corin's face.

Corin licked his lips, mind racing. Then he raised his hands high and shouted, "We're unarmed. And we surrender. Take us before the king."

(**15**)

Across the plaza, Ephitel's face twisted in a cruel grin. He came forward at the same slow advance.

"This is your plan?" Avery hissed.

"It gets us in the palace," Corin answered under his breath.

"In the dungeons! That is not the same at all."

"Can you think of something better?"

"Yes! You should have left town! Hidden in some manling farmer's barn for a week while you made some connections and plotted something that might actually work."

Corin swallowed his first sarcastic response. He said, "Maurelle believed the Nimble Fingers would be connections enough."

"Not to challenge Ephitel. Oberon himself might not be connection enough."

Ephitel's arrival ended that conversation. For a long moment, he sat in judgment over them, his cohort spread out in tableau.

Then he spoke. "Avery of the House of Violets. While under charge, you have further dared to despise the custody of the Royal Guard. And here's your pretty sister, Maurelle of the House of Violets. A conspirator in your crimes."

Avery's whole body tensed in anger and fear, but the gentleman did not dare object. Corin had no such restraint. "She's done no—"

"And you," Ephitel boomed, smiling even as he voiced his grim displeasure. "Corin Hugh of Aepoli, a manling vagabond far from home now meddling in the affairs of his betters."

Corin staggered at those words. How had Ephitel learned his identity? The answer came to him in a moment. "Aemilia..."

Corin barely breathed the name, but Ephitel nodded. "You have led me on a merry chase, slinking fox, but the moneylender made for docile prey."

But she's escaped your net, Corin thought. He strove to hide the flash of satisfaction from his eyes, but Ephitel reacted. He spurred his stallion forward, knocking Corin back, and kicked aside the open carriage door. He stared inside. Corin itched to have some weapon—the sword he'd left behind, or even the crude knives he'd nearly borrowed from the kitchen earlier. For one long moment Ephitel left his back turned on Corin, and the pirate yearned to bury three feet of sharp steel in it.

Maybe not *too* sharp.

Then the prince wheeled in a fury. "Where is she? Where has the druid gone?"

One of his lieutenants pressed forward. "She must have slipped away with the crowd."

"Impossible!" Ephitel shouted. "She carried a draught of the druids' own sleeping potion. That would have rendered her as useless as these fools upon the road." His eyes narrowed in sudden suspicion. "What has happened here?"

Panic burned behind Corin's breastbone. He couldn't let Ephitel suspect the druids' involvement. Corin pushed forward and raised his chin. "I came to rescue Avery."

"I have seen something of your tricks," Ephitel said. "This is not your handiwork."

"It is!" Corin shouted. He pointed to the guard he'd overcome earlier. The unfortunate soldier was stirring now, groaning softly, and matching bruises blacked both his eyes. Corin darted toward him. "Ask this one. I fell upon him like a storm at sea."

Ephitel followed Corin until he sat staring down at the stirring soldier with the same disdain he had shown to Corin before. "Yeoman Kellen. I should not be surprised to find you embroiled in this affair."

Yeoman Kellen stopped stirring, although he did give one more heartfelt groan.

Ephitel leaned one arm against his pommel and asked icily, "Do you need aid, Yeoman Kellen?"

"No, sir," the fallen soldier said. His eyes snapped open, and Kellen winced once, then began the laborious process of climbing to his feet. "No, Lord Ephitel. I am able."

"Hardly," the prince said. "What happened here?"

"Riot, sir. There might have been a thousand angry citizens—"

"Rebels," Ephitel growled.

Kellen swallowed hard, then shrugged. "As you say. Torches and stones."

"What was their intent?"

Kellen swallowed hard again, and this time he looked away. "I couldn't make it out."

"Ha!" Ephitel leaned back and shook his head. "You've never had a spine, Yeoman Kellen. I feel your time among my men is at an end."

The yeoman hung his head in shame and gave no answer.

"And what of my other brave jailers?" Ephitel cried, apparently hoping to stir more of them. "So much disturbance, and still they sleep, though I see no mark upon them. One might even think these others suffered the effects of druids."

Ephitel's lieutenant called out, "Sir!" from where he knelt beside one of the fallen men. "Even so. These are the druids' poisoned darts." He brandished one of the shiny projectiles Corin had seen before.

"Aha," Ephitel said, "proof at last of their treachery."

"No," Corin cried, inventing wildly. "That's my doing, too."

"Impossible."

"Not at all. I...the druids took me in. As you well know. And...while I was in their care, I stole these trinkets."

"Is that so?" Ephitel asked, a strange, hungry look in his eyes. "You are quite the resourceful one. Yeoman Kellen! Tie him up."

"Tie him, sir? There are chains in the carriage—"

"Chains he has already defeated once, you will find. As I said, he is a resourceful one. Tie him with an elven knot." He turned aside for a moment, running his eyes over his other prisoners. "We should have a knot for Lord Avery, too. Chains will suffice for Lady Maurelle."

"No!" Avery cried. "Let her go!"

Ephitel spurred his horse two quick steps closer to Avery, then answered the angry thief with an armor-plated kick to his unprotected stomach. Avery folded double, then collapsed in a whimpering pile. Ephitel spat down at him. "Watch your tongue when you speak to the lord protector." He turned dispassionate eyes back to Kellen. "Well? Tie them!"

The soldier sprang into action. He uncoiled a cord from around his upper arm, something fine and gilded that Corin had taken for decorative braiding. But as Kellen unrolled the cord and drew out a measured length of it, Corin recognized the hair-fine thread. In his time it was an artifact, a relic of the ages when elves walked with men. But he was in those ages now, and Yeoman Kellen approached to bind his hands with a delicate thread that could have held an anchor through any gale. Now two loops went over each hand, and Kellen pulled the knot tight with a simple gesture, but Corin found no slack, no loose edges, no angle to escape the bindings.

"There's a handy trick," Corin said. "Why use manacles at all?"

Ephitel moved closer, eyes narrowed. "It is strange the things that you don't know. And, then again, the ones you do."

It took only a moment before Corin understood. The dwarven powder. Maurelle had told him Ephitel craved the stuff. Corin shook his head, "I am just a manling vagabond—"

"Rich in mystery and richer in defiance," Ephitel said. "We have a place set aside for such as you." He jerked his head toward the coach. "Take them to the palace dungeons. And you! Take thirty men and hunt down the traitor druids."

Halfway to the carriage, Corin wrenched against his captors' grip to shout back, "No! The druids had no part in this!"

"You are a wretched liar," Ephitel answered. He told his lieutenant, "Go. Now." Then he turned back to the jailers' carriage as two of his soldiers forced Corin into its confines. "Two insignificant children from the House of Violets, and one mysterious manling from out of time," Ephitel mused, almost to himself. "What can you have in common?"

Corin suppressed his angry response. He said, "Innocence?"

"Hardly." The prince stepped back half a pace so Yeoman Kellen could heave the groaning Avery up into the cab with Corin and Maurelle. Ephitel considered them all for a moment, then nodded slowly. "This shall be interesting. I must speak with Oberon."

"I would speak with him, too," Corin said. "Shall we go together?"

Ephitel's brows crashed together. "*You* shall go to the darkest prison I can find for you."

"I demand an audience with the king."

"It is not your right to demand such a thing."

"Avery, then—"

"No. By its association with you, the House of Violets has lost such rights as well." Ephitel grinned. "Oh, you may prove useful to me after all."

"Gods' blood!" Corin snapped. "What have they done against you?"

"Be careful of the threats you make," Ephitel answered him. "Yeoman Kellen! Are the prisoners secure?"

"Yes, Lord Ephitel."

"Very good. You will accompany them to the dungeons."

"Yes, Lord Ephitel. And who will join me? The rest of my unit are still upon the road."

"So they are," Ephitel said. "I believe you will go alone."

Kellen looked into the confines of the carriage, and a little shudder shook him. Corin understood. Once the carriage was in motion it would become an island, isolated, and on that island Yeoman Kellen would be much outnumbered by his charges. Even with their hands bound, they could do him no small damage. Jailers always preferred numbers until their prisoners were safely in cells. This was near enough a suicide order, or must have seemed so to the yeoman.

He swallowed hard. "Alone, sir?"

"You have your orders."

For a moment he seemed prepared to argue. Then he meekly bowed his head and reached to retrieve the truncheon that had fallen from his grip. Ephitel urged his horse forward, and a steel-shod hoof slammed down on the haft of the hardened club, reducing it to splinters. Kellen barely kept his hand.

The yeoman leaped back, looking to his lord protector in shock. Ephitel nodded pointedly at the sword on Kellen's belt. "A soldier of mine should not fear a little bloodshed."

Kellen nodded, defeated, then turned and climbed into the carriage. A moment later the door slammed shut, and everyone within it could hear the locks on the outer doors slamming into place. Outside, Ephitel sniffed. "Ease your heart, Yeoman Kellen. I would not trust these prisoners to your charge for all the gold in Oberon's coffers. There will be forty of your stalwart companions riding along outside." Then he shouted a command and the carriage jerked into motion, dragging them all toward the palace dungeons.

(**16**)

For some time silence reigned within the carriage while Corin plotted. He had learned much in the brief exchange between the lord protector and his reluctant guard. This Yeoman Kellen seemed hesitant to execute Ephitel's cruelty, and that could prove a boon. If Corin could just find the best approach, he might make an ally of their captor.

But Avery spoke first. He leaned forward, hands still bound by the elven knot, and fixed his jailer with a vicious glare. "So," he said, "this is Yeoman Kellen, the famous coward of the Royal Guard!"

It seemed a foolish provocation. Corin looked sideways at his hero.

Kellen rested his hand on the hilt of his sword. "Be careful how you address me, Violets. You are still bound."

"And you are still a coward."

Corin said softly, "Careful."

Kellen nodded. "You should listen to your accomplice here. You've given me more than one reason to make you bleed."

Avery laughed. "I doubt you have the nerve."

Shocked, Corin turned to him. "What are you doing?"

Kellen answered for him. "He's lashing out. His actions cost his house its standing, and he hates the lord protector for enforcing Oberon's law."

"A mere pretext," Avery spat. "Ephitel despised my father long before I started making waves."

Corin sighed. These were the politics he'd so hoped to avoid. But now he needed some cooperation between these two. He caught Avery's eyes. "And why do you hate Kellen for Ephitel's actions?"

"I hate all his little toadies," Avery sneered.

"Yet he has never said a word," Kellen answered. "Except he's heard my name, and he thinks I am toothless."

"I've heard your name, for it was you who clapped my father in his chains," Avery said. "When your father had once been my family's friend."

Kellen bit his lip. That told Corin all he needed to know. The yeoman turned away. "I had my orders. I could not disobey."

"And so I'll say again, you are a coward."

Corin rolled his eyes. "You are a bore." He turned back to Kellen. "We have no quarrel with you, Yeoman. In fact, our enemy and yours might be the same."

Kellen frowned. "Who do you mean?"

It was a gamble, but Corin was a gambler. He shrugged. "I mean your master, Lord Ephitel."

Kellen shook his head. "He is not my master, merely my superior. I have no master but King Oberon."

Corin hid his grin. He scooted to the edge of his seat. "Then even more you should consider us your friends. Our only goal is to protect the king. Lord Ephitel has made himself a threat."

"These are courageous accusations," Kellen said. "Ephitel is powerful, and he is trusted by the king."

"Perhaps, but the lord protector keeps his secrets. Do you know that he is hoarding writs of provender?"

Kellen frowned. "Why would he do this?"

"To field an army. To defy the king. The druids have recognized the threat he poses, and now the lord protector turns his malevolence against them."

"How does that concern you? You are not a druid."

"They have asked me to carry a warning to your king."

Kellen frowned. "You show great foolishness, sharing your intelligence with a soldier in the Royal Guard."

"I count it little risk," Corin said, "for you are loyal to the king, and Ephitel has shown how poorly he esteems you. We would show you more respect—"

Avery interrupted. "Speak for yourself, manling. Some of us know the Kellen name."

Kellen's eyes flashed fury.

Corin stopped himself from kicking Avery's shin, but just barely. He kept his attention fixed on the yeoman. "If you but help us—"

"Help you?" Kellen demanded. "Assist the lord protector's enemies? I would have to be a brave man indeed to take that risk. I prefer the company of honorable men."

"There was no honor in your lord protector's accusations. How can you serve such a man?"

"There are words," Kellen said, "and then there are actions. I bear the mark of the respect you offered me."

Corin shook his head, frantic. "We could not have known you were loyal, while you stood with Ephitel in opposition to our efforts for the king."

Kellen raised his chin. "You argue well, but I have never known a criminal without a smooth tongue. You will have a chance to make your case, but it will not be here before me. Keep your silence."

Avery sighed. "What else could we expect? I'd leave another mark upon him if I could."

Corin turned to him. "It does not help our cause to gain this man's enmity."

"Trouble yourself not," Avery said. "It would not help our cause to gain his favor, either. No, we will have to find our freedom by another means."

Kellen shook his head. "You will be lucky to find freedom at all. No one leaves the lord protector's dungeons."

Corin tried to apologize, but Kellen silenced him with a firm shake of his head. "I will hear no more from either of you!"

Silence fell again, and Corin brooded. Avery had shown some talent. There was one small mercy. But his arrogance now made an enemy of a man who might otherwise have been a useful friend. An ally in the Guard would have served them well.

But Corin only sighed. Such was his fortune in this place. He'd found no more aid from friends than he'd received from his own crew within the cave. The druids had recruited him, then sent him off all on his own. True, they'd shown up for his jailbreak, but only...

No, he realized. They had not shown up for him. They could not have known what Corin planned. The riot had been a project of their own, with no other aim than to rescue Aemilia. When Corin appeared, they had let him break into the jailers' carriage for them, then left him high and dry, at Ephitel's mercy.

So why had he fought so hard to guard their secret? Why had he lied to Ephitel to protect those who had betrayed him? He chewed his lip, considering, and it was not until he raised his eyes to Maurelle that he found his answer. She huddled in the corner, silent through all the argument between her brother and her captor, but her eyes burned on Corin with a feverish hope—a desperate need to make things right.

And there was his answer. In all this wretched city, they alone dared to defy Ephitel. She saw it in Corin, and he saw it in the druids. Corin had no hope that he might be the man who killed a god, but whatever he could do to serve the druids, if it hobbled Ephitel, he would gladly make the sacrifice.

But what was *he* to do? He'd hoped a plea might be enough to gain him a royal audience, even if it were a trial. With that avenue cut off, he'd have to manage an escape. The raucous clatter of hoofbeats outside the coach's walls proved Ephitel had kept his word. The prisoner transport traveled with a healthy escort. Easier then to wait until they'd been forgotten in some stinking cell and escape from chains and bars.

It would not be the first time Corin had accomplished such a feat, though he'd never faced a palace dungeon before. He could have some aid from Avery, but—for all the damage they had done Kellen—the reviled soldier still seemed their last, best hope. Corin tried again. "Yeoman Kellen—"

He got no further. Faster than a blink, the soldier drew his sword and pressed its tip to Corin's throat.

"Not another word," the soldier said, his voice as hard as the blade's edge, "or I'll betray my pledge as your secure steward and likely win a commendation for it."

"That you would," Avery said softly, sounding a bit impressed. "You very likely would."

Corin held his tongue. A moment later Kellen nodded, satisfied, and laid the blade across his knees. He didn't sheathe it, and no one spoke for the rest of the rattling ride.

When they stopped at last, the open doors revealed not the grand front gates or a majestic palace entrance, but a barred and fortified carriage yard somewhere else within the palace grounds. Somewhere far more...military.

The escort was there as Ephitel had promised it would be—easily half a hundred men, crowding the courtyard and bristling with pikes and crossbows, all of them aimed at the three prisoners. Ephitel himself came forward to watch the prisoners leave the carriage. Corin watched him, wary. The strutting lord should have gone off to see the king. It was unsettling to see him here.

Kellen was the last out, and he stumbled when he saw the lord protector. "My…my lord! I understood that you intended to go directly to the king."

Ephitel didn't meet the soldier's eyes, but still he answered. "I have had time upon the journey to reconsider. I would prefer to have some answers from the miscreants before I attempt to make a report to Oberon. Come."

He turned, and the crowd of soldiers opened a path to a heavy door, barred in iron and secured by half a dozen locks. It opened with a groan and revealed a stairway walled with stone that plunged down into the darkness underneath the palace. The soldiers jostled Corin, Maurelle, and Avery until the prisoners fell into a single-file line, which was all the narrow stairway would allow. Yeoman Kellen went on ahead, Corin close behind him, and from the sound of footsteps Corin knew that only one more escort accompanied the brother and sister behind him. He never doubted who that might be.

Once or twice along the long descent, Corin passed a narrow landing before the path turned back and down. At each such landing, a pair of wardens stood attentive beyond a gate of iron bars, armed with heavy crossbows more than able to cut down any prisoner attempting an escape from below. Down and down they went, deep beneath the earth, until at last Corin stepped onto a landing that had no further descent. Here, too, a gate looked out onto the landing, and Kellen approached it with all the dignity and authority Ephitel had denied him before.

He saluted the two wardens standing watch, then called out in a strong, clear voice, "Three prisoners, upon the mercy of the king, arrested under order of Lord Ephitel for breach of peace."

In the wider landing, Avery stepped up beside Corin. He spoke under his breath. "I could garrote him with his own elven cord. How funny would that be? I guarantee those guards would only watch and laugh."

Maurelle stepped up beside Avery and clutched at his arm. Irritation and worry creased the lordling's brow. It only grew worse when Ephitel stepped past them and into the wardens' torchlight.

"Calm yourself, Kellen," Ephitel said smoothly. To the wardens, he said, "These are troublemakers who must be well watched. And I count not three, but four."

"My lord?" Kellen asked, a quaver in his voice.

"As I said, I had time upon the journey to consider. What I discovered looked too much like a plot. Five good men rode with you to bring back my druid and my elf. Five of them are convalescing now, sick with druid poison. But you alone suffered only superficial blows—"

"They were hardly superficial! I'll vow I've suffered more than those sleeping from a nettle's sting."

"Yet you were not incapacitated, when all the others were. You stink of complicity."

Kellen trembled with a futile rage. "I *detest* these criminals."

"And we return the sentiment," Avery offered.

Ephitel casually backhanded the gentleman, never moving his gaze from Kellen. "Yeoman, I cannot believe that one manling vagabond and the worthless daughter of a dishonored house might have overcome a squad of my best men. Not without some aid."

"I would never—"

"Nonetheless," Ephitel said, "this matter bears close scrutiny, and I will not risk your liberty before it is settled. Find a cell."

Ephitel nodded to the wardens. They turned a heavy key and swung wide the landing's gate. Kellen stood for a moment, jaw working without words, then turned on his heel and slunk through the open gate. Beyond, a narrow passage separated half a dozen tiny cells, all empty. Kellen chose the second from the left, trudged inside, and slammed the heavy iron door behind him.

Ephitel turned to the other prisoners. "And these," he said. "Before you see them in cells of their own, strip them of whatever tools they may possess. They have proven themselves resourceful to a surprising degree. You may leave them their clothes, but nothing more."

The jailers immediately set to the task, one of them searching all the many pockets inside Corin's cloak. Ephitel watched with an apparent hunger, but the most interesting thing the warden found was Parkyr's lockpick set. The soldier offered it with a victorious flourish, proof of Corin's villainy, but Ephitel dismissed it with a wave.

Red-faced, the younger jailer suffered Maurelle the indignity of a close search. Avery snarled to see his sister groped by such ungentle men, but one raised eyebrow from Ephitel was enough to silence him. Avery was searched as well, though he clearly had been disarmed before his prior arrest. Then a jailer pointed toward Kellen's cell. "And him?"

Ephitel laughed. "Kellen?" He approached the soldier. "Yeoman! Yield to me your sword."

Utterly defeated, Kellen unbuckled his sword belt and passed it through the bars. Ephitel tossed it aside to clatter against the stone floor near the wardens' station. "Even that was probably unnecessary," he said. "I've never seen this one draw blood. He is lucky his father served Oberon so well, or he might have to find some *useful* occupation."

Ephitel turned back to the jailers. "Lock them up. But not this one. I would have a word with him yet." He caught Corin by the collarbone and dragged him some short distance back toward the stairs. There was no room for privacy—this place was not designed for such things—but Ephitel cast an imperious gaze around the landing, and the wardens at least pretended not to be listening.

If Ephitel was even talking to him, Corin had a chance. But even absent Kellen's sad display, Corin knew better than to play the meek prisoner. Strong men were always brash, and Ephitel's sort had no respect for any other kind. Corin gave a weary sigh. "What do you want of me?"

"I want you to understand the cost of defying me. Do you see how vagabonds are treated in my city?"

"Your city? I understood it was Oberon's."

"The king has tasked me to keep the peace. In this regard, at least, it is my domain."

"And you show so much attention to every vagabond?"

"Not at all. Most are beaten senseless and left outside the city walls."

"Hospitable."

"But most do not walk around with a thousand livres of dwarven powder in their pockets. And none would dare employ it against the innocent patrons of an honest tavern."

Corin shook his head. "I know of no such powder. But if I did, I would have employed it against you, not the innocent patrons."

"A dangerous statement," Ephitel said. "You would not want me for an enemy."

"And yet I seem to have you all the same."

Ephitel stepped closer and lowered his voice. "But perhaps you may find another way to employ the dwarven powder."

Corin frowned. "How is that?"

"For all the threat you pose, for all the damage you have done, I could yet be willing to turn you loose, if you prove useful to me."

"I have heard offers like this before."

"Not like this," Ephitel said. "And never from such as me."

"What do you require, then?"

"A large supply of dwarven powder."

"But the city, as you say, is your domain. Can you not acquire that supply yourself?"

"There are...limitations," Ephitel said. "These same limitations should make it impossible for a manling like you to acquire any such powder at all. And yet you carried a full bag."

"Did I? I don't recall."

"Don't toy with me. I know you had a hoard of powder. That tells me one of two things: you have a compromising friend among the dwarves, or you have the skills and knowledge to acquire the powder despite them. I would reward you well for either resource."

"I'm afraid my resources would be of little use to you."

"Likely," Ephitel replied. "Likely that small bag was the limit of your abilities, where I need crates. But I have resources of my own. Show me where to start, and I will find reward enough for us all."

"It's no small thing you ask of me, to defy the orders of Oberon and betray the secrets of the dwarves."

"Ah, but yours is no small crime that I am prepared to forgive."

"I'm sorry, Ephitel. Forgiveness is not reward enough for me."

The prince lowered his brows. "Then what would satisfy you? A pile of gold? A name? An estate within the city? I can give you all these things."

"But will you?"

Ephitel showed his teeth in what was meant to be a smile. "I give my word."

"And all you ask of me?"

"A name. A place. Whatever lead it takes to gain access to their storehouses."

"You have a deal," Corin said. "I'll give you the name for a thousand pistoles."

Ephitel grinned and clapped his hands together. "A princely sum!"

But Corin shook his head. "That's not all. You must also free Maurelle and Avery." He hesitated, then added, "And Yeoman Kellen."

"The elves are no concern of yours."

Corin crossed his arms over his chest. "I regret to say that I must insist."

Ephitel sighed. "Maurelle I can give you. And Kellen, though I cannot imagine why you'd want him. But Avery's name has already been committed to a warrant. It would be no small matter to arrange his release."

"Nonetheless, it is a matter you must attend to. I will not leave here without Avery."

Ephitel narrowed his eyes. "Be careful how you answer me. I am not known for my generosity."

Corin shrugged. "And I am not known for leaving my crew in dangerous waters. You have my answer."

"Then I will give you mine," Ephitel shouted. "You may rot in here forgotten! If I come back for you at all, you will wish I hadn't."

While Ephitel swept up the stairs, the jailers came for Corin. He went quietly. There were not cells enough for the guards to fully follow Ephitel's demands, but they had seen enough of his treatment of Kellen that they did not consider him a true collaborator. So Corin had the first cell on the left and Avery the third with Kellen separating them. Across the corridor, Maurelle had the center cell alone.

The jailers checked the lock on Corin's door, and all the others', too, but they seemed easily satisfied. They soon resumed their places by the gate, half-turned to watch the landing and the prisoners at once. Corin waved to them, then took a seat on his narrow cot and leaned his back against the wall, trying hard to look completely unambitious.

Kellen interrupted his pretense. "He means it, you know. You would not be the first to rot, forgotten, in these cells. You should have taken his offer."

"I have no faith in the promises of Ephitel."

"Do you hold hope the druids will come save you? They can't. They have no access to these dungeons."

Corin shook his head. "They wouldn't even try."

Kellen nodded slowly. "So you hoped to escape on your own?"

"I did," Corin said. "But this is no easy prison to escape. Even without the fortified courtyard up above, every landing on the stair is a guarded checkpoint."

"As I said, you should have taken Ephitel's offer."

Corin had no answer. The yeoman fell silent for a while, but he was clearly troubled. He wrung his hands and shifted on his cot, then finally he spoke again. "Why did you ask for me?"

Corin shrugged. "You do not deserve to be here."

"You do not know me. You could have asked for more in gold. Why speak my name?"

Corin turned to face him for a moment. The pirate sighed. "I have a special fondness for anyone despised by tyrants. Such men are my friends, even if I do not know them yet."

Kellen nodded slowly over Corin's words. He stared at his hands, then gave a smirk. "You should not have asked for Avery. Even Avery agrees."

"I need Avery."

"For a thousand pistoles, you could have bought a better man and changed his name."

Corin laughed. "It doesn't matter. Ephitel would not have paid. I would rot down here no matter what I said."

"How can you know that?"

"You heard his words. He wants a secret from me, and it is not a secret he can risk out in the world."

Kellen chuckled, though there was no joy in the sound. "It is a poor secret if he discusses it where we all can hear."

Corin held his eyes for a moment, then repeated what the yeoman had told them in the carriage. "No one leaves the lord protector's dungeons." The pirate glanced toward the wardens and frowned. "Although this does not look good for them."

Kellen shook his head. "He might just trust that we don't understand. I heard his words, but they meant nothing to me. I barely grasp what's going on."

"You heard how freely Ephitel defies the king."

"Yes, but I cannot guess why."

"Then I will tell you," Corin said. "Ephitel seeks dwarven powder. Do you know what that is for?"

"Everyone knows. It's used in holiday rockets and for excavation. Perhaps Ephitel means at last to carve a road through the Elpan Mountains."

"Why would he not ask the powder of Oberon then? No. I'll grant you rockets and excavations, but I'd wager everything he wants it for cannons and guns."

"Cannons *and* guns?" Kellen asked, looking confused. "They are not the same? I have heard of cannon…"

"By guns, I mean firearms. Muskets. Flintlock pistols." The bafflement on the yeoman's face told Corin everything he needed to know.

"You don't have guns. There are no guns. Yet. Oh, gods' blood!" Corin hissed. "Ephitel is bringing guns to Jezeeli! That is how he means to overthrow the king."

(**18**)

Horror gripped Corin at the thought. He hated guns almost as much as he hated Ephitel. The one was distant and terrible, the other sharp and close at hand. If ever a weapon had been made to kill a god, surely it was the flintlock musket. He shuddered at the thought.

It changed nothing. That thought alone comforted him. His only goal was to go back home. He'd made a promise to share the news, and now the news grew far more grim, but he had every hope of being gone before Ephitel could kill the king. Delaen had said it would take weeks or months to spend the writs of provender. That was more than time enough.

He took a calming breath and turned his attention back to their escape. Throughout it all he kept his eyes upon the wardens, but for now, at least, their attentions were still fixed upon the outer landing. By all appearances they trusted the cells to hold the prisoners. Still, Corin lowered his voice to something just above a whisper. "We must get to the king. Do you have any friends among the guards?"

Kellen shook his head. "You've heard how they consider me."

"We may be running thin on fortune. This is a tougher dungeon than I've faced before, and we are out of allies."

The silence stretched out for a while. When Kellen spoke again, Corin barely heard the whisper. "Come closer to my cell. Show me your wrists."

Corin did as he was told, scooting closer to the wall between the two cells. He felt a spark of hope as soon as he understood. The elven knots that only Kellen could undo! Ephitel had placed his trust in them.

And, as it happened, he had placed too little suspicion on Yeoman Kellen. Corin watched, astonished, as Kellen drew a heavy knife from his belt. The yeoman breathed some quiet word in his own tongue, then sliced through the unyielding cord as though it were cobweb. As Corin's bindings fell away, the pirate caught the soldier by his sleeve. "And Avery as well."

Kellen shook his head.

"We cannot do this without Avery," Corin insisted. "I need his help."

Kellen frowned, but at last he nodded. Corin nodded back. "Good. See to that, but not right now. They will watch with some suspicion for an hour, but then they'll settle in for the long wait. That is when we move."

Kellen's eyes darted to the guards. His hands shook. "I cannot wait that long."

"You can," Corin said. "Be valiant as your father was. For Oberon!"

It was a gamble, but it worked. Some spark of noble pride flared in the yeoman's eyes, and he nodded.

"Good," Corin said. "In half an hour—"

A shout from one of the wardens interrupted him. "You two! Break it up!"

Corin glanced that way, then slunk back to his cot with his wrists still close together. The warden still stared at him, suspicious. Corin shrugged and showed a sheepish grin. "I thought perhaps a member of the Guard might know how to escape this place."

In his cell, Kellen gasped, but the warden merely laughed. "You picked the runt of the litter, but even old man Bryer here couldn't help you. There's no way out but up!"

He rang his sword against the metal bars of the landing gate, and the clatter that it made echoed in the narrow dungeon.

The older of the two, sharp-faced Bryer, caught the other guard a lazy backhand. "To your post," he growled. "And you! Keep still and keep to yourself. That goes for all of you. I've never yet earned the lord protector's ire, and I don't intend to do it over such a sorry lot."

Corin shrugged again and settled back against the wall. From the corner of his eye, he saw Kellen's nervous expression. Corin made calming gestures, all composed, then closed his eyes to slits and, minutes later, started snoring.

It was a good snore, starting low and irregular but building over time. Soon the stone walls growled with it. Corin kept it up for five minutes, maybe ten, then cut the snores abruptly short. Silence fell across the dungeons, broken only by a relieved sigh from somewhere down the line. The pirate let the silence spin out, heartbeat after heartbeat, then he smashed it with a *snnrkkrt*.

Warden Bryer snapped. He bellowed, "Cut that out!" and hurled a battered tin cup at Corin's head. Its handle clanked against the bars as it was passing through, or it would have caught Corin just above the ear. Instead, it skipped off the ground with a whining ting and leaped right into his cot.

"No more snoring!" Bryer yelled. "No more! If I have to carve your flesh to keep you awake, I will. I swear by postulates and proofs!"

Corin blinked as though through bleary eyes and offered his jailer an apologetic shrug. Then he shifted in his cot, sinking down to a more comfortable position—wrapping his body around the tin cup as he did so—and pretended to settle into a gentler doze.

The snore was mostly meant to rattle nerves, and it had certainly done that. It was a trick he'd learned from Sleepy Jim and, with time enough, it almost always drew a similar effect. The tin cup had merely been a lucky break. Luckier still that Bryer's aim had damaged it, because Corin had little trouble prying at the cheap, twisted metal of the handle until it came loose. That gave him a tool. With time and care, he could make a decent lockpick of the thing or sharpen its edge into a decent shiv.

For now, Corin simply needed the weight. He snuggled under his cloak, pulling it tight around him, then reached into the lining of his cloak and worried free the end of a long, thin wrapped wire that Ephitel's jailers had overlooked. He drew it out, inches at a time, until he had a cord most of four paces long.

He tied one end around the weight of the cup's handle, then looped some of the rest around his wrists, a crude disguise to imitate the elven knot. The larger loops he tucked beneath his arm where the cloak would hide it well.

Then he judged it time to act. He struggled upright, swayed for a moment, then found his feet. With his hands close together, near his waist as though they were still bound, he moved to the cell door and shouted. "Jailer!"

The younger one met Corin's eyes and gave a lazy blink, but otherwise they made no response.

"Jailer!" Corin called again. "I would have a word."

"You would have a bruise," Warden Bryer barked. "Take a seat and get back to your rotting."

Corin cursed. There was nothing he could do from this distance. While he was still searching for some plea that might draw a jailer over, Avery shouted from down the line. "His hands are free! Look, guards! Use your eyes! His hands are free now. Stop him!"

That caught their attention, but not in the way Corin had hoped. The younger jailer grabbed his sword and dashed toward Corin's cage, but old man Bryer held his place at the outer gate. He reached beneath the table there and brought out a loaded crossbow.

Corin cursed. He'd hoped for shock, a quick attack against one guard that might have won him a hostage. But Avery had helped—gods bless him—and now Corin had one blade coming at him and a heavy crossbow bolt on its way. He had to act. He stabbed his arms between the bars of his cage and snapped his wrist, casting the little bit of tin out in a tight arc behind the charging guard. He threw it low so the wire curled around behind the jailer's knees, and when the bit of tin came back around, Corin caught it in his other hand. With one end of the wire in each hand, he planted his feet, gripped tight, and dove away from the cell's door.

He twisted as he flew, trying to see how Bryer had reacted. The hardened guard had not wasted a moment on panic. He'd drawn the bow, and when he saw Corin's flashing arm, he fired.

But he hadn't anticipated Corin's backward dive. Corin watched the heavy bolt flash past his nose and smash to pieces on the wall above his cot. Bryer bent immediately to load another bolt, but Corin couldn't watch. The wire jerked taut, digging into Corin's callused palms, but it transferred the full force of Corin's dive into the backs of the jailer's knees. Already rushing at full tilt, the sudden tug upended him, and he fell in a clatter of armor and sword that ended with a noisy crash against the bars of Corin's cell.

Corin dropped the wire and rolled away from where it had fallen. A moment later, another crossbow bolt ricocheted off the stone floor and clanged between the bars and into Kellen's cell. The yeoman had the sense to duck. He cowered in one corner, as far from the fight as he could get, but Avery was on his feet, leaning against the bars of his cage with a fire in his eyes. The gentleman rogue stared down the hall at old man Bryer.

And in his right hand, he held Kellen's knife.

Corin shouted, "No!" but not in time. Avery's arm extended with a fluid grace, sharp-edged steel flashed by torchlight, and the heavy knife buried itself to the hilt in Bryer's gut. It was a perfect toss, with all the cool precision of a dedicated enthusiast, demonstrating relentless hours spent in the practice yard attacking training dummies.

It was also a violation of a Nimble Fingers law: never kill a hired guard. Avery himself had set that law, though clearly that had come with later experience. A closer look told Corin that his hero had broken another law with that throw as well: if you must kill at all, kill fast and clean. Black blood stained the warden's belt and leggings, but it was not a gush, and he was still moving.

Corin cursed and scrabbled over to the younger jailer, unconscious in a heap against his door. The pirate kicked the warden's sword away, then heaved him up to tear the keys from his belt. Behind him, Avery let loose a sickened cry.

Corin looked over at Bryer again, but the old warden was slumped against the wall. His arm twitched, and Corin realized with a start that, even with a palm's length of steel in his gut, Bryer was readying another shot.

Corin wasted just one try before he found the key to open his door. The lock gave a noisy clank as it turned, and across the narrow hall, Maurelle let out a muted cheer. But Corin had no time to celebrate. He shoved the door and the fallen jailer aside with a mighty heave, then he dashed across the gap. He dropped into a slide as Bryer raised the crossbow, then snapped a kick that tore the weapon from his hands even as Bryer pulled the trigger.

The bolt buzzed past Corin's ear. His own weight bowled him into the bleeding guard, and Corin rolled, springing up top of him. Then the pirate did with two vicious blows what Avery's well-thrown knife had not accomplished.

19

Panting, lungs and throat both burning, Corin found his feet. He moved with practiced efficiency, checking pulses, searching for weapons, and sliding the bodies out of sight. The crossbow lay in pieces where it had smashed against the wall, but Corin stole the younger soldier's rapier and scooped up Kellen's from where Ephitel had dropped it.

The younger jailer was still breathing, though he showed no signs of waking soon. Corin dragged him to the farthest cell and bound him with the shackles he removed from Maurelle's wrists. Then he locked the door, recovered his lockpicks and other effects from the table in the corner, and turned his attention to the other men.

Avery still leaned against the bars, where he had been when he threw the knife. But he had fallen to his knees, and he was trembling. The fancy gentleman had gone all pale, and he was gibbering beneath his breath.

Corin turned the key in his cell door and approached to lay a hand on his shoulder. "It's easy to call a man a coward who hesitates to do what you've just done," Corin said.

Avery turned his stricken gaze to Corin. Tears shone in his eyes.

Corin nodded. "Then you do it once, and you think differ-ently. Stick to sleight of hand. Leave the murder to crooks and kings."

Avery flinched at the word *murder*, but a moment later he drew a shuddering breath and began to pull himself together. Corin left him to that task and went to gather Kellen.

To his surprise, the yeoman was in no such state. Perhaps his face was paler, perhaps his brow a little drawn, but he accepted his sword belt calmly and buckled it around his waist. "Corin, take the lead. You three go in single file. Pretend your wrists are bound. I'll come along behind like I'm your escort. My uniform should be enough to get us past the other wardens as long as we move quickly."

He stopped talking when he noticed the surprise on Corin's face. The yeoman nodded in recognition and said simply, "For the king."

"For the king," Corin echoed. He turned to Maurelle and Avery. "Are you ready?"

They nodded, though without much vigor. Gone was the naive thrill that had lit the lady's eyes. Gone the condescending pride that had stiffened the lord's spine. Now they both looked apprehensive of the real risks they faced. But neither one broke down. Neither one gave up.

Corin offered them a soldier's salute, then turned and led them away. He held his breath as they approached the first land-ing, every muscle tensed, and he jumped when Kellen shouted from below him, "Prisoner transfer! Three to go before the king!"

But the wardens at their stations merely turned away when they saw the yeoman's uniform. Up and out the prisoners marched, unchallenged even when they left the carriage yard. Someone called a gibe at Kellen, but he went stoically ahead, and somehow, as a brilliant dawn exploded over the strange city, Corin found himself at liberty upon the palace grounds.

They left the cobbled, siegeproof prison yard and emerged into a wider barracks, surrounded on all sides by a high stone wall lined with long, low buildings and spotted with roped-off yards where soldiers trained in combat. Kellen led them on a beeline across the barracks and toward another inner gate in the stone wall. The silver palace climbed high into the sky just beyond that wall.

But when they passed through the arch, they stepped into a luscious garden. Living things were everywhere, bright and beautiful and dancing to a gentle song woven of a thousand pleasant noises. Water rolled and leaves fluttered and singing birds gave voice. It was a park drawn out of dreams.

Corin could scarce enjoy it. His eyes darted, searching ceaselessly for some sign of threat. He sought the palace, too, expecting another carriage yard or some broad, marbled boulevard approaching its high doors. Then, through a gap in the thick green canopy above, he happened to glance up and see the shining gold-and-silver walls directly overhead.

He jerked his gaze back down, expecting to see walls within a pace or two, but there was only the flowered path. On the left, a handful of lords and ladies lounged around a quiet pool fed by a babbling brook. Ahead and to the right, a pair of guards in uniform stood in quiet conversation, but they paid the prisoners no mind.

They left the sentry guards behind, and when Corin judged it safe, he slowed his pace so he could ask Maurelle, "Where is the palace?"

She frowned at him. "Here!" Her gaze drifted, and as it roamed, the anxiety drained from her expression. A wistful ease settled in its place.

Corin risked a glance back at Kellen and hissed, "This is not a palace! This is a bower!"

Kellen shook his head. "This is the court of Oberon. What else would you expect of the king of fairies?"

Slowly, Kellen's meaning sank in. There was no handiwork of man here. There were no walls or doors, though the glamour of a kingly castle hung over the place. Still, Corin saw the avenues among the elms, the corridors and sitting rooms laid out by hedge and creeping vine. He even saw a banquet hall, where willow branches twisted together overhead, and a single sprawling granite slab made a table for a host of hungry lords.

He walked the halls of Oberon's living palace and wondered what manner of king he would find upon its throne.

Kellen interrupted Corin's awe with a curt command. "Take her arm."

"What?"

"Take Maurelle's arm. You're her plaything."

Corin and Avery responded in perfect time. "*What?*"

Kellen rolled his eyes. "We can drop the act of prisoners now. It's only making you conspicuous. But Corin should take Maurelle's arm—"

"*I* will be her escort," Avery insisted.

"No," Maurelle answered, just as stern. "We two together would be recognized. The House of Violets is out of favor. But if you do not draw attention..."

"I can hardly hide my face," Avery said.

"Turn it to Kellen," Corin suggested, while he offered his arm to Maurelle. "Share a quiet conversation. It makes a good excuse for ducking, and if you look engaged, even those who recognize you are less likely to interrupt."

Avery stopped, stunned. For a long moment he favored Corin with an appraising gaze, but then he started walking again. "You have a gift, manling. I would fain know where you learned these things."

From the Nimble Fingers at Aepoli, Corin thought, but he kept that to himself. He leaned his head toward Maurelle. "Can you lead us to Oberon?"

"In my sleep. In my fairest dreams." She sighed, content. "It's just this way."

Corin let her lead him while he discreetly strained to hear the conversation between Avery and Kellen. He'd feared another trade of jabs that he would have to interrupt, but instead he heard a heartfelt question from Avery.

"What manner of man draws duty in the lowest of the dungeons? That whole floor was empty until we arrived."

Corin winced at the question, for he could guess the answer. And Kellen did nothing to soften the blow. "Heroes who deserve a spot of rest. And fools who cannot be trusted anywhere else. Most often, there is one of each."

They walked ten paces in gloomy silence, until Corin feared he would need to remind them of their ruse. But Kellen spoke again. "A fortnight gone, I was the useless fool."

"You have not been useless today," Avery said. "You have given us our freedom. I...I regret the things I said before."

Kellen grunted. "I require no apology. What I do now, I do for the king. It seems you do as well. That is all I need to know."

Four more paces passed in silence. Then Maurelle squeaked a tiny, startled, "Oh!" and Corin moved on instinct. He tugged her off the path, slapping Kellen's chest as he passed. By the sound of it, Avery was the first to understand, driving Kellen after Corin with a rustle and a grunt.

They darted into one of the verdant sitting rooms, a wide, low grotto beneath the canopy, spotted here and there with trees and bushes bearing aromatic fruits. Corin darted from the entryway and down the hedge to peek back out upon the path. Avery joined him right away while the other two hovered nervously behind him.

Through a narrow gap in the interwoven branches, Corin watched Lord Ephitel come storming down the palace corridor. He had a lieutenant at his elbow, and as he stomped along, Ephitel rattled off orders the lieutenant couldn't hope to keep track of. Ephitel spoke of dwarves and regiments and writs of provender, but between every irritated order, he paused to curse the druids and the king.

Corin grinned at that. The prince would add more names to that list when he learned what had happened in the dungeons, but for now he hadn't spotted them. Corin watched Ephitel pass their quiet grotto, never slowing, too distracted by his irritation.

"Fortune favors us again," Corin said. "Now come, let us see the king."

20

It was not far from there to Oberon's throne. The king of Gesoelig held court within a clearing more than a hundred paces end to end. At its heart grew a single oak tree, its trunk reaching at least three stories high before the lowest branches broke away.

The limbs of that mighty oak stretched out over the breadth of the palace, and its peak soared high into the sky. From underneath, Corin saw the strands of gossamer draped all across its boughs, glittering with dew that twisted sunlight and cast the distant image of a man-made palace. From where he stood, the tree alone seemed far more majestic than that illusion of marble and gold.

And at the base of that elder oak, its roots rolled and crowded into a knot above the earth, taller than a man and folded lovingly around a throne carved into the tree itself. On the throne sat something like a man. Corin had expected the friendly, timeworn face he'd seen carved into the cliff. Instead, he saw a monster out of nightmares. Taller even than the elven lords and ladies, the king had the fur-clad legs of a goat. His bare chest boasted a thick mane of red-brown hair. It bristled in his beard as well, and covered his crown in thick curls. Around his brow he wore a wreath of lily blossoms, and from his temples jutted two great antlers.

Courtiers by the hundreds surrounded him, a vast sea of beautiful creatures dressed in all the shades of a flower's petals. Ripples ran among them, whorls and eddies as they spoke among themselves or paid their tributes to the king, but clearly they were here above all else just to be here. To see and to be seen in such proximity to the king.

The king himself paid them no mind at all. He lounged within his living throne, staring out across the broad expanse beneath the oak tree's limbs. From half a hundred paces distant, his eyes fixed on the four newly arrived, and he started to his feet.

"What is this?" he boomed, a gleeful anger in his tone. "I see the son of Kellen Strong upon my threshold. And a pair of wilting Violets! And they have brought a manling. Bring them here to me!"

At his words, two hundred courtiers turned at once toward the place where Corin stood. Lords in flowing robes and ladies with flowers in their hair surged forward like an ocean swell. They crashed around the newcomers and raised a frothy babble among themselves, asking senseless questions or conjecturing what might have brought a Kellen and a pair of Violets together.

Corin rode the wave, anxious just to stay afloat, but nothing in his life had prepared him for this. He would scarce have been at home in the court at Aerome—or even at the Vestossis' supper table—but he liked to think he could have found his way. This, though...this was not a stately gathering of posh buffoons.

It wasn't even what he'd come to expect of the elves—condescending lords and ladies sullying their dignity to interact with a mere manling. No, these were fairies from the stories of old. They were dreamlike chaos, animal frenzy playing at humanity. They giggled and hissed, they ogled and jeered as they chivied Corin and his three companions toward the throne of Oberon.

Corin cast for a plan. He'd told Kellen to come warn the king, but he had not expected such a crowd. It would be dangerous to denounce Ephitel before this throng. He would need a private audience. But staring at the creature on the throne, Corin wasn't certain he could handle that.

Strong hands propelled him until at last, a dozen paces from the throne, the courtiers suddenly withdrew. The four companions stood alone, hemmed on one side by hundreds of courtiers and on the other by the beastly Oberon.

The king surged to his hoofed feet, towering twice as tall as a man. His eyes danced, manic, and his words came out wrapped within a giggle. "Kellen, son of Kellen. I was told that you were buried."

The yeoman fell to his knees and pressed his forehead to the mossy turf. The ring of courtiers snickered, but Kellen paid them no mind. "Your Majesty, I have betrayed my command, but only out of loyalty to you."

"Ha! Ho! How so?" The king spoke in a lilting chant, but it ended with a snarl. "Your command is mine. I am your lord. You cannot obey by disobedience!"

Corin stepped forward before Kellen could say anything more. "Please, King Oberon, we would have a private audience. It is of matters most severe and delicate."

"Ooh. That does sound painful. But I've never known a private audience. One does require ears to hear."

For a moment, Corin could only gape. This was wise king Oberon? This was their noble creator? He seemed more like a madman. But this strange beast was Corin's only way home. If he would not allow a private hearing, let it be a public one.

"I have come to beg your aid," he said. "Only your magic might send me home."

"But who are you to speak to me?" Oberon asked, condescending. "Who are you to ask me anything?"

"I am your humble servant," Corin said. "And I bring you news well worth the boon I ask."

Oberon frowned. "What news is this?"

"Grim news, Your Majesty. The lord protector betrays your trust. He plots rebellion in dark corners."

Astonished gasps and murmurs ran like ripples through the crowd, but Corin's attention was all on Oberon. The king glanced up sharply at Corin's pronouncement. The dark, animal eyes flashed surprise and fear, but not, Corin realized, at the news. It was at the courtiers' reaction.

Corin saw perfect understanding in the king's eyes. Oberon thought as Corin had before: it would have been far better if these tidings were not shared out loud, but anything at all was better than silence.

Still, Corin stepped closer and lowered his voice. "I apologize, Your Majesty, but we could not afford—"

The king cut him off. Oberon tossed his mighty antlers, threw back his head, and brayed a laugh that sawed against the nerves. That silenced the courtiers. They watched the king as he danced a little jig, *clip clip clop*, then Oberon fell exhausted back onto his throne and looked on Corin with those wild eyes again.

"What is this manling who brings such tales to my court? Is he a pet of yours, A. Violet? Or pretty M.? Do you bring him to entertain me with a farce?"

Kellen staggered to his feet. "It is no farce, Your Majesty."

The king arched one bushy eyebrow, and that was enough to silence the meek warrior. Oberon spoke in a whisper that might have carried to the farthest corner of the hall. "No more words from you, Yeoman Kellen. We will have words, but the time is not yet come."

The warrior paled and shrank away, hiding behind Corin. Maurelle found the courage to step up in his place. She curtsied low, then cleared her throat. "He is no pet, my king. He is an emissary from your druids. Lord Ephitel tried hard to stop him coming here—"

Oberon clapped his hands together with a boom that left her mute. His eyes glittered with fury, but he spoke with that same mad glee he had shown before. "Ooh, a *complicated* performance. See how well they set the stage? I'd no idea the House of Violets was now a troupe. How far you've fallen. And are you a trouper in their ranks, too, Kellen, telling tales since you no more troop for me?"

Avery snarled. "My sister tells no tales. She has risked much for you, who did nothing to protect us. Do not—"

This time Corin interrupted before the king could. He threw wide his cloak in a grand flare that just chanced to muffle Avery. Then Corin turned to bow toward the audience. He turned back and bowed to the king. "Aye, my lord, you have the right of it. We are a complicated band with a chilling tale to tell. Would you hear it?"

Those eyes...one moment they danced with madness, and the next they cut like knives. They fixed on Corin now, even as the king feigned a wide, long yawn.

"No," he moaned. "No, I tire of your antics. I can't believe you bring me tales I haven't heard before."

There. It was an invitation. For all his wild appearances, the king was shrewd.

And terrified.

This was all a sham. Corin saw it in an instant. This whole court, perhaps Oberon's whole persona, was a sham to buy him time. If he was weak and wild, Ephitel need not rush to overthrow him. The traitor could take his time. Corin could not guess how many months the ploy had bought, but it was spent now. Ephitel was moving.

So Corin pressed his case. "Good king," he cried, "you have heard wild tales and speculation. You have heard myths before, and silly rumors. But I bring you *news*! I bring you tidings of great change. The story of a revolution grim and gory."

Oberon hesitated, weighing his decision. Fear won out. Or caution. Either way, he shook his head. "I have no time for tragedies."

"But mine—" Corin tried.

"No buts! No tragedies. No trials. Go away, and I will watch you slip the noose. I will see how you outrun the dogs. That will entertain me enough, I think."

Corin understood—or thought he understood—the hidden meaning. They were free to go. Oberon would see them off, unmolested by Ephitel. It was almost a generous offer.

But Corin had nowhere to go. He needed Oberon to send him home. Wasn't that why he had come here? Delaen had sent him...with instructions...

He'd forgotten her instructions. Corin met the mad king's eyes and said, "No tragedies, my liege, but may I tell a fantasy? It is a dream made real! I am not just a storyteller. I am a traveler. I am an anomaly."

"I've made my choice," Oberon said, but Corin spoke over him.

"I am a man out of time," he said. "And I bring a tale you've been waiting for."

Silence fell within the strange cathedral. All the courtiers watched to see how their king might discipline the impudent manling. Avery looked curious, too. Maurelle and Kellen trembled. Corin only watched the king.

Oberon leaned back, lounging in his throne. He feigned another yawn, then shrugged one shoulder.

"Tell your tale, little man. If I do not enjoy it, I'll feed your entrails to my dogs."

(21)

"Once upon a time," Corin said, "there was a man named Corin Hugh. Corin was a peasant, born in Aepoli beneath the reign of Cosimo Vestossi, and in his time the name of Oberon was not known. In his time, Ephitel was thought a god among the manling nations."

A shock rolled through the listening crowd at that, but Oberon silenced them with a raised hand. "Tread with care, manling."

Corin swallowed hard, but he pressed on. He told the tale of how he'd found the ancient map, how he'd studied long-forgotten legends to find the final resting place of bright Gesoelig. And when he came to the end of the story, when he told Oberon how Ethan Blake had betrayed him, he bent the truth.

"Blake was my second-in-command," Corin said, "whom I'd long esteemed. Whom I even had suspected, but whom I never thought would strike me down so boldly. He gathered rumors and traded in promises. He cast away my loyal followers and belittled those who would have stood for me. He waged a private war against my trusted advisors, including the desert rose Iryana. I should have worked harder to protect her..."

Corin trailed off, an unexpected lump hard in his throat. He whispered, "Iryana..."

And above him, the monstrous king whispered, "Sweet Aemilia..."

Corin's head shot up. The king saw the parallel! Corin cleared his throat. "Aye, my lord. For all his noble blood, my second-in-command was the blackest of villains I have ever known. He found a hoard of dwarven powder and made a weapon of it. He struck a spark, and the explosion sent the ancient city up in flames. The traitors slipped away, but I was left marooned within the cave. And when the fires overtook me—"

Oberon sprang forward in his seat. "Yes?"

Corin shrugged. "I woke up in this world."

The king cheered and raised a great applause, and all the court followed his lead. Corin swept a gracious bow, but he was otherwise unmoved. He held his place and held his gaze upon the king.

When the applause died down, Oberon, still chortling, cried out, "Well told! Well told! A well-imagined farce. I'll hang a silver bracelet from your wrist as your reward."

Corin stood his ground. "That is not the favor I would ask."

"Ah! Indeed. For you were injured in the struggle with your treacherous lieutenant. I see the handiwork of my faithful druids on your hoof there, but I know better tricks than theirs."

He snapped his fingers, and a shock of perfect agony stabbed through Corin's damaged ankle. Corin screamed, collapsing to the ground and wrapping himself tight around the pain. But before he'd even finished falling, the pain was gone. Inside the strange boot, Corin's foot was whole again.

Corin knelt there, gasping for his breath, and Oberon nodded beneficently. "Have this gift, and I will still offer you that bracelet—"

"No!" Corin gasped. "I need more."

"What else could you want of me? Half my kingdom?"

"None of it," Corin said. "I want you to send me home."

The laughter fled from Oberon's face. His brows came crashing down. "The tale-telling time is done."

Corin pressed closer, speaking just for Oberon. "It is no farce. I am not where I should be. Please send me home."

Oberon answered just as quietly. "You ask a sleeping man to change his dreams. What control have I?"

"You are Oberon." It was answer enough.

The king straightened in his throne. His gaze flicked out to the audience and he gave them another chortle. "Let it not be said—never in my court—that a manling played at farces better than King Oberon. Let us all pretend your tale is true. Let us all pretend there was an honest thief named Corin Hugh. Let us all pretend the fires of a dead Gesoelig brought him to my kingdom. How could I even know that you are he?"

Corin floundered. "I…well…you have heard the tale I told. Could anyone but Corin Hugh have said it as plainly?"

"Anyone among his crew," Oberon replied. "They were all there. And what if Corin got away? What if *you* are one of his villains? What wretched kind of king would I be to send you back?"

Corin licked his lips, baffled. "I…I could find someone to vouch for me?"

"Someone? No. Some*thing*. The legendary thief Corin Hugh would have no trouble stealing the whistle from a summer breeze or the wickedness from a cat's dark heart."

"You would have me steal something?"

Oberon laughed, and the court laughed with him, though Corin could tell from the tenor they were just as confused as he was. All together, they played along with Oberon.

The mad king's laugh subsided. "No. You told the story wrong. The Corin Hugh you've told me of would not have come to Gesoelig helpless as a babe. He would have lifted the cutlass from his wretched first mate's belt. Show me the sword, and I will send you home."

Corin gaped. He shouted, "No! That never happened!"

"It should have," Oberon said, but he shook his head and corrected himself. "It shall have." He shook his head again. "It will." At that he nodded, beaming.

Corin whispered fiercely, "I *didn't* take the sword. Please. Help me!"

But Oberon turned his head away and rolled his shoulders. "Without the sword, you are nothing but a liar. I grow bored of farces."

"Please! Your Majesty!" Corin begged, but Oberon flapped a hand in weary dismissal.

"Take them away and bring me no more mummers evermore."

The wave crashed in again as it had before, a hundred courtiers surging forward to close around Corin and his three companions. It was an undertow, a riptide Corin couldn't swim against, and in a moment he was hurled up on the shore, outside the living cavern of Oberon's court. He tried to dive back in, but the outer edge of courtiers closed up, solid as a wall, and no matter how he tried, Corin could not get around them.

"Save your strength," Maurelle told him sadly. "I've wasted weeks outside the edges, and I never found a crack. When you are cast outside the court, you stay outside."

Corin sank down on his knees, weak and weary. "But I *need* his aid."

She shrugged. "Then you had better find that sword."

"No, you don't understand! I don't have the sword. There is no sword. I don't know where to find it!"

Yeoman Kellen bit his lip, then after a long moment he let out an explosive sigh. "I do. I know where. And this will not be fun."

Corin rubbed his eyes. "You're not listening. There *is* no sword."

"Of course there is," Kellen said. "In your story—"

"That was masterfully done," Avery said. "I've spun a fancy thread from time to time, but never such a parable as that."

"Precisely," Kellen said. "With you for Oberon, and Ethan Blake for Ephitel—"

Maurelle clapped her hands together, delighted. "Don't forget he mentioned us! The advisors Blake dismissed? That makes me Iryana! Avery, you can be Sleepy Jim—"

"I think he meant the advisors to be Oberon's druids," Avery said.

"It could be both," Maurelle insisted. "I could be Iryana."

"It's not a made-up story!" Corin shouted. "It is my life. Those people are real people, and Ethan Blake still wears his cutlass on his belt while he drags Iryana and Sleepy Jim away in chains." Corin stopped himself, panting. Maurelle gave a frightened squeak. Avery stepped closer, peering into Corin's eyes. "You really believe this?"

"I do," Corin said. "And the druids do as well. It was they who sent me to ask Oberon for help."

"They knew it was not a metaphor?"

"Of course they did. I had to change some details to make that work for Oberon."

"Ah," Avery said.

"And that," Kellen said, "is how I know there is a sword."

All eyes turned to him. He grimaced and loosened his sword within its scabbard. "Oberon only heard the parable. And he is not a fool. He doesn't want the sword of Ethan Blake. He wants you to get Ephitel's."

A shocked silence reigned until Maurelle creased her pretty brow and said, "But…Ephitel doesn't carry a sword."

All three men answered her as one. "He does."

"No," she said. "I've seen him oft at court, and I have never seen him with a sword. He keeps a silver-chased baton for formal functions, a riding crop for fetes, and a Dehtzwood bow when he goes off to war. It has a green case of hardened leather and a quiver to match."

All three men stared, dumbfounded.

Avery found his voice first. "Remarkable."

She shrugged. "I do pay attention to the things that matter."

"I do, too," Corin said. "And I saw the sword he wore upon his hip when he went to see Aemilia yesterday. It looked fit for a king."

"He wore it still when he arrested you," Avery said.

"It's true," Kellen said. "I noted it as well, but the lady isn't wrong. Despite this evidence, the lord protector never wears a sword."

Corin shook his head. "A man might make an exception for that blade."

"What blade was this?" Avery asked. "I only saw that he was armed."

"A relic, by the look of it," Corin said, remembering it fondly. "Daemescin blue the blade, traced with whorls and serpents. A Rikkeborh guard, if I had to guess, but with a Castelan crosspiece chased in silver, and a ruby in the pommel—"

"Larger than your thumbnail," Avery finished for him.

"So you did see it?"

Avery shook his head. "I know this sword by legend, if not by sight."

Corin frowned. "You have legends?"

"Doesn't everyone? This sword is more than most. It belonged once to a warrior."

"Aeraculanon," Kellen cut in, eyes bright with sudden understanding. "Proofs! The prince is wearing Aeraculanon's sword?"

Fear closed tight around Corin's heart. "No! That cannot be. My people have this legend, too. You cannot be telling me that Ephitel owns the sword *Godslayer*!"

Kellen shrugged. "It doesn't have a name."

"Though that's a good one," Avery said. "Aeraculanon forged that blade to slay the pagan lord of war. I had heard some rumors Ephitel owned the blade, but no one really thought it true."

"But when could he have gotten it?" Corin asked.

"From Aeraculanon?" Kellen guessed. "They served together in the Hivernan War."

Corin frowned. "How long ago was that?"

"Six hundred years?" Kellen looked to Avery for confirmation. "Seven hundred? Something near to that. My father earned his name holding the Pyren Pass while Ephitel and his regiment laid siege to Maedred."

"And Ephitel has owned it all this time?" Corin asked. "Why wouldn't he have shown it long before?"

"You have seen the blade," Avery said. "Would you wear that where it might be lost or stolen? As you said, it is a relic."

"And yet he wears it now."

"Wore it." Avery frowned. "He had it when he took us to the dungeons, but not when he stormed out of the palace."

Kellen chuckled. "Would you wear a legendary sword of god slaying to go before King Oberon? Especially if you had real plans in motion?"

Corin groaned. "But that explains the timing. It is more than a trophy. Ephitel means to wage war with Oberon. It could begin at any moment, so he wears the sword in readiness."

"Age of reason," Avery cursed. "This is more than just your fever dream. This may be real."

"It's real," Corin said. "And for all his silly rhymes, Oberon is wise enough to see it."

"That's why he bade you fetch the sword!" Kellen shouted.

"Aye," Corin said. He dragged a hand across his brow. "But I would have no part in this. I am not meant to wage a war. I just want to go home."

Kellen clapped him on the back. "You have been at war since the moment I met you."

Avery nodded. "I would follow you into the fray."

"But—"

"For glory," Maurelle said. She wiped a tear from her eye. "For Iryana."

Corin looked around the circle, considering each in turn. He sighed. "I *would* love to get my hands on that sword."

"Excellent!" Avery said. "Now...how?"

"He didn't have the sword when he went before Oberon," Corin said. "Would he have trusted his lieutenant to hold it for him?"

"Ephitel trusts no one," Kellen said.

"Then he has stashed it somewhere."

Kellen nodded. "He has an estate here in the city."

Corin tried to judge how much time had passed while they were locked within the cells. He shook his head. "It would have to be close."

"Just across the bridge."

"Perfect," Corin said, sarcastic. "I suppose it's well secured?"

Avery nodded. "I have never seen anything like it."

"We won't stand much chance in a fair fight," Corin said. "How do you suggest we take it from him?"

"Quickly," Avery said. "You heard him at the palace. He said he was late to a meeting with the dwarves. Their nearest chapter house is halfway across the city in the opposite direction."

"Still, he might have stopped for *Godslayer*."

"Not a chance. For two reasons: dwarves prize punctuality, and no one—lord or king—has ever gone armed into a dwarven chapter house."

"That's promising," Corin said. "But how do you know Ephitel went to them? Couldn't the meeting have been here in the palace? Or at his...what?"

All three stood staring at Corin as though he were mad. He raised an eyebrow. "I am a man out of time! Just tell me what I'm missing."

Maurelle said, "Dwarves do not leave their chapter houses."

"They are not allowed," Kellen said. "By Oberon's decree."

Avery nodded. "For their safety, as much as anything. The dwarves who do not live in distant mines travel under high security and only between chapter houses."

Corin shrugged. "See how easy that was? Next time, just explain it to me."

For a long moment, he stood thinking. Robbing Ephitel did have a certain appeal. That sword made a worthy target, too, even before he'd known it might be *Godslayer*. But now he had a chance to steal a legendary artifact from Ephitel, king of gods, with the aid of Avery of Jesalich, king of thieves. In his own time, Corin would have leaped at any part of that adventure, and here it was his only way of getting home. He had to do it. For Iryana, and for glory.

"Very well," he said. "Show me the way."

A wide, slow river brought fresh water to Gesoelig. It rolled between the city's many hills and curved protectively around the fertile spit of land that held the palace. Like everything else about the place, the bridge that crossed the river looked a mighty structure crafted of stone from any distance, but approaching from the palace side, Corin saw it as a living thing. The texture was rough and knotty, like ancient bark, though its main surface was worn smooth from years of traffic. Corin puzzled over it as he walked, and he was nearly to the other side before he figured it out. Then he spun in place, horrified, and stared back more than a mile to the palace. "Impossible!"

Kellen drew his sword. Avery searched their trail with darting eyes. Maurelle just cocked her head and asked, "What?"

"It's a root," Corin said.

Kellen sheathed his sword, Avery grumbled something and turned back toward Ephitel's estate, but Maurelle beamed. "Oberon always wanted Hurope to have a world tree. It is nothing like the real thing yet, but give it time. It will be marvelous someday."

It will be buried in a mountain, Corin thought. *Or can I stop that happening? What did happen to this place?* It was as much as he'd considered the question in all the time he'd been here. Time.

That was the key. There was never any time—not to plan, not to explain, not to ask questions. He was always running.

And now was no different. He had no wish to try his skill at pickpocketing against an armed Lord Ephitel. He had to get the sword while the prince was otherwise engaged. Perhaps when that was done he'd find the time to ask a question or two about the nature of reality. For now, he turned his back on the incredible tree, offered Maurelle his arm, and hurried down the busy street in pursuit of Avery.

As he went, he thought about the palace. About the strange gardened courtyard and Kellen's earlier comment. *What else would you expect of the king of fairies?* He thought of the strange behavior of the courtiers and the mad monster on the throne. He ducked his head toward Maurelle.

"Why is he like that?"

"Who?"

"The king. Why does his palace look like a palace from the outside, and like a park from within? Why do the courtiers…" He shook his head, unable to describe them. "Why aren't you like that? Or Kellen? Or Ephitel?"

Sadness touched her eyes so they drooped at the outer corners, and her lip trembled. "We are not allowed. That is one of the rules of this world. If we want to play here, we must play by its rules. And it has so many rules. Only those at court can ever truly let their hair down."

Corin stared at her. "You want to be *more* like that?"

She gave a solemn nod. "Cause and effect can be so tiring. I miss the dance."

Corin turned away, continuing down into the city. But as he went, he shook his head. "I like you better like this."

"Of course you do," she said, bumping his shoulder playfully. "You're just a manling."

Their easy path grew more difficult once they reached the city streets. Perhaps the night had thinned the crowds a bit, but they'd returned with sunrise. Corin struggled to find a path for Maurelle. Avery's black clothes and Kellen's uniform were easy enough to spot, but Corin and Maurelle fell farther and farther behind until he feared he might lose them completely.

He asked Maurelle, "Do you know the way?" but she couldn't hear him.

"Hmm?"

He leaned close and still he had to shout. "Do you know the way to Ephitel's estate? Your brother has left us."

When she caught his meaning, she laughed. She stretched on tiptoes to point to a plaza some short way ahead, then jerked her thumb to the right. Corin judged it north, by the position of the sun, and he understood her meaning. North off the plaza, and presumably close by. Corin showed her his gratitude with a smile, then pressed doggedly on.

They reached the intersection—another grand piazza half a mile on each side and lined everywhere with expensive storefronts and gaudy townhouses. Everywhere except the north edge. There the plaza was bounded by a tall, wrought-iron gate with spear points done in silver. A tended hedge grew behind the gate, and a graveled drive bisected it, extending from the plaza down a tree-lined avenue toward a distant mansion.

Corin stopped and stared. "Is this another glamour?"

Maurelle wrinkled her nose. "Not in the least. Ephitel likes his precious *things*. He's very nearly as bad as a manling."

Whether from disdain of *things* or out of fear of the tyrant, no one went very close to that end of the plaza. Everywhere else this city's streets were packed cheek by jowl, but Ephitel's front gate commanded twenty paces of respectful, empty space. Most in the crowd wouldn't even look that way. In fact, Corin slowly realized, *no one* did. Even Maurelle had turned away to stare toward some merchant's wares. Corin frowned, trying to guess whether this was some sort of elven magic, when Avery spoke in his ear. "Very subtle. You might just as well stroll right up to the gate and offer them your card."

Corin turned to Avery, trying not to show embarrassed haste. "I did not expect you to wander off."

"I did not suspect you could get lost. But come. Kellen has found us a handy vantage point."

Corin caught Maurelle's hand and followed close on Avery's heels this time. They pressed toward the northeast corner of the plaza, then into a bustling wine merchant's shop. Avery nodded toward a proprietor in a wine-stained apron, pointing him out to Corin. As soon as the man was engaged with a customer, Avery slipped along a side wall and out a rear exit.

Corin and Maurelle darted after, unseen, and emerged into a quiet little garden bounded on three sides by the high marbled walls of the plaza's storefronts. The north side, though, held only a small cottage—probably the winemaker's—and an alley that led past the cottage. Corin followed Avery down the narrow path and came out on a shady lane. On the right, trees and underbrush grew wild right down to the river's edge. On the left, Ephitel's wrought-iron gate stretched straight as an arrow to the north horizon.

Kellen stood waiting in the shade and silence. The other three ran up to him, then Corin spun to look back the way they'd come. He turned again. "By all the gods, Kellen, how did you find this place?"

Avery laughed. "I asked the same thing. I guess all the guardsmen know it, or somewhere like it. It pays to spy upon your master."

"A prudent soldier is not caught unawares," Kellen said, a little irritated. "That is not the same as spying."

"Bless your heart, Kellen," Avery said. "But you are naive at times."

"Pay him no mind," Corin said. "You have done well. We can learn much from here."

"Indeed we can," Kellen said. "And you are not going to like any of it."

Corin cocked his head, confused by Kellen's certainty, but instead of explaining, the yeoman beckoned to them and set off quickly down the fence. He went perhaps a hundred paces, then showed them to a gap in the hedge. Corin moved up first, anxious to see what so troubled the young soldier.

From this spot he had a narrow view across the lawn to the mansion's front doors. The graveled driveway ended in a wide circle there, and parked at the front steps was a plain brown carriage.

Corin frowned. "That isn't Ephitel's coach."

"No," Kellen said. "Ephitel's coach just dropped him off, shortly after Avery went to fetch you here. It's probably in the stables already."

"Then whose—" Corin started, but he cut short when the carriage door swung open. Three nervous figures climbed down, twitching to look left and right before they hurried up the steps and into the house. Corin didn't recognize the faces, but he knew them by their stature.

He turned toward the pale-faced Avery watching by his shoulder. "Tell me one more time about the dwarves and their chapter houses."

A ll is lost," Kellen said.

"No," Avery insisted. "No, there's still time, as long as we act *quickly.*"

Corin shook his head. "I have no desire to face Ephitel in person."

"We shouldn't have to," Avery said. "He'll hardly keep his guests waiting while he goes and buckles on a sword! No. Now's the perfect time to sneak in there, while he's distracted with the dwarves, and steal it right out from under him."

Maurelle frowned. "Will we have time for that?"

"We should," Corin said. "Dialogues with dwarves are never over quickly. Especially if they have something you want. Ephitel might not be out until tomorrow."

"*We* have time," Avery said, "but not you, sister. You are going home."

"I'm certainly *not!*"

"I will not see you in this kind of danger."

"I have already been in prison today, *brother*, and it wasn't *I* who murdered a distinguished hero there!"

Avery gasped and staggered half a step. "How dare you—"

"How dare *you* pretend to care for me? Now."

"Maurelle—" Corin started, soothing, but she went right on.

"All you had to do was drop your silly club a month ago, and I would still have a life. You chose this fate for your family, Avery. I'm just following through."

Avery could not meet her eyes. He stared at the toes of his boots, breathing in shuddering gasps. When he spoke, his words were eerily familiar. "You must go home. We may well tangle with Ephitel's private guards, and they are not good men."

Before Maurelle could lash out again, Corin caught her hand. "I have a use for you."

"No!" she snapped angrily, even as Avery did the same.

Corin ignored them both and went on. "We will need a distraction here. Something to draw off Ephitel's guards while we sneak in."

"That *would* simplify things a bit," Kellen said.

"But what am I to do?" Maurelle asked.

Avery said, "Go home!"

Corin silenced him with a glare, then answered the lady. "Go to the druids. They meet in a shady tavern off Piazza Primavera. I'll give you directions."

"I don't know what they told you," Avery said, "but the druids will not be much help in a raid on Ephitel's estate. They are not that kind of organization."

"No," Corin said. "But their organization is key. Find Delaen. She is the one with long white hair. Tell her we need another riot. Send a mob to Ephitel's front gates, and we will sneak around the back."

"Can they really do that?" Kellen asked, doubtful.

"They raised the mob that delayed Avery's trip to the palace dungeons," Corin said. The soldier's eyebrows climbed his brow, and Corin grinned. "Aye, they have their uses."

"But *will* they do that?" Avery asked. "For you?"

"Not for me, but they'll do it for Oberon. Tell them everything we know—that Ephitel is meeting with the dwarves to buy gunpowder with his writs of provender, that he has been wearing the sword *Godslayer*, and that he is moving quickly. Tell them they must move more quickly still."

"I can tell them all that," Maurelle said, though she sounded intimidated by the burden.

"For glory, and for Iryana," Corin said.

She grinned at him.

"And what if they refuse?" Avery asked. "What if they cannot raise a mob in time?"

"Then we will walk away. We'll slip out of town, find some barn to hide in, and wait till this blows over while we make another plan. We'll just have to hope the king survives that long."

Kellen cleared his throat. "I cannot accept that risk."

"Honestly, I can't either," Corin said. "So let us put our faith in Maurelle and in the druids. And in the people of Gesoelig."

Avery watched his sister walk away, head held high, until she disappeared beyond the cottage. Then he hung his head. "Proven postulates!" he groaned. "We're doomed."

"We aren't doomed," Corin said. "Maurelle shows remarkable tenacity. And I think Delaen will listen to her."

Kellen drummed his fingers on the hard leather of his scabbard. "What do we do until then?"

"We wait and watch," Corin said.

Avery sighed. "Sounds dull."

"Most of thieving is," Corin said. He considered Avery for a while, then asked, "How did you come to form the Nimble Fingers?"

"It was just a hobby," Avery said. "No. Not even that. An interest. I had heard stories of the thieving fairies of yesterworld, and of manling heroes there renowned for their burglaries."

"Wait! What is the yesterworld?"

Avery frowned. "Nothing. It is nowhere."

"Is that where the druids come from? Ephitel called them outlanders."

"He should not have used that name," Avery said. "We're not allowed to speak of yesterworld to manling mortals."

Corin wanted to ask more, but Avery looked wretched at what he had let slip, and Kellen stood behind him with a white-knuckled grip on his sword's hilt. Corin couldn't imagine the gentle soldier employing the weapon, but the gaffe had clearly upset them both.

"Forget the yesterworld," Corin said. "Tell me more about the Nimble Fingers."

Avery cocked his head. "Why should I tell tales when you are from tomorrow? Shouldn't you be telling me?"

Corin shrugged. "What questions do you have?"

"Who is king of Gesoelig in your time?"

"It is as I said in the story. There is no Gesoelig. This whole city was lost and forgotten somewhere along the way."

"Very well," Avery said. "Then who is king of Hurope?"

Corin shook his head. "There is no king of Hurope. Hurope is divided into near a dozen kingdoms. Ithale may be the most powerful, Rikkeborh the wealthiest, Raentz the cleverest..."

"Ithale the most powerful," Avery said. "And you claimed Ephitel is king there?"

"Worse," Corin said. "He is their god. The manling family Vestossi reigns at Ephitel's pleasure, but everyone within the land trembles in fear of Ephitel."

"That does not sound so different from Gesoelig," Kellen muttered. "They do not remember Oberon at all?"

"He was hidden in the oldest texts," Corin said. "Lost in forgotten languages. But I found his name, and others could. I will remember him and tell the world, if I can but get back."

Gloomy silence settled on the three until Corin grinned and said, "You are remembered, Avery." The black-clad gentleman gave a start, and Corin laughed. "Aye. In all the land, though they call you Avery of Jesalich."

"Better than A. Violet," Kellen said.

Avery shot him a glare, but turned quickly back to Corin. "How do they know me? Why?"

"By the Nimble Fingers," Corin said. "It became far more than a hobby. It is your legacy."

"The Nimble Fingers?" Avery's brief laughter became a suspicious glare. "You are teasing me."

"Not in the least. I owe my every talent to your teachings passed down through the years. You have been something of a hero to me, ever since I was a boy. It will be an honor to rob a god with you."

Avery grinned at that. "It will be fun to try."

"And what of me?" Kellen asked. "Am...am I remembered in your time?"

Corin shrugged and looked away. "I'm sorry, but I do not know your name."

"What of Maurelle?" Avery asked. "Or Parkyr?"

Corin shook his head. "There aren't elves within the lands of men. I was astonished to see so many lords and ladies in this place. There are old stories of your people, and rumors of distant, mystical islands where elves still live. But mostly you are just stories for our children."

After a stale moment, Kellen heaved a sigh. "It is likely just as well that I'm forgotten. I doubt I'd be pleased to know how I was remembered."

Corin shook his head. "You are a hero, Yeoman Kellen. I will remember you as nobly as I remember Oberon. If I can find my way home, I will tell them how you stood against a tyrant. That is courage."

Kellen smirked. "I have not stood yet."

"You will," Corin said. "I see it in you."

Avery's ears perked up. He sat a little straighter, then sprang to his feet. "And soon, perhaps. It seems I misjudged my sister. And your druids."

"Have they come?" Corin asked, but a moment later he heard it himself. From away to the south, the clamor of an angry mob tore at the morning stillness.

"The guards are on the move," Kellen said, from his place at the gate. "It's working. Age of reason, it's working!"

"Keep calm," Corin said. "This is our plan." He looked up toward the top of the gate and the cruelly sharp spikes that topped it. "Is this our best way in?"

Kellen shook his head. "There's a river birch some way down that leans over the gate. It's nearer to the stables entrance, anyway."

"Then let us move," Corin said. "I don't know how long Delaen's mob will hold against Ephitel's guards."

Kellen led the way, darting north along the gate's path. He moved with the same easy grace as Avery, but his eyes flickered nervously, and he never stopped chewing his lip.

Corin asked, "What troubles you?"

Kellen snorted. "Everything? What are we to do once we're inside the gate?"

"We find a way into the house. With any luck, undetected."

"And then?"

Corin nearly missed a step. "Well…we find the sword."

"How?"

Corin shrugged. "There is some reason to the way a house is arranged. Once we're inside, we should be able to guess where Ephitel might keep his valuables—"

"But won't those places be well guarded?"

Corin had to shrug. "Perhaps."

"Then we will fight."

"No. Not if we can avoid it. Fighting only draws attention. We'll try to find something cleverer." He brightened. "Perhaps you could pretend to belong. It worked in the dungeons."

"Only because I belong in the dungeons. No. Ephitel's house guard wear a different uniform, and…" He sighed, miserable. "They all know Ephitel would never choose me."

Corin slapped him on the back. "You'll make him pay for that. I've never been the favorite, Kellen. Never in my life. And yet somehow I've always managed to come out on top."

The yeoman brightened. "We'll make him pay. I like the sound of that."

"Me, too," Avery said from behind them. "Now quit gossiping like courtiers and pay some attention. This is careful business."

As they approached the birch that Kellen had mentioned, Corin recognized it instantly. It grew out at an angle from the ground—a long, straight trunk just wide enough to scamper up, and tall enough to overhang the iron gate by perhaps a pace. It happened to loom over a lightly forested corner of Ephitel's estate as well, which offered them some cover for the approach.

Corin went ahead, climbing the smooth trunk almost as easily as the rigging back on his ship, *Diavahl*. As soon as he was past the gate, he dropped lightly down and darted into the shade beneath a blooming cherry tree. Avery came right behind him, then Kellen landed with a muffled crash and a violent curse, but in a moment he was up again and standing with the others, peering out toward the mansion.

"I don't see any guards," Corin said.

"Maurelle's commotion at the gates must have drawn them," Kellen said. "No one ever disturbs this property."

"I noticed. The people wouldn't even look toward the house."

"Ephitel has a fearsome reputation."

Corin shrugged. "Well, today it serves us well. Let us move while they are still distracted."

He went ahead, leading a darting path among the cherry trees, then dashing over twenty paces of open lawn to flatten his back against the stable wall. From there no windows on the property gave view, so he caught his breath while Avery and Kellen joined him. As soon as they were all together, he slipped down the back of the stable, listening for the sound of some attendants in the bays, but it seemed even they had gone to see what caused such ruckus at the front gate. Still, he eased his way around the end of that wall, peering into every shadow in the stable yard, then he dashed across the yard into the shelter of the house's stable door.

Avery came after him, padding lightly as a cat, but Kellen tromped like a soldier in his heavy boots. Corin ground his teeth, but he said nothing. They were fortunate to have such a powerful distraction. He glanced around the yard one more time, saw no one watching, then tried the handle on the door.

He looked to Avery. "It's open."

"Then go ahead."

"I cannot guess what's on the other side."

"One way to find out." The gentleman stepped past Corin, unhesitating, and turned the handle. He threw the door wide and darted through, hands raised before him as though ready for a fight.

No one waited in the hall. Corin followed after Avery, and no matter how he strained his ears, he could hear no one in the house.

"We saw the dwarves come in, didn't we?"

"They're here," Avery said. "Keep your focus. And, for your fear of reason, keep quiet."

He threw a glare at Kellen, then slipped away down the hall.

"Why is he so mad at me?" Kellen asked, in a tone too near a normal speaking voice.

"He has a gift for stealth," Corin said, pointing down to Kellen's heavy boots. "You do not."

The yeoman looked crestfallen, but before he could apologize, Corin shook his head. "You're doing your best. Just…keep doing better."

Corin darted after Avery, down the corridor and past a busy kitchen, unnoticed. The hallway branched to left and right, and Corin followed the flash of Avery's black boots to the left. That felt right, anyway, moving toward the mansion's heart, somewhere sturdy and secure. Somewhere far from windows and other prying eyes. But for a treasure like this sword, somewhere wide and tall. A library or some inner den.

He caught up with Avery at the threshold of a sitting room. The elven thief hid in the shadows of the doorway, but Corin could see what had given him pause. The room beyond offered stairways up and down—to the private chambers up above and the sturdy cellars down below. Corin whispered, "Down."

Avery's mouth tightened in a grim smile. "I was just think-ing up."

"It could be either," Corin said. "But downstairs we are less likely to get caught. We might have time to search, and even if we come up empty, we'll still be able to make another attempt."

Avery shook his head. "That's well considered, but it costs too much in time. We can't afford it. We should split up."

"Absolutely not," Corin said. "We risk too much as it is."

"But less without the lumbering ox around," Avery said, roll-ing his eyes back down the hall behind them. "I swear, if Kellen keeps that up—"

"Keeps what up?" Kellen asked, from right behind them.

Corin was as surprised as Avery. He'd heard the same heavy, clomping boots just down the hall behind them.

"Guards," Corin whispered.

Kellen's eyes shot wide. "What do we do?"

Before Corin could find an answer, a pair of Ephitel's house guards came around the corner behind them. They spotted Kellen instantly and froze in a moment's uncertainty. Another pair appeared down the hall opposite, across the sitting room, and they were not as hesitant. They drew their swords and broke into a sprint.

Kellen bounced on his toes, almost whimpering. "What do we do?"

Corin and Avery answered as one. "We run!"

(**24**)

Corin had no desire to split up now, so he darted for the stairs leading up. Apparently pursuing the same line of reasoning, Avery dashed the other way. Corin tried to correct his route, but Kellen was too close behind him. The yeoman's legs tangled with Corin's, and both went crashing to the floor. Corin caught one glimpse of Avery, head still above the landing, looking back in worry. The gentleman hesitated, for just a moment, then he disappeared.

Corin couldn't blame him. Four guards were charging after them, and as Corin looked up, he spotted another hurrying down from the upstairs landing. Corin scrambled to his feet, hauling Kellen after him, then he leaped toward the cellar stairs.

But Kellen couldn't follow quickly. The soldier limped, clearly favoring his hip, and before he'd made it halfway to the stairs, all five guards were in the sitting room. Steel rasped as they drew their blades, and Corin saw understanding in Kellen's eyes.

The yeoman drew his sword. Corin shook his head frantically. "Don't be a fool. Get over here!"

Kellen turned in place, still backing slowly toward Corin, but he spent most of his attention on the guards. "I'll hold them off."

"You'll get yourself killed," Corin said. "Drop that thing and try to run!"

Kellen looked back over his shoulder, holding Corin's gaze. "Find the sword," he said. "Protect the king. And remember me a hero."

Corin wanted to pummel Kellen then, to drag him bodily down the stairs, but there was no time. With that limp, the soldier likely wouldn't have made it if he tried. He might buy Corin time to get away, though. Furious, the pirate captain tore himself away and threw himself down the narrow stairs and into the cellar's gloom. A moment later, steel clashed on steel overhead, and someone cried in pain.

Corin forced himself to run on. He could not have fought five men. Not without some trick, and he was out of tricks. His only choice had been to run. Anything else would have only gotten two men killed or captured instead of one. It was Kellen's noble right to sacrifice himself. And for the greater good.

Not a word of that made running easier. Corin fought himself for every step until the narrow passages and the heavy stone walls cut off the sounds of fighting behind him and above. Then for the first time, he took some stock of his surroundings. This was not the wide, airy wine cellar he had expected of such a mansion. These were catacombs, close and cold, walled with ancient stone. The corridor was not more than a pace across, and every dozen paces it branched off to the right and left, or else it opened on a room filled with old crates or moldering documents or bones.

Every crossing corridor looked just the same, every storeroom identical. This might be a fine place to secure a precious relic, but Corin couldn't guess where to begin. He saw no sign of Avery, either. The gentleman was well and truly gone. Corin cursed, showing aggravation to hide his fear, and moved deeper among the passageways.

Corin stepped into one of the storage vaults at random, out of sight, and stood for some time straining to hear any useful noise over the pounding of his heart. He could imagine the distant clang and crash of weapons, but he heard nothing else at all. No footsteps. No voices. No pursuit.

Perhaps Kellen was winning.

Corin dashed the thought. It was not worth hoping for. Kellen the Coward? Cruel though the reputation was, a soldier didn't win such a name through battle prowess. Corin forced down the hope and focused on making the yeoman's sacrifice worthwhile.

For now, he was mostly hiding. The catacombs made an excellent place for that. Strange magic flames provided some illumination at every crossing corridor, but shadows lay heavy between them, and the darkness in the vaults was almost complete. Only Corin's well-trained eyes allowed him to recognize the shapes of crates and shelves.

The darkness made for excellent hiding but lousy searching. So, too, the extent of the catacombs, which at a glance seemed to cover at least as much ground as the sprawling mansion. Corin could easily have spent days searching among the vaults before he could find the one that held his object.

But it was not so difficult a thing as that. He knew that Ephitel had moved quickly, rushing from the dungeons to his home and then back to the palace. If he'd come into the cellars, he would not have wandered far or aimlessly. He would have chosen some special vault, or one that was nearby and handy.

Corin didn't dare return to the rooms nearest the stairs, but they seemed unlikely candidates anyway. Too easily accessed.

Corin set his hope on a more secure stronghold and, still straining his ears for any recognizable noise, he set off deeper into the gloom.

He'd made two turns in his first hasty flight, just to get out of sight, but now that he was farther from the stairs, he worked his way back toward the central corridor. That did seem the most likely. As he approached it, he paused again and again, expecting some sign of searchers, but there was none. He peeked around the corner when he reached it, then eased his stolen sword within its sheath and slipped onto that path.

No one met him, but at the next room he passed, he felt a little thrill of vindication. While the doors of the others stood open through empty stone archways, the rooms along this hall were sealed with iron doors. He felt the pockets of his cloak, searching out the flimsy lockpicks he'd borrowed from Parkyr, and tried them against the first door he came to.

The lock's mechanism was not a complicated one, but it was heavily made and tough to turn. Corin quickly found the combination to the lock's tumblers, but when he tried to turn the lock, Parkyr's miniature tension wrench snapped across its middle. For one long, miserable moment Corin stood staring down at the easiest lock he'd ever failed to open. Then he remembered the torn handle of old man Bryer's tin cup. He found it in a pocket of his cloak and bent it to the task. With a little force and an unfortunate metallic *skreek*, the heavy iron door fell open.

Corin darted into the room and pushed the door very nearly closed. He dropped the tin handle into the gap to keep the door from closing all the way, then turned away from the door and waited for his eyes to adjust.

What he found, to his surprise, was paper. Stacks and stacks of the stuff. Most of it was tied in bundles, wrapped in coarser parchment and bound with twine, but nearer to the door he found some open packages. Paper. Expensive material, by the feel of it. Soft and thin. Corin might have expected it for some manner of counterfeiting—perhaps to draft more of those writs of provender—but the sheets were too small. Any given piece was barely larger than Corin's hand.

He wasted no time puzzling over it now. His goal was to find the sword, and it wasn't in this room. The corridor outside was still deserted. Corin was able to force the next lock much more quickly, but inside that room he found only barrels. They were heavily sealed, and none of them tall enough to hold the sword, so he left them unexamined.

The next door opened smoothly, its lock newer or more carefully maintained, and Corin found a little workshop. A table against one wall held a set of heavy tools, an extinguished lantern, and a scattered pile of the small sheets of paper. On the left side of the table, stacked in a neat pile, were small bundles of the paper, wrapped into careful little cylinders that Corin could have easily concealed within his palm. He picked one up, surprised at the weight, and gashed the paper with his thumbnail.

Heavy grains spilled out across the back of his thumb, and the sulfur scent immediately warned him of danger. Dwarven powder. Not the fancy starlight stuff Corin preferred, but the explosive black powder that drove his ship's huge cannons.

Tucked inside the paper packet, with a neatly measured dose of powder, was a single iron ball. This was a shot. Every packet was a shot, ready to cut a man down at sixty paces, and easier to load than anything known even in Corin's time.

Corin remembered the stacks and stacks of paper. He remembered the crates he'd seen nearer the stairs. Were those full of musket shot? He groaned under his breath. The barrels.

How much powder did Ephitel already have? How much more did he need from the dwarves to arm his regiments?

Too many questions. Corin had to carry word to Oberon. There was no more time for farces, no more time to play at madness. If the king did not act quickly, he was doomed. Corin grabbed a handful of the packets to take back as proof, but something panicky and hot burned behind his breastbone as soon as he did. He had no love for dwarven powder. Especially this sort. It had only burned him once, and only superficially, but it was devilish stuff. He settled for one packet and tucked it carefully into an inner pocket. Then he tore the rest apart, some minor strike against Ephitel's plans, and scattered their dust across the floor.

For a heartbeat he wished he had some flint and steel, some spark, that he could use this bit of powder to reduce all the precious paper to so much expensive dust. But paper was not hard to come by, and Corin's heart quailed at the very thought of lighting the powder. No. He would settle for this scattering. He gulped a calming breath and turned back to the door.

And saw the shadow of a man. His panic redoubled, but Corin fought it down, stealing closer to the door for a better view. He just had time to recognize Avery before the figure began to move again, back toward the stairs where they'd left Kellen.

Before he could go more than a step, Corin whispered, "*Pssst. Nimble Fingers.*"

Avery spun, stopped himself from crying out, then dove toward the door. Corin let him in, then eased the door almost shut again. He waited for a count of ten, then heaved a weary sigh and asked quietly, "Avery...why are you crying?"

The gentleman didn't sob. He dabbed a handkerchief to his eyes and answered gravely, "Because we're going to die. Ephitel gets to be a god, and we all have to die. There's no justice in it."

(25)

I'd like to slap you," Corin said. "You and Kellen both. Keep calm and keep quiet. Isn't that what you told Kellen?"

Avery shook his head. "That was before."

"Before what? What have you seen?"

"Heard," Avery corrected. "I found Ephitel."

"Down here?"

"Indeed. And he has the dwarves."

"That's good," Corin said. "They'll keep him busy while we—"

"You don't understand. He *has* the dwarves. They've already made a deal. He gets all the powder his wretched heart desires. The sneaking gnomes are even making him his hand cannons."

"Guns," Corin said, but Avery shook his head.

"That name isn't large enough. I heard how Ephitel spoke of them. I saw Ephitel *smile.*"

The gentleman shook his head in tired melancholy, all the fight gone out of him. Corin sighed and stepped closer. "So?"

"So we are lost."

"And that's the end of it? Do you really want to die down here?"

Avery shrugged his shoulders.

Corin crowded closer still. "Do you want Maurelle to die? Because that is what comes next. A battle in the city streets."

Avery narrowed his eyes. "Of course I don't."

Corin jabbed a finger in his chest. "Do you want Ephitel to *win*?"

"No!" Avery snapped. "I want him dead!"

"Good. Then we have work to do."

Avery nodded, a spark finally catching in his eyes. "Of course! You've found the sword. That's why you were waiting here."

Corin had to sigh. "Alas. I haven't found it yet. This is...just a storeroom."

"Perhaps he's wearing it. We could go and check."

"You *saw* him?"

"From a distance, yes. He has another room like this, but wide as Oberon's throne room. He's meeting with the dwarves there."

Corin frowned. "A room that large for Ephitel and three dwarves?"

Avery swallowed hard. "No. You must come and see."

Now that he was in control, the elven thief showed an uncanny sense of direction in the gloomy maze. Corin tried to track the turns, but Avery moved as if on instinct. He picked a path deep into the cellars, until Corin felt confident they must be out beneath the lawn by now. Perhaps beneath the teeming plaza, though Corin had no guess which direction they'd traveled. What was west of Ephitel's estate? Or north? The edge of the city?

He was pondering these things when Avery abruptly stopped. The gentleman's voice shook a little as he said, "It's just ahead. Around that corner. Move with care."

Corin eased forward, and his straining ears picked up the sound of distant voices, blurred to a murmur by the earthy echo.

He slipped around the corner and into a corridor that ended at an open iron door much like the ones Corin had picked before. This was another storage room, like all the rest, but the far wall had been torn down. The work had been done recently, for crumbled mortar and broken stone still littered the floor. Corin stepped past it, his attention drawn to the gallery beyond.

Despite what Avery had said, this room was nothing like the other vaults. It was an artificial cavern, wide and low, its unfinished walls of dirt, not masoned stone. Pillars every ten paces propped up a latticed ceiling of heavy wooden beams. Attached to every fourth or fifth pillar was one of the small barrels Corin had found in another vault. Black powder. Terror froze Corin in his tracks while his eyes picked out dozens of the little barrels, reaching deep into the distant gloom.

"He's undermined the city," Corin breathed.

"The Piazza Autunno," Avery answered. "All the way to Marvolo's, I think. And to Green on the west. And nearly to the palace bridge."

"But how?"

Avery nodded toward the distant sound of voices. "As I said, he has the dwarves."

Corin moved in that direction, flitting from pillar to pillar but avoiding any with a barrel at its top. As he moved toward the sound of chatter, he also found more and more light, not from the eerie magic flames, but from lanterns. Dozens of lanterns. Hundreds. Thousands. Corin pressed himself against a heavy pillar, showing the narrowest sliver of his face as he looked out on an army of dwarven miners, hacking away at the city's bedrock. Ephitel and the three dwarves from the carriage stood watching them work.

"How can you claim this is not enough?" one of the dwarves demanded. "All seven of the Dehtzlan mines are sitting idle while we work for you. Three of our clans will starve if you do not deliver!"

"It is not your work that I find wanting," Ephitel replied with the aggravated air of a man repeating himself yet again. "I need more powder!"

The dwarf rolled his eyes like a panicked horse. "How can you need more?" He sounded desperate. Terrified. "We have stocked this mine. We have stocked your troops, and more waits in your cellars. You must have enough by now!"

Ephitel's lip curled as he looked down on the wretched dwarf. "For today, perhaps," he said coldly. "But when I show my force, consider who will come against me. I need more for tomorrow."

"Ask the heavens for more stars! Ask the seas to make more waves. We have buried you in powder—"

"There must be more. Find me more. Everything depends on powder."

The dwarf scrubbed his hands over his face. "We have stripped the world of it. We have gained the suspicion of every clan by buying out their stores. Our alchemists work day and night—"

"And yet some filthy manling walks into my city with half a pound of the stuff in a leather bag."

"I have told you, that would not have been our work. No one has sold powder to a manling."

"Then he stole it. Where are there still stores to steal? I'll send thieves of my own—"

"There are no stores. I swear by sand and stone. Search everywhere within this world, and you will not find another grain."

Ephitel stood for a long moment glaring down at his confederates. He growled low and animal. "Make me more. Find me more. And do it quickly, or I will see that more than three clans starve."

The dwarf went pale at that, and stammered, "No. No, my lord. Give us time. We will…we will find some way."

"There is not much time to give. You have your orders."

The exchange was quickly coming to a close. Corin pulled away, slipping far enough into the shadows to hide from sight, but still close enough to keep an eye on Ephitel.

Avery rejoined him, silent as a shadow by Corin's shoulder until he whispered, "You see? What are we to do?"

"We must warn Oberon," Corin said. "We shouldn't even have come to see this. We must warn the king and quickly."

"Warn him of what? What do you understand?"

"I understand that Ephitel has guns. He has the banned black powder—barrels and barrels of the stuff—and he's asking the dwarves for more. The only thing I do not understand…" He trailed off, his gaze drifting up a nearby column to the powder keg bound up against the ceiling joist. "What does he have planned for those?"

Avery sighed, distraught. "I have been considering that. As I said, this cavern reaches nearly to the river bridge, and that's the direction the dwarves are extending it. When the lord protector's troops are ready, he'll gather them here, explode the powder, and bring down the ceiling, opening a path straight to the palace."

"Oh, no," Corin said slowly, a new horror sinking into his heart. "No, that's not his plan. He *is* the lord protector. He doesn't need a secret tunnel through the city. He could march right in."

"Not with ten thousand men."

"Perhaps," Corin said, thinking of the narrow doorway from the catacombs into this chamber. "But he could not bring that many men through here, either. And he doesn't need that many men when he has guns."

"Then why all this? It was no easy task to tame so many dwarves."

"He means to bring it down," Corin said. "He will collapse the plaza and everything up to the bridge. *After* his riflemen are in the palace. The regiments won't be able to come to Oberon's aid. No one will be able to reach the palace for hours. Maybe days."

Corin thought of the crushing press of bodies in the plaza, the always-busy streets of the city, and a fire kindled somewhere in his belly. "He will kill how many thousand innocent people in the process? Gods' blood, this will not end well."

"I told you," Avery said, his voice edging toward melancholy again.

Corin made no effort to soothe him this time. His eyes were on the imposing figure of the prince, moving now. The ruby on *Godslayer*'s pommel flashed and burned within the gloom. Corin watched the dancing flame cross the wide cavern, leaving all the dwarves behind. The pirate let Ephitel gain an easy lead, then dragged Avery after him.

"Aye," Corin said. "You told me right. We are all going to die."

"Then why are you smiling? What do you intend?"

"I intend to take that sword."

"We don't have time. Believe me, Oberon will grant an audience—"

"I need more than an audience. I need that sword. It's the only way I can escape the madness that is coming."

Avery stopped, stunned. "You think taking that sword may let you save Oberon's life?"

That hadn't been his meaning at all. Corin had no more hopes of thwarting Ephitel. But if he caught the prince off guard, if he could just wrest that sword away and run, he might yet leave this place before the waves came crashing down.

He could hardly say as much to Avery, though. Instead he nodded and said, "Aye. I think it is the key."

"Then we must find a way to take it from him."

Corin stalked after the distant shadow of the prince. He drew his stolen sword, which brought a startled hiss from Avery. "Not here! Not now!"

Corin didn't even answer. He quickened his pace. The sound of dwarves at work was distant now, but still enough to provide some muffled cover for the sound of Corin's footsteps. Fear burned in Corin's belly, and he stoked it till it glowed, gripping the rapier's hilt so hard his hand began to ache. He fell into an easy jog and then a trot as Ephitel neared the cavern's entrance.

Thirty paces still, maybe forty, but Corin felt close enough to lunge. Avery hissed some desperate caution, but Corin ignored him. He hoped to slash the sword belt with one clean cut, then bowl the lord protector over from behind and scamper down the hall while Ephitel was sprawling. He only hoped the gentleman could follow his lead. Corin raised his sword and burst into a silent sprint just as Ephitel emerged into the catacombs. The pirate followed, not five paces behind him now, and noticed only as he ran into the vault that the iron door was closed. The room was brighter than he'd left it, too.

And crowded. Half a dozen of the house guard were packed into the room, waiting for their master. Corin had a single instant to recognize Kellen—badly bruised but still alive, tied up in a wooden chair off in one corner.

All these things unfolded over Corin in an instant. *This*, he thought, *is why the Nimble Fingers have rules at all.*

Then he crashed into Ephitel, and both men went sprawling.

(26)

Surprise at seeing Kellen fouled Corin's strike. He'd tried at the last moment to bring the sword to bear, but it glanced off the prince's shoulder. As the two went spilling across the cellar floor, the sword was torn from Corin's hand.

Still, he was no stranger to infighting. He kicked and jabbed, aiming blows at any soft target, but there was nothing soft about the lord protector. Though Ephitel wore no armor, Corin bruised his knee trying for a kidney shot and split his knuckles on the elf's hard jaw. The man seemed made of iron.

Corin grabbed for the belt on Ephitel's waist, still hoping to get the sword, but Ephitel twisted under Corin, squirming like a snake, and closed one hand like a manacle around Corin's left shoulder. He closed the other on Corin's right hip, and as they slid to a stop, Ephitel heaved without apparent effort and slung Corin across the room. The pirate crashed against the stone wall at the feet of a pair of guards.

Ephitel roared in offended anger. "You little piece of trash! You dare invade my home?"

Corin didn't try to trade banter. He rolled out of the reach of the stooping guards and sprang toward the sword he'd dropped. Ephitel came to meet him, but at a walk. Corin beat him to the blade, snatched it up, and leaped to his feet. Ephitel didn't draw; he sneered. "Who do you think—"

Corin didn't let him finish. He lunged. He likely could have cut the sword belt then. He could have caught the sword and run. The door wasn't locked, and there were enough distractions. But the sight of noble Kellen, bruised and battered and tied up here for questioning, was enough to stop him. So was the thought of all that powder underneath the city. He remembered what he'd asked Avery before: *Do you want Maurelle to die? Because that is what comes next.*

He didn't. He wanted Ephitel to die. So he forgot the fancy sword he'd come to steal and aimed his blade at Ephitel's heart. He lunged and drove the sword with all his strength, hoping to end the tyrant god with one fell strike.

The prince slapped the blade aside with a casual backhand. "Guards! This grows tiresome."

Corin darted left and slashed back to the right, a vicious strike toward the prince's unprotected neck. Ephitel caught the blade in his bare hand. He held it for a moment, immobilizing the blade no matter how Corin wrenched at it.

Then with a casual pressure from his thumb, Ephitel snapped the blade in two. He tore its ruined grip from Corin's hand, flung it across the room in a show of rage, then knocked Corin to the ground with a crushing backhand.

"I am Ephitel of the High Moor!" he shouted, enraged. "I am a lord of war and prince of all Hurope. You cannot hurt me, but you are making me *most annoyed.*"

Sprawled on his back, Corin aimed a kick at the elf's right knee. Ephitel didn't even try to dodge. He took the blow with no reaction, but Corin felt the shock of it all the way to his hip. He tried to roll away, but Ephitel caught his ankle so he was brought up short, facing back toward the dwarves' cavern.

Every eye was fixed on Corin. Three guards by the left wall, standing over a terrified Kellen. Three guards by the right wall, just now stepping away from the table where they'd been waiting. In the bright light of the guards' lantern, Corin saw what he had not when he first passed through this room: that the table held the hand cannon that Avery had mentioned before.

It was a flintlock pistol fit for a prince. Gorgeous dwarven craftsmanship, with a stock of polished bone, its grip and barrels plated gold. And at a glance, it looked to be loaded, half-cocked and primed. Corin felt a flash of hope.

And another when he saw a wash of motion. Every eye was on Corin, so only Corin saw Avery now creeping into the room. Still hanging half-suspended, Corin met Avery's eyes, then shot a glance at his broken sword, and then turned to Kellen.

"Kellen!" Corin shouted. "Kellen! Help me!"

The poor yeoman could not have answered, but the ruse shifted the guards' attention from Corin to Kellen.

Behind him, Ephitel barked a condescending laugh. "The coward can do nothing for you, manling." Then he took Corin's captured foot in both hands and twisted.

If not for the druid's strange boot, Corin's ankle would have shattered for the second time in as many days. Instead the whole boot spun, tearing painfully at Corin's knee for a moment before he hurled himself up and over, twisting with the motion. He folded his knees and bent at the waist, grabbing for Ephitel's wrists, but the prince was already turning, half a spin, and he released Corin to fly across the room.

This time Corin's head bounced off the stone wall and nauseating lights flashed behind his eyes. He rolled when he landed, out of instinct more than any clear intention, but he fetched up short against some piece of furniture.

The table! Ephitel had clearly thrown him *away* from the ally he'd tried to call upon, but in the process, he'd thrown Corin within reach of the pistol. Surging on a thrill of victory, Corin leaped up—and instantly collapsed again. His right knee throbbed, and whether from the pain or the blow to his head, Corin's vision swam. He grabbed the table leg to stay upright and blinked against the sickening blur.

Avery was in the room now, silent as a cat. Corin only saw him as a splash of black, and perhaps the guards saw little more because he moved so fast. The gentleman thief dove toward the broken sword, reaching with his left hand even as his right lashed out. He must have found some bit of stone within the excavation, because it smashed into the soldier's lantern with a crash of breaking glass, and most of the light fled from the room.

The guards cried in surprise—then one of them in pain—then Corin heard the sound of ropes snapping under strain. He saw the new blur of motion, too, in the colors of the Royal Guard's uniform. Kellen was free! Another scream, this one cut short with a thud, and Corin knew the yeoman had joined the battle.

Ephitel had turned at the disturbance. "Age of reason!" he shouted, furious. "Is that a Violet? Will you let yourselves be beaten by a Kellen and a Violet? Kill them! Kill them all!"

Corin's vision cleared at last, and even in the darkness he saw Kellen on his feet, the broken leg of his chair in one hand and his empty scabbard in the other—both heavily battered. Avery stood back-to-back with him, armed with the broken sword and Kellen's heavy work knife. Both blades dripped black with the soldiers' blood. Two of the guards were on the ground, and another three were limping from blows already taken. None looked anxious to approach the pair at bay.

None but Ephitel. The prince went like an avalanche, a living doom approaching with a roar. He had the legendary sword of Aeraculanon raised, noble *Godslayer* ready to slay two base knaves, but Corin seized the chance. He heaved himself upright, leaning hard against the table, and grabbed the heavy gun. It was indeed a flintlock pistol, but unlike any he had seen before. Six separate barrels extended from its stock, the topmost evenly aligned with the gold-plated lock.

Strange though the contraption was, its operation was obvious enough. He leveled it at Ephitel, fighting down a surge of panic. He hated guns, but he hated Ephitel even more. He aimed it center mass, at Ephitel's black heart, and squeezed the trigger.

The pistol jerked within his grasp like a thing alive, wrenching at his shoulder even as it let off a deafening boom within the confines of the stone-walled room. A dragon could not have outdone its roar, nor the pace-long lick of flame that stabbed toward the prince. That flash lit the room red for one terrible instant.

The shot from the dwarves' hand cannon ended Ephitel's charge. It pierced the prince's back just left of his spine and exploded out his chest, ripping a fist-sized hole out of his fancy-dress uniform. The flash burned out as quickly as it had come, then time and darkness rushed back in to fill the gap.

Ephitel fell. Corin saw it in vague silhouette, shadows against gloom. The prince fell to his knees, *Godslayer* limp within his grasp. The four guards still on their feet took flight, throwing down their swords and dashing from the room. Avery and Kellen stood ashen-faced and motionless, every bit as frightened as the departed guards. They had never seen a firearm in use before. Corin hadn't seen it often, and never from this close.

But he felt no sympathy for Ephitel. The beast had still not fallen. Even with a hole clean through him. He sat upon his heels with his chin drooped down against his chest. Remembering the powder barrels in the cavern, Ephitel's dark plans for the city, Corin aimed the gun and squeezed the trigger one more time. Corin had half suspected this strange gun, with all its extra barrels, might fire other shots, but nothing happened. The pirate shrugged, almost glad, and went to fetch *Godslayer*.

Before he'd gone one step, Ephitel's corpse shook with a violent tremor. Avery and Kellen shrank away, and even Corin hesitated. When nothing happened, Corin took another step. This time Ephitel fell forward, bowing prostrate to the other two. His frame began to shake, and through the ringing in his ears, Corin heard what he took at first to be a death rattle. And then a cough. And then he cursed.

"The sword!" He threw aside the gun and sprinted forward. "Get the sword! Gods' blood, get the sword!"

The others didn't move, too baffled or afraid. Corin dove forward, scraping over the rough stone floor beside the fallen elf. He reached with both hands, grabbing for the legendary blade.

But Ephitel wrenched it away. Corin leaped on top of him, grabbing at his wrist with both hands, and beneath him Ephitel shook and shook with laughter.

"It didn't work!" he boomed. "Even guns cannot defeat me!"

Corin wrapped arms and legs around Ephitel's arm. He planted one foot against the prince's jaw and the other against his rib cage. He grabbed the crosspiece on *Godslayer*'s guard in both hands. He strained his legs and heaved with all his might, and for one crushing heartbeat he feared it still wouldn't be enough.

Then the godling gave a groan and the sword slipped from his grasp. As hard as he'd been pulling, Corin flung the sword away. It rang out when it struck the stone floor, throwing sparks, then skipped off into the darkness of the cavern.

Corin tried to scramble after it, terrified. Nothing he had done had stopped this monster, but his every hope lay in capturing that sword. He made it to his feet as Ephitel roared. "Nevertheless!" Then the lord protector curled his hand into a fist and bowled Corin across the room with one blow.

As Corin sprawled, Ephitel climbed unsteadily back to his feet. His shirt and pants clung to his frame, slick with blood, but beneath the gap torn in his tabard, he had only pale flesh, smooth and perfect as new-quarried marble. There was no wound at all. "I am Ephitel of the High Moor! I am a lord of war and prince of all Hurope! You cannot hurt me!"

(27)

A very and Kellen darted over to check on Corin. He saw the terror in their eyes, and it was no surprise. The last three minutes had contained three of the most horrifying things he'd ever seen. But if they didn't act fast, Ephitel might add three more.

Corin waved a hand toward the prince resurgent and hissed toward the others, "You're both elves. Can you do that?"

Kellen and Avery both shook their heads, the yeoman's bruised complexion answer enough.

"But Ephitel and Oberon—"

Again they shook their heads. Kellen said, "The only one I've ever heard of who could survive a blow like that is…"

He didn't finish the sentence, but he didn't have to. Corin's people knew that legend, too. There had been a pagan lord of war named Memnon, invulnerable in battle. He'd been slain by the hero Aeraculanon, who had forged the sword *Godslayer* to the task.

Then Corin understood why Oberon had sent him for the sword. It was not to save him from the traitor, but so the traitor might be cut down. Perhaps he'd meant that task for later, but Corin would take care of it right now. He knotted a fist in Avery's shirt and jerked himself upright. Nose to nose, he growled, "Get the sword!"

Avery waved helplessly toward the gloom of the cavern. "It's lost!"

"And without it, so are we. *Find it!*"

Avery blinked, then turned and fled into the cavern. Kellen caught Corin under the arm and helped him to his knees. "What about me? What do you want of me?"

"We keep him talking," Corin answered quietly. "Bless his wretched heart, he loves to talk. So we buy time. And when Avery gets back with the sword, we do everything we can to bury it in Ephitel."

Ephitel was on his feet now, prodding curiously at his uninjured chest. "That is…interesting," he said. "I don't believe I've ever died before."

Leaning on Kellen, Corin climbed to his feet. The motion drew Ephitel's attention, and Ephitel took a moment to consider them. "So. He is a shrinking Violet. I can't pretend I am surprised."

"He has gone to warn the king," Corin said. "He's slipped your trap twice now."

"Three," Ephitel said, bored. "But that was before your time."

"When was that? Is that why you knocked his house from favor?"

Ephitel waved an admonishing finger. "I will ask the questions. Who are you?"

"A manling vagabond," Corin said. "No one of importance."

"But the druids think that you are outside time. There are prophecies, you know."

Corin frowned. "Prophecies. I thought they were just rumors."

"When they come from the lips of gods, they're all the same." Ephitel stooped to retrieve the spent pistol. He weighed it in his hands and shook his head. "You taught the coward Kellen how to use his sword. You convinced a Violet to enter my domain. And you know what to do with this. The druids call you Corin Hugh, but that is a false name if ever I heard one. How did your father call you?"

Corin didn't know the honest answer, but he seized the chance to confuse Ephitel. If there ever were a future, if Corin ever found his way back home, he didn't want the lord protector to remember him. So now Corin hung his head and offered a dramatic sigh. "Very well. I hoped to preserve my family's honor, but you have found me out. I'm Ethan Blake of House Vestossi."

Kellen snickered. Corin didn't kick him, but it was a close thing.

Ephitel missed that exchange. His attention was focused more closely on the gun Corin had shot him with. "Ethan Blake. I will remember that. You are draped in infamy. You've barely been inside my city for a day, and already you have firebombed a public house and assaulted royal guards. Back in the dungeons, you killed old brave Bryer in cold blood!" He chuckled. "But that only saves me the effort. His young partner Pau will be easy to destroy."

"You monster!" Kellen shouted. "Traitor! Knave!"

"The coward Kellen speaks," Ephitel said. "Wonder upon wonder. But if you call me knave again..." He grabbed the bundled barrels of the strange gun, turned them easily, then pressed a new barrel against the lock with a clear click. He caught a little leather pouch from off his belt and tipped a bit of powder in the pistol's priming pan. Then he cocked the gun and lowered it at Kellen.

He smiled at Corin. "Well, you knew *most* of what to do with this."

Kellen's face was ghostly pale and his voice wavered when he spoke, but he said, "I will repeat again, you are a knave."

Corin elbowed him. "You do not have to goad him."

The yeoman raised his chin and addressed the prince still. "I marvel that you didn't balk at *traitor*. Shall I call you worse? Bastard. Villain. Scientist."

Ephitel screamed, enraged, and fired. The shot took Kellen in his right shoulder, spraying blood and bone. Kellen screamed and hit his knees. His body shuddered. He caught his breath to scream again and didn't stop. Ephitel just rolled his eyes and spun the barrels of the gun.

"That was not a miss," he said, raising his voice above Kellen's wail. "I have been practicing. I could kill a frisky cat from fifty paces. I've three shots left. Enough for each of you."

Corin forced himself to forget Kellen's pain. He had to keep the prince talking. "But Avery is gone. I told you, he is heading to the king right now."

"Unlikely," Ephitel said. "I suspect he's safe in the hands of my loyal dwarves."

Corin shook his head, showing his genuine surprise. "How did you win the loyalty of dwarves?" *In my time, they hate your name.*

"Bought and sold," Ephitel said, while he primed another shot. "They're hungry little curs, and I had food."

"You used your soldiers' rations? How did you feed the regiments?"

Ephitel laughed. "They are all enterprising men. I let them feed themselves."

Just like a Vestossi, Corin thought. *This is how tyrants reason.* He pretended surprise. "Does that not risk the anger of the farmers?"

Ephitel sneered. "What do I care for some manling's ire?"

"But Oberon—"

"He's lost his grip," Ephitel said. "That's the beauty of my plan. I bought the resources I need with rations Oberon gave me, from dwarves made desperate for food by choices Oberon has made."

"What choices?"

"You don't know? Oh, yes, you are a manling outside time." He laughed. "Oberon always feared the dwarves. He feared the change that comes with guns and cannons. He feared their powder would lead to another yesterworld."

"But isn't he the creator? Why make dwarves if he feared them?"

"Make dwarves? Ha! Only manlings can be made. He *brought* the dwarves, and he brought them because he needed their artifice to build Hurope. He hoped to limit their threat by limiting their numbers. He embargoed trade in food and left them hungry, or I never could have bought the powder that will end Oberon's reign. There's a pleasing poetry, don't you think?"

"I'll call it treachery and nothing else," Corin said. "Even with the gun, how can you hope to beat a god?"

Ephitel hesitated. His gaze flicked toward the cavern, and Corin realized he'd made a mistake. He'd hoped to learn some of the prince's plans, but he'd reminded him about the sword.

"Where *has* your Violet gone off to?"

Corin's mind raced, desperate to find some other distraction, but he could think of nothing.

Kellen moved. He'd stopped screaming some time ago, and now he struggled to his feet. He had to use the wall to support his weight, leaning awkwardly against it as he forced himself up in erratic jerks. His right arm hung limp, the sleeve soaked with blood. Corin started over to him to offer aid, but Ephitel said, "No. Stand where you are."

Corin would not have obeyed him, even with that terrible gun trained on him, but Ephitel now aimed at Kellen. When he saw Corin's complacency, the prince nodded. "I want to see what Kellen has become."

A hero, Corin thought. Every motion clearly pained him, but the yeoman held his feet, burying his agony behind an arrogant stare for Ephitel. He risked his life to buy a bit more time for Avery.

"I am only what I've always been," Kellen said. His voice was weak and ragged. "I am my father's son, and I am loyal to the king."

Ephitel spat. "You are a coward who has never bloodied his inherited blade. I should have dismissed you long ago."

Kellen held the prince's eyes. "I have bloodied it now. I felled three of your men upstairs before some...some *coward* threw a blanket over me." He grinned, relishing the word. "You have stained my name in all Gesoelig because I hesitate to steal a farmer's food. Because I hesitate to beat your enemies to death. Because I'm loyal to the king and to the law. But I will not hesitate to fight your treachery. I will spend my life defying you."

With his head to one side, Ephitel stared at the yeoman. "You really mean it, don't you? Well. Your father would be proud. I never thought I'd say that to a Kellen."

Kellen groaned, sinking lower down the wall as his strength faded. Ephitel chuckled. "So very like your father. Did you know I killed him, too?"

Kellen's eyes went wide, though from surprise or pain, Corin didn't know. The yeoman sucked a ragged breath and wheezed.

"You did not. He died a hero. In the Pyren Pass. You were at the siege of Old Maedred."

Ephitel nodded. "Playing cards and drinking tea. It is a boring task, sitting a siege."

Kellen shook his head. "No. You warred against the heathens—"

Ephitel smiled. "We *watched* the heathens. We sat and waited while they starved. And when reinforcements tried to come by the Pyren Pass—"

Kellen sobbed, sinking farther down the wall. He was bent double now, every breath a labor.

Ephitel's grin widened as he watched the yeoman suffer. "I have never told a soul, but I received your father's message."

Kellen shook his head, the only answer he could muster.

"I did," Ephitel said. "That attack was no surprise. I could have spared a hundred men to hold the pass, and no one ever would have known your father's name. Instead, I made him a hero, and you became the penance for my sin. If I had ever guessed there was true mettle in you, I would have made you something useful."

"No!" Kellen growled. "I would never serve you!"

"Then I would have killed you long ago and saved myself the shot now." He lowered the gun to finish the task, and Corin tensed himself to spring, hoping he could knock the gun aside.

But Ephitel withdrew the gun. "No. I needn't bother. You're dying from a flesh wound. How pathetic."

"I...am not...done yet," Kellen gasped.

"Nor am I," Ephitel said. "You'll get to watch your little manling die, for one."

He lowered the gun again, this time at Corin. And this time he didn't think it over. He pulled the trigger.

Caught up as he was in other plans, Corin didn't think to dodge until it was too late. But Kellen moved as soon as Ephitel made his threat. The yeoman straightened with a cry of agony and hurled himself forward. He didn't aim for the prince's firing arm as Corin had considered. The soldier was too weak and much too far away. Instead, Kellen the Coward dove between Ephitel and his target. The shot meant for Corin struck the wounded soldier somewhere in his torso, and Kellen crashed down to the floor.

Ephitel rolled his eyes. "How many times do I have to kill you?" He spun his barrel and reloaded the gun.

Frantic, Corin looked to the far corner, but Kellen's sword would not save them. He looked back into the cavern, hoping desperately to find Avery waiting with the legendary blade, but he saw only shadows. He watched Ephitel tip a bit more powder into the priming pan...

And he had an idea. A gunshot hadn't killed the invulnerable elf, but it had staggered him. It had hurt him, clear enough. Perhaps the same again could buy them time. Corin lunged toward Kellen, throwing his cloak up over both of them just to complicate the prince's aim. Then he grabbed for the inner pocket where he had stashed the clever little paper shot. He tore the paper with his thumbnail, then peeked past his cloak just as Ephitel lowered the gun. Corin twisted, throwing his pitiful half handful of black powder straight at Ephitel's face.

Ephitel flinched even as he pulled the trigger. Another crack of harnessed thunder, another flash of tamed hellfire, and this time there was a cloud of dust to catch the flame. It exploded like a solstice rocket in the prince's face.

Ephitel screamed. It was a banshee's maddening wail. Corin knew the feeling all too well. Nothing burned quite like dwarven powder. It seared sharper, deeper than any normal flame, and left a wicked stain within the mind. He hadn't fired a cannon since the accident off Spinola's coast. He avoided even getting near the stuff.

Now it was the prince's turn to burn. Even if that wound would heal, it seared right now. Ephitel dropped the gun and batted at his own face, panicking. He shuddered like a tree caught in a gale. Then, with a dreadful wail, he spun and sprinted off into his catacombs, leaving Corin and Kellen there alone.

Corin fought to catch his breath, trying desperately to guess what he should do first. Kellen was clearly dying. Avery was lost. Corin had to find the sword and warn the king. But Ephitel might regain control at any time. His guards might come. All the dangers spun in Corin's head like a tinker's child's toy while he sought how to use this tiny chance.

Then a voice spoke from the darkness behind him. "Pardon me, manling." From very near behind him. "But *that* was our master."

Corin dropped his cloak and turned to see who had found him. It was the dwarf who'd done the talking earlier. And he was not alone. The others stood behind him. *All* the others. A dwarven army caught in treachery, and none of them looked happy.

Corin spotted Avery among the dwarves, his hands and feet tied up and a gag over his mouth. He saw the sword as well, held reverentially by one of Avery's wardens.

Corin fought against a feverish laugh, bottled it up, and met the lead dwarf's eyes with all the sincerity he could muster. "I'm sorry. You should find a better one."

The dwarf leader came into the vault. He stood for a moment, looking around the room. He took note of the fallen house guards and all the abandoned weapons. He went forward to retrieve the fallen pistol, then turned to consider all the spattered blood—from Ephitel in the center of the room, and from Kellen on two different walls. Then he lowered his gaze to Corin and the dying yeoman.

"My name is Ogden Strunk, and I am chieftain of the Dehtzwood clan."

"Corin Hugh, and I am captain of the *Diavahl*. Or…I was. I will be."

The dwarf gave a heavy sigh. "Toplanders are too soft. The percussion from the powder stirs your brain stuff. I've always said as much."

Corin frowned. "Strunk? You said Strunk. I think I know your grandson."

The chieftain shook his head. "I have no grandson."

"Benjamin, he's called. He said his granda was the last of the respectable Strunks, because his father was a loser."

The chieftain's eyes narrowed to dark slits. "My mewling baby's name is Benjamin."

"Ah," Corin said, as the spinning in his head began to settle. "I guess it was the Ephitel business that brought you down."

Ogden frowned. "I think I should be offended." Then he hung his head. "But then, you have a point at that. You have a strange way of making it, but it's a fair point all the same. Ehrin, Durhl, come see what you can do for this poor sod. Biffin, cut the slick one loose."

One of the others who had come with Ogden in the coach bustled forward and grabbed his chieftain's coat. "What are you doing?"

"What we should have done a week ago. Or from the very start."

"But Oberon will have our heads!"

"He'll have 'em all the same," Ogden said. "Or Ephitel, if he wins out. You heard how he talked of the jailers, and they're his men. They're his own kind. He wouldn't treat us well once his need is done."

"You're right at that," Corin said. "I have seen it more than once."

"But the payment!" the other dwarf cried.

Ogden shook his head. "It was never worth the price. And now he's demanding more than we could ever give."

The other dwarf licked his lips and avoided glancing Corin's way. "Perhaps...in exchange for these prisoners..."

"I thought the same when we caught the slinking Violet," Ogden said. "But you saw how this yeoman stood against the prince. You saw how he took a bullet even when he knew the price. There isn't food enough within the world to buy that kind of valor. It isn't ours to sell."

"Then you will let us go?" Corin asked.

Ogden nodded. "Aye."

"With the sword," Corin pressed. "We have to have the sword."

"That, I think, we'll keep," the chieftain said. "It's the only piece we'll have to barter our salvation."

"That sword has valor of its own," Corin said, playing to the dwarf's strange sense of honor, but Ogden cut him off before he could say more.

"I know well this blade's pedigree. And the purpose to which the prince had hoped to put it."

Corin sighed. "Then you know why you must—"

"Relent there, manling. You'll need your strength to get away alive. Don't waste it on a haggle you can't win."

Avery came forward then, freed from his bonds. He clapped Corin on the back by way of greeting. "Listen to the dwarf. I've tried to talk them round before. It never happens."

Corin rounded on Avery. "We cannot go before Oberon empty-handed." He turned back to the chieftain. "But if we have that sword, he will listen to us. Give it to me now, and I will tell him how you served us at the last. Then he will conquer Ephitel, and I will see that he is not unkind to you."

"Ooh, I like that!" Avery said. "You may trade it for redemption here and now."

When the chieftain appeared to consider the offer, his second grabbed his coat again. "Don't do it, Ogden. Would you put us at their mercy?"

"Not theirs," the chieftain said, but then he pointed down at Kellen. "But at his I would. If we can raise him, if he will give his word, then I will yield the blade to you and call it done."

"I appreciate your consideration," Corin said. "But time is short. Ephitel could return at any moment with a regiment behind him."

Ogden shrugged. "Then we will leave by the other tunnels."

Corin brightened. "You have other tunnels?"

"Aye. What, did you think we brought three clans down here one carriage at a time?"

"I had not considered it."

"We have," Ogden said. "And we've considered more than once what a twisting viper Ephitel can be. We have our plans for terminating this arrangement."

"Do they involve a pile of those powder kegs in a vault beneath his mansion? And a very long fuse?"

Ogden gave a low whistle. "They hadn't until now. I like your style, manling."

"Call me Corin."

"Would you know where to find this vault?"

Corin blinked. "I didn't really..." His eyes fell on Kellen, breathing slowly now but still unconscious. Still far too pale. Corin nodded. "Yes. I think I know the way. And I left the door unlocked."

"Glad to hear it," Ogden said. "Biffin here can run the fuse, but once he lights it, run."

Corin shook his head. "There will be others in the house. Cooks and servants. Decent guards."

"We'll set off a couple warning blasts before, then. Give them time to all clear out, then bring the sinkhole down."

"You're serious," Corin said.

"We're double-crossing Ephitel. We have to be."

"I understand that," Corin said. "But the risk—"

"It will stop him coming after us," Avery said. "It will bury whatever cannons he has down here—"

"Alas, but most of those are with his troops," Ogden said. "I saw to the deliveries myself."

"What troops?" Corin asked.

"A regiment in Ephitel's colors," Ogden said. "Camped with all the others outside the city."

"That's where he'll go," Corin said. "If we cut off this venue, if we bring down his house, the only move he will have left is to get to that regiment and bring them into the city. He'll march on the palace."

Avery nodded. "He might be heading there already."

"How long will that take?"

"It depends upon the traffic in the city, but knowing Ephitel… two hours? Three at most."

"We have to stop him. He'll use those guns against the citizens."

Ogden gaped. "That seems too much, even for him."

Corin raised his eyebrows. He pointed out into the cavern to one of the powder kegs mounted on a supporting pillar. "What do you think he intended for those?"

"A last resort, in case we were discovered."

Avery snorted. "This is the ground beneath the Via Autunno, right to the palace bridge."

Corin nodded. "He meant to move against the king, then sink the plaza and cut off any aid across the river."

Ogden cursed. Even his second swore an oath. "I never meant to aid in this."

"No," the dwarven chieftain said. "We'll have no part in it. Take down the powder kegs. Brick up the wall and earth it in. We'll take the prisoners to topsides and be done with them."

"And the sword?" Corin asked.

"That still depends," Ogden said, "on if your valor lives or dies."

That meant Kellen. The dwarves moved Kellen, Corin, and Avery out into the cavern, and then they set to work. For half an hour Corin divided his attention between their construction and the fate of the wounded soldier.

He watched a wall go up in an amazing time. Stones were carved and shaped and slotted into the demolished wall without a seam. When the work was done, Corin could not have guessed which bricks were new and which were old. It looked as though the ancient wall had never been torn down.

But the dwarves did not stop there. They brought barrow-loads of dirt from elsewhere in the excavation, dumping, piling, shoring up, until the wall was buried behind a dozen paces of earth. A cannon could not have cleared a way into the cavern from the cellars. The mansion was sealed off.

But as rewarding as that process was to watch, Corin spent far more attention on the other. He watched the dwarven medics as they probed the yeoman's wounds. They extracted both lead shots— horribly deformed from their brief flights—and bandaged all his wounds. They applied unguents from small clay pots and chanted prayers to pagan spirits of the dark. They spent every bit as much in toil and energy as their brothers moving earth or breaking rock, but with half an hour spent, they had nothing to show for it. Kellen still breathed—if irregularly and only in panting wheezes—but he hadn't stirred. His pulse was feeble and his skin burned to the touch.

When Corin judged that half an hour had burned away, he dragged Avery to hunt down the dwarven chieftain. Ogden brightened as the two approached. "Has your valor wakened?"

"Age of reason!" Avery grumbled. "I have the better part of valor!"

Corin shushed him with a gesture and answered the dwarf. "He hasn't stirred. He makes no sign of progress."

"Oh, well," Ogden said with a forced cheerfulness, "these things take time. We'll know more by tomorrow."

"We don't have until tomorrow!" Corin said.

The chieftain shrugged. "I understand you're worried, but you must consider my position. I have a thousand lives looking to me—"

Corin waved him down impatiently. "I know, I know. I understand your requirements, and I will stay here until Kellen wakes. I only ask that you take Avery on ahead. Have someone show him to the surface so he can take a warning to the king."

"Why me?" Avery demanded. "You should go. I'll stay here with Kellen. I'm just as concerned for him as you are."

Corin rolled his eyes. "No, you're not!"

"No?" Avery threw a look back toward the wounded soldier, then he turned back to Corin. "Even so. Even so. I do want the sword as much as you do."

"Not even close," Corin said.

"I'll argue with you there. I have every reason to hate Ephitel for what he's done in the last year."

"One year?" Corin asked. "Talk to me again when you can claim a thousand."

Avery stepped back, his jaw hanging. "Honestly?"

"Aye. Maybe more. And all of it a tyranny that I would see undone."

The gentleman dropped his head and shrugged pathetically. "I won't contest you then. But even so, the king will not see me."

"With the news you have, I think he will."

"Ah, but there's the catch—until he sees me, he won't know what news I have."

"Avery, we don't have time for this."

"Then we don't have time to waste on foolish errands."

Corin shook his head. "I suspect your sister will already be here. I just need you to take the latest news."

"But if she's not…"

Corin caught Avery by the shoulders and turned the thief to face him. He recognized the fear in the other man's eyes. Avery was out of his element, baffled by the unrecognizable mess his world had become within a few short hours.

Corin remembered that feeling well, and he remembered how he'd overcome it. "Remember who you are. You're Avery of Jesalich, legendary founder of the Nimble Fingers."

"Yes, but—"

Corin cut him off. "You want an audience with Oberon? Go and steal one."

(**29**)

It wasn't quite so simple as that. Corin and Avery stepped aside, scheming between them as to *how* the gentleman thief might infiltrate the impenetrable wall the courtiers formed.

"Is there another route into the throne room?" Corin asked. "A servants' entrance, perhaps?"

"Oh, I don't know. I never really learned the palace grounds."

"That is unfortunate. We'll need deception over stealth, then. Could you manage some distraction?"

Avery only shrugged, his attention fixed on something far away.

Corin ground his teeth. "Avery! This is important!"

"Nothing more in all the world," Avery said, still not meeting Corin's eyes.

The pirate sighed. "Perhaps he'll fall for the same trick twice. He didn't seem too attentive, either. Announce yourself as a man out of time."

Avery nodded and strained up on his toes to peer past Corin's shoulder. "Yes. Yes. There's never enough time."

"Or just pretend you have the sword! That might be—gods' blood, Avery, what has you so distracted?"

Avery flushed red and stammered an apology. Corin spun, expecting to find chests full of dwarven gold or perhaps the legendary sword. Instead, he saw half a dozen dwarven lanterns gathered in a ring to illuminate the injured yeoman.

Kellen was pale as a sheet, his face drawn, his torn clothes now sodden with his blood. Dwarven medics worked around him, fretting ceaselessly, but for all their effort, Corin saw no sign of improvement.

Corin mumbled, "Oh." He turned back to Avery. "You really *do* care about Kellen?"

The thief shrugged one shoulder. "Of all of us, he shouldn't be the one who dies. We watched your fight with Ephitel, you know. We saw it all. The dwarves were waiting to see who would win, and Kellen..." He trailed off, choked up.

"He'll make it through," Corin said. "Heroes don't die like this."

"He *is* a hero." Avery sighed with deep regret. "I called him a coward, just last night, and he proved more a hero than any of us."

"He'll come back," Corin said. "The dwarves are master craftsmen, and their healers are no exception. They'll bring him back."

Avery forced a sad smile. Corin sighed. "You stay with him. I'm sure it won't be long. Bring me the sword."

Avery wrung his hands. "But you said—"

"No. This is best. I should have seen it from the start. The king will see me before he would see you. Just...take care. And do come quickly once you have the sword."

"Of course! Of course!" the gentleman stammered. "Thank you, Corin Hugh. You have a noble heart."

Corin couldn't answer that. He left Kellen's fate to fortune and the dwarves, and went off in search of Ogden Strunk. He found him not ten paces off, pretending not to listen. Corin forced a grin. "Avery is staying. I go to see the king. Can you find someone—"

"Aye. And someone's me. You seem to be a man worth talking to, and there'll be time while we walk."

Corin watched while Ogden bustled over to his fellow dwarves. The chieftain spoke with them a while, then came back with a bundle tucked beneath his arm. He said nothing of it, merely headed off into the cavern's depths, but the pirate's curiosity wouldn't stand for that. Ten paces in, Corin asked, "What's in the rags?"

"A gift to make amends," Ogden said. "You could call it a reward."

They walked in silence for a while, the dwarf offering nothing more. Corin grunted. "I hope it's something edible. I'm half-starved."

Ogden didn't laugh. "You're talking to the wrong folks for that."

"Oh. Aye. I suppose I am." Corin licked his lips. "I'm sorry. I can speak to Oberon about that, too."

Ogden cocked his head. "Can you really? Are you such good friends as that?"

"I can't make any promises, but the king owes me a favor." Corin looked back over his shoulder, toward the injured yeoman and the gentleman thief sitting anxious by his side. "The king owes a lot of favors."

The chieftain snorted his agreement, but he said no more. For some time they walked beneath the city's streets, until they left the sounds of voices and the workers' lights all far behind. Ogden's lantern was their only light, an eldritch thing that glowed without a flame.

While they walked, Corin made his plans. He would carry a warning to the king and beg transportation back to his own time and place. If the sword was really needed for that magic, Avery would bring it soon enough. But Corin suspected it was no such thing. Oberon had used him as a pawn against the lord protector. He had sent the four of them to find a lord of war.

Corin frowned. The four of them. Avery, his lifelong hero. Maurelle, the sister of his hero, whom Corin had chanced upon within a crowded plaza. The coward Kellen, an enemy of the House of Violets and yet a noble man, and one they'd needed to confront Lord Ephitel. There was too much of chance in all of that. If he considered this a plot, just how far did it reach?

Ogden interrupted his musing, though he never looked Corin's way. "What can you tell me of Benjamin?"

"What?" Corin asked, caught off guard. "Ben—"

"My son." Ogden kicked a stone, which skittered off with a hollow rattle that hung in the still air. The chieftain cleared his throat. "You said before that you knew my son. You come here from another time. What can you tell me of my son?"

Corin had no wish for small talk. Enormous things weighed on his mind, and this idle question only made it worse. What chance was it that he had stumbled across Ben Strunk's father? But Ogden was yet an uneasy ally, and such things needed care. The pirate licked his lips. "I don't...the druids said it isn't wise—"

"Friya take the druids. I care little for their games. Just tell me what you know about my boy."

"Ben Strunk. In my time, he is...an honest man," Corin said, fabricating wildly. "Rich in valor. Honored for his handiwork. Everyone in Aepoli knows his name." That much, at least, was true.

The chieftain wrinkled his nose. "A city dweller, then? Ah, I suppose it's not so bad if he's found fame."

Infamy, more like, the pirate thought, though he kept that to himself. He'd never known a dwarf more desperate for drink or worse at playing cards. Between the two, he was a useful man to know. But Corin wanted done with this discussion, and a generous fiction would serve them both. "I rarely go a week without paying him a visit," Corin said. "And I always regret it when I do."

The chieftain took the lies with all the naive pride of a new parent. "It warms my heart. It's good to know he has a future, despite the things I've done."

That struck a spark of guilt in Corin's breast, and he could find no answer. Ogden seemed happy with the silence for a while. He led Corin on among the pillars, until at last they reached an earthen wall stretching off into darkness on either side. The dwarf had come unerringly to the only breach in the wide, clean-cut wall. A rounded passage angled up through the earth, for all the world like a man-sized rabbit hole. Or...*not quite* man-sized.

"It may be a tight fit," Corin said.

"Oh, aye! Good thing you're hungry, eh?"

Corin sighed. He ducked his head toward the tunnel, but Ogden stopped him with a hand on his elbow. "This is as far as I go. We must make haste if my people are to survive the coming days. But I would give you this." He held out the small hand lantern, and Corin accepted it gratefully.

"And this."

Corin took the cloth-wrapped bundle. He'd hoped against reason that it would be the sword *Godslayer*, but it was far too small. Curious, he folded back the dirty rags and gasped to find the gleaming gold-plate stock of Ephitel's revolver.

"That is a piece of master craft," Ogden said. "Borrowed from the lore of yesterworld. There's not another like it in the world."

A gift of dwarven master craft. Corin was stunned. "I...I don't know what to say."

Ogden shrugged. "'Thanks' is pretty popular. Or 'Give it here, ya stinkin' dwarf.' It's probably fifty-fifty."

Corin turned the pistol in his hand to catch the light. He remembered how the thing had felt when he'd fired on the prince—powerful and wicked and alive. Priceless treasure though the weapon was, Corin was not sure he could trust a thing like that in battle. He certainly had no desire to carry bags of its black powder with him.

It was just as well. He could see the glint in Ogden's eye, the desperate, unspoken hesitation. Corin took his knee to meet the chieftain eye to eye. He had never bent his knee to god or king before, but he suffered nothing for the chieftain's pride. "Why do you give me such a gift?"

"It's a trophy won in battle. You left it on the field."

There was some ritual to giving master craft, and Corin saw that it would take some ritual to reject it. He shook his head. "Not if it is dwarven master craft. Such things cannot be owned by men unless they're given by their makers."

Ogden grinned. "Well. Little Benny taught you something." He cleared his throat. "Aye, well, that's the heart of it. I made it as a heritage for Benny."

A tension loosened in Corin's chest as he pushed the bundle back toward Ogden. He had tried before to rob another people's history, and it had ended badly. He could hardly rob a friend. "Then it belongs to Ben. I cannot take what you would give to your own blood."

Ogden made no move to take the package. "You're an honest manling, Corin Hugh. But you show more respect to my handiwork than I ever did. I broke the maker's bond for greed when I offered Benny's heritage to Ephitel. Greed and sin and—"

"Hunger," Corin interrupted. "That is not a sin."

"Be it what it is," Ogden said, "I made the gun a gift to Ephitel, and now whatever falls, Oberon will learn of it. Even if you find us some clemency from him, he will not allow a gun the likes of that within my clan."

"But Ben—"

"Will grow just fine without a weapon in his hand. I'll teach him axes if it comes to that."

Broken bottles would be better, Corin thought, but he held his tongue again.

Ogden went right on. "And if the tale you tell is true, if you can somehow go back through future ages to a time when little Benny is a friend, you may pass my heritage along to him if it please your heart."

"You place a great deal of trust in me," Corin said.

"I would. But no. If it never sees my son's hands, that is my sin, not yours. If you keep it to your hoard, I can't complain. You are a more worthy owner than the one I sold it to."

Corin drew a heavy breath, sighed, and nodded. "Very well. If that's truly how you feel, then give it here, ya stinkin' dwarf."

Ogden barked a laugh of sheer surprise, then he clapped Corin warmly on the shoulder. "You have a task I wouldn't see delayed, but if you'll tarry one more moment, I will show you how to use the thing."

The chieftain taught him how to load the barrels, how to prime the pan and set the safety cock. He showed him how the revolving mechanism worked as well, though Corin had received ample education watching Ephitel.

Still, out of courtesy he waited through the demonstration—grateful when the dwarf refrained from firing the last live shot—then he expressed his gratitude with more sincerity, said his good-bye, and slithered up the rabbit hole.

It was no easy task, but he emerged into a bright midmorning. The songs of sparrows seemed like strident screeches after the ancient silence underground. The gentle sunlight seemed a searing blaze. But worst of all, by contrast, was the rushing tide of time.

Midmorning already. Time had felt imaginary underground, but based on the sun's position, Ephitel must have gained an advantageous lead.

Corin cursed and caught his bearing. The bridge stood south, along the nearby riverbank, not half a mile down. Corin frowned, calculating. He didn't recognize the place, but this could not be far from the path Kellen had shown him. That meant Ephitel's mansion would be near enough to see…

He turned that way, in time to see the windows on the first floor light up red and orange, exploding outward in a rain of glass. The walls followed a moment later, firing bricks across the lawn like cannon shot. The second floor went half a heartbeat behind the first, and then a plume of fire lifted the shingled ceiling up into the sky.

So, he thought, *I guess they found the storerooms.*

The thunder of it hit him then, and Corin turned his back before the debris could start to fall. He threw his cloak over his head and started south beside the riverbank, heading for a meeting with the king.

(30)

Corin's knee still twinged. His head pounded, and everything ached, but he was strong enough to walk. He pushed through the underbrush along the riverbank, climbing higher, and soon he broke free onto a narrow walking path. As he went, he worried at the questions he'd encountered underground. What was this place? What was this city, with its twisted fate? He traced the strange path of his journey here, considered all the strange events, and the more he thought on them, the more certain he became that there was some guiding force behind it. Some manipulating hand.

That thought lit a fire in his gut and drove him forward. He followed the secret footpath back to the winemaker's shop, and this time he spent no time on subterfuge. He strolled through the back door, waved a greeting to the startled owner, and then went out onto the plaza near the palace.

Everything had changed. The crowd was pressing hard against the north gates, rattling the iron bars and shouting cheers while they watched Ephitel's mansion burn. Corin scanned the crowd for some sign of Maurelle or the druids, but he found none. He did find evidence of Ephitel's handiwork. There were bruises everywhere, bleeding wounds and black eyes where Ephitel's guards had responded to the mob. Corin saw the fist-sized stones littering the courtyard, and he marveled that the crowd hadn't flung them back. The people of Gesoelig were too kind.

There was no sign of Ephitel or his guards now, only rioters flush with victory, marveling at the bonfire atop the hill. That was no sure victory, though. Not while the wretched prince was still alive. Corin left them cheering and headed for the bridge.

When he reached it, soldiers barred his way. They did not seem hostile—not Ephitel's men, then—but they were stout and they watched the thick black smoke with nervous eyes. Corin approached them at a stroll, trying hard to look uninteresting despite his limp. Despite the bundle in his arms and his mud-slick hair and clothes. He must have looked a sickly pauper, and the guards responded automatically with raised eyebrows and lowered pikes.

"Halt!" cried their commander. "The bridge is closed. No one's to pass until that mess is sorted out."

Corin went straight to him, heedless of the iron spear points aimed his way. "I'm on a mission for the king. He bade me bring him this"—he raised the bundle—"with every haste."

The commander shook his head. "Orders were clear. *No one's* to cross the bridge."

Corin ground his teeth. "Very well. Send a messenger for me."

The commander shook his head. "Come back tomorrow."

"If I wait till then, we'll all be rotting corpses," Corin growled. "I have the answers you are waiting for. I can explain what happened over there, and I bring news of far worse things than that! Send someone to the king to tell him Corin Hugh—"

"You're Corin Hugh?"

The burst of excitement in the soldier's voice took Corin aback. He nodded slowly. "Aye."

"You should have said! I didn't recognize you under all that mud. Come through! Let him on through!"

Corin went mechanically, still shocked that it could be so easy. "Oberon's expecting me? The king will see me?"

"Oh, not much chance of that. The king's in a right pique. But you can wait with Lady Delaen and the others. They said you would be coming."

Lady Delaen. The name curled Corin's lip.

But the commander didn't seem to notice. He frowned, lost in thought. "Where's the other two?"

"They'll be here shortly," Corin said. "Send them on through, *even if* they're dirty."

The commander chuckled, his cheeks a little red. "I will. I will. I'll see it done. But you go on to the Midnight Grotto. That is where they're waiting."

"To where?"

"Oh! Ha. She said you'd need a guide. Pothamer! Show the man the way, and make it quick. We wouldn't want to keep the druids waiting."

The Midnight Grotto proved to be the same chamber Corin and the others had ducked into before to hide from Ephitel. Corin's escort pointed out the doorway, clearly hesitant to approach the room, and when Corin nodded understanding, the soldier turned and scurried back toward the bridge.

Corin watched him go, then steeled himself and slipped into the room. His gaze went to the distant corner, where delicious-smelling fruit had grown before, but now the bushes were picked bare. Corin sighed and turned himself to business.

Maurelle was there, and Corin was glad of that. The lady's hair was disheveled, her sleeve ripped, and a scrape across her temple was just now beginning to bruise.

She was not alone. Aemilia was there as well, stretched out on the grassy floor, apparently asleep. And there, of course, was Delaen, expression grim beneath that stark white hair. She was watching Corin with appraising eyes, and as he considered her, he felt a rising tide of anger.

He stalked toward her. "Good morning, druid. You won't—"

Maurelle wrecked his stormy entrance. As soon as she turned his way, she screamed, "Corin! You're alive!" and wrapped him in a crushing hug.

"I'm alive," he said, smoothing down her hair. "And Avery as well."

"Where is Avery? And Kellen?"

"Together," Corin said, not yet prepared to tell that tale. "In a cavern underneath the Piazza Autunno."

Delaen spoke up. "There is no cavern under the piazza."

"There is now," Corin said.

Maurelle gasped in shock.

Corin nodded. "Ephitel's handiwork. Just one of many ugly surprises he had planned."

Delaen narrowed her eyes. "I hear a note of accusation in your voice, but I cannot guess what you mean to imply."

Corin pushed away from Maurelle so he could face the druid. "Then I will tell you plainly. I begin to see a guiding hand at my every turn. Someone sent me to the Piazza Primavera at just the right moment to encounter the sister of Avery of Jesalich. Someone helped me when I went to rescue Avery. Someone arranged for me to pass the blockade on the palace bridge—"

Delaen tossed her hair. "If you object to friendly aid—"

"You do not aid *me*," Corin said. "You use me like a puppet—like a blacksmith's hammer—and I grow tired of the pounding."

The druid frowned. "I don't underst—"

"You sent me to the king! You told me what to say. You promised it would get me home, but instead he sent me on an errand."

"The king has unpredictable—"

"No!" Corin snapped. "You did this to me! From the moment I arrived in this city, someone has been twisting my fate. One of your druids took me in? Oh, and *just* as Ephitel was at her shop? You showed me his tyranny. You gave me over to one of his pretty, pitiful victims—"

Maurelle squeaked in objection, but Corin paid no mind. He felt a throbbing fever in his temples, and he gave it vent.

"You handed me to Avery, whom I've admired since I was a child. You paired me with a noble warrior badly used. You primed me like a pistol so that Oberon could fire me upon your foes."

Delaen arched an eyebrow. "Are you opposed to fighting Ephitel?"

"This is not my war! I only wanted to go home. But you have broken me."

"I have done nothing," Delaen said. "I could not arrange a tenth of what you say."

"So it is chance? Pure chance I met the ancient father of the only dwarf I know in all the world? All my life I've walked with fortune near at hand, but even I cannot believe…what?"

The shock and fear in Delaen's eyes stole Corin's fury. He trailed off, then asked again, "What have I said?"

"I could not arrange these things," Delaen said, her voice far off. "But there is one who could."

Corin didn't have to consider long. "Oberon?"

"Oberon. His will can tug the threads of fortune. He has been known to twist a fate."

"I am done with being twisted," Corin snapped.

"Then on your own, you would not have challenged Ephitel?"

"I never would have dreamed to! No!"

"And now that you have dreamed?"

Corin's chest heaved, but he could not easily answer that question. He furrowed his brow, thinking hard, and when he spoke his voice rang hollow to his own ear. "That is why I rage. My heart is mine. It is not yours to manipulate, and it is not Oberon's."

"But you do not want to fight Ephitel?"

"I want to see him dead!" Corin shouted. "Like I have wanted nothing else in all my life. I want to kill that wretched snake…"

"And yet?"

"This is not my home. This is not my world at all. You have abducted me, and I may never see my home again."

"Or Iryana," Maurelle said, speaking to Delaen. "That's what really troubles him. He loves her, and she does seem something wonderful."

"I barely know her," Corin growled. "But I owe her a debt. I should be focusing on that. I should be back in my own time."

Delaen came forward and laid a gentle hand on Corin's arm. Her voice was just as soft. "But you are here. It must be for a reason. If Oberon brought you here, he has a plan."

"He's mad!" Corin shouted. "I've spoken with him once, and his is not a wisdom I would trust to rule a household, let alone a kingdom. Let alone a world!"

"The elves do not think as we think—"

"He doesn't think at all! He is a fool."

"He is under such a strain."

"And still he plays these games. Still he shuns his dedicated friends. Why are you waiting in this room while rebellion builds? Why won't he grant an audience even to you?"

"He must have his reasons. We bide until—"

"No," Corin said. "We bide no more. This kingdom is about to tear in pieces. I won't just sit here."

He headed for the throne room, and both women trailed after him. "I've told you," Maurelle said, "it's no use to try. You can't get in unless they let you."

"They will let me," Corin growled. "I've brought a present."

Maurelle brightened. "Oh? Did you bring the sword? That's what we were waiting for."

"Games," Corin grumbled. "His head is on the block and he plays games!"

Corin burst around the corner onto the landing overlooking Oberon's distant throne. The king was seated there, but he sprang to his feet as soon as he saw Corin, hope glowing like starlight in his eyes. One glance told him Corin didn't have the sword, and that spark died as quickly as it had kindled. He clapped his hands together, no words spoken, and the courtiers formed their unbroken wall, locking Corin out.

Delaen sighed, clearly disappointed. "This is why we wait. You should have brought the sword."

"I brought something better," Corin said. He drew his bundle, shook the rags loose from Ogden's pistol, and raised it overhead. He fired straight into the air.

The powder flashed unnaturally bright, flaring red and angry in the living cavern. The thunder crack rolled out, breaking all the careful decorum of the synchronized courtiers. Some screamed. Some fainted. No one held his ground. They broke apart like ocean swell against a ship's bow, peeling back in a frenzy until a path opened between Corin and the throne. The king alone stood unmoved.

He stared at Corin across the gap, then raised his voice. "Ethan Blake never owned a sword like that."

"No, he didn't," Corin called back. "But Ephitel did. And he has more." He held the monster's gaze for one heavy heartbeat, then he started down toward the throne. "Clear the court. It's time we had a talk."

(31)

Oberon clapped his hands together, and the courtiers poured from the room. Maurelle stuck close to Corin, hanging on his arm, while Delaen watched the gun with nervous fear. The pirate ignored them both. He didn't run to meet Oberon. He went at a walk, head high, while the gun exhaled its noxious smoke in his wake.

Ten paces out, Corin stopped. He met the mad king's black eyes. "You have a problem on your hands."

"An armed intruder, marching on my throne?"

"As it happens, yes." Corin carefully stowed the gun beneath his cloak, then raised his gaze to Oberon again. "But it isn't me."

"The prince."

"Aye. Ephitel of the High Moor. A lord of war."

"He called himself that?"

Corin nodded.

Oberon sighed. "That was the title Memnon took when he posed a threat to my city. I saw he was destroyed."

"No, my lord. You *watched* him be destroyed," Corin said. "I know the story. Aeraculanon slew him."

"In my name."

"Yes. But by his mortal hand. By his will."

The elf king shrugged. "I rewarded him most kindly. I elevated him to the gentry, made him a place at court—"

"You used him," Corin said, marveling. "Just as you used me."

Oberon arched an eyebrow. "Just the same? I had not heard that Ephitel was dead."

Corin shrugged. "He *was* dead. I shot him through the heart. But no. He yet lives."

"Impossible!"

Delaen pressed forward. "'Tis true, Your Majesty. We saw his carriage force a way through the crowds outside his mansion, nearly two hours ago now."

"The crowd?" Oberon asked, chastising. "That is a rather friendly name for the mob you raised."

"It was a friendly act on your behalf!" Corin snapped. "You owe her gratitude, not rebuke."

Maurelle gasped and shrank away. Delaen frowned and shook her head, but Corin wasn't through. "Your kingdom balances upon the brink of ruin and you do nothing. You dare to despise the ones who do. That is as much a tyranny as anything that Ephitel has done."

The king drew himself to his full height, three paces tall and thick with wild power. He threw his head back and roared, but Corin didn't flinch. Corin screamed into the madness. "Do you want to be king? Do you want to be king? Then stop playing foolish farces and *do your job!*"

The king subsided. He stumbled back a step and collapsed into his chair. "Y—you dare demand of me—"

"Not of you," Corin spat. "You're a shell game. You're a parl trick to buy some time. You are not a king at all. But if there king, a true and loyal leader anywhere beneath that cheap fa then yes. I do demand of him."

For a long time the monstrous king stared down at Corin. Then he heaved a weary sigh and clapped his hands. Something like a summer breeze rolled down upon the throne, splashing out across the clearing and carrying with it a multicolored fog that quickly burned away.

Behind it, on the throne, the goat-legged monster was replaced by an ordinary man. He had been tall, once. He had been handsome. And by the breadth of his shoulders, he had been powerfully built. But now he just looked tired. Old. Kind. Corin recognized the face from the sandstone cliffs at the edge of the Endless Desert.

"Oberon," he said.

Maurelle gave a squeak. "It was all a glamour? All these years?"

Delaen didn't look surprised at all. Corin took note of that. But she seemed to look more kindly on the poor old man than she ever had the beast.

True to his character, Oberon paid her no mind. He looked down at Corin. "How did you know?"

I didn't, Corin thought, but he kept that to himself. He'd never guessed the strange appearance was a ruse, just the wild behavior. But it little profited him to tell the truth, so he shrugged and said, "A liar always knows."

"So he does," Oberon said. "So he does. But if we're done playing at farces, tell me plainly: What does Ephitel intend?"

Corin shook his head. "You owe me an accounting first."

"There is no time. Tell me—"

"No. In all this land, I alone am no subject of yours. You can-command me, elf king. You will give me an accounting, or withhold my own."

"ou would risk the lives of all my people?"

"That choice was never mine to make. It is yours."

The old man tapped his foot impatiently. "I should have known. You are a pirate after all. How much gold will satisfy your greedy heart?"

Corin shook his head. "You do not have enough gold to satisfy me."

"I *create* the gold."

"And still you do not have enough. It is not a ransom I demand, but an accounting. Tell me what you've done to me."

"Done to you?"

"You stole my destiny. You twisted fate. You threw me in the paths of Avery and Ogden. You sent me after Ephitel—"

"I'll take the blame for everything except the last. *You* went after Ephitel. *You* used Avery for good and found the valor in poor Kellen's heart. You had your chance to take the sword and run, and that was all I ever asked of you. But you, out of the good in your own heart, chose to defy the prince."

"I am not a righteous man. I defy Ephitel for no more noble reason than hatred. I hate the things he's done, the evil he's promoted."

"Then you are good enough for my name's sake."

Corin frowned. "How can you know these things?"

"This is my kingdom. How could I not know?"

"You know, and you do nothing?"

"Tread carefully where your eyes barely see. I am not a wicked man. I work in ways you cannot even guess at."

"More glamours? More silly games?"

Oberon shook his head. "I hold a world within my head. That is no small feat. I change one tiny pattern, and it breaks a million others. I cannot end Ephitel, but I gave you Avery. I changed a thousand years of history in subtle ways to give you Ogden Strunk."

"You can do these things, but you cannot stop Ephitel from buying guns? You can't stop him hoarding writs of provender? You can't feed the starving dwarves?"

Oberon looked away. He seemed so small within the monster's throne. "Once the story's told, it becomes real. I cannot shape it. Once Ephitel became a legend, I could not undo him. Once the sword *Godslayer* gained a name, I couldn't give it to you. You had to find it on your own."

Corin ground his teeth in anger. "How can you be so powerless over your own creation?"

"How could you suffer mutiny to Ethan Blake? No matter how you play your hand, free will may always thwart you."

"But still you sent me for the sword," Corin snapped, focusing on something he hoped he might truly comprehend. "So tell me plainly. Why is that sword so important? Do you intend me to kill Ephitel by its blade?"

"Would you do that?" Oberon asked quietly. "Are you another Aeraculanon to serve me?"

"What else could you want it for?"

Oberon shrugged. "To send you home. That was what you asked of me."

"You...you need the sword to send me home? You truly meant to send me home?"

"That is how the story has to go."

"But...what of Ephitel?"

"The Ephitel out there...the one you've faced within this city...he is my concern, not yours. You've done more than any subject could be asked to thwart the traitor's plans. You have earned your just reward."

"But Ephitel is coming! He is real. He brings a regiment with guns against the city."

"We can confirm that," Delaen said. "Jeff and Kirk are on surveillance. Ephitel is with his regiment right now. He's given orders to the others to stand pat."

"Then they will be outside the fire," Oberon mused. "That is good."

"But if you bring them in, they could stand against Ephitel's men," Delaen said.

"They would be cut down," Oberon said. "If Ephitel has guns, my other regiments would be no more challenge to him than my chefs and linen maids. No. Leave them where they stand."

"But we need them—"

"We might have needed them," Oberon said, "in another time, when the story went another way. They might have been useful rescuing survivors from the ruins of the Piazza Autunno explosion. But our friend prevented that disaster." He looked to Corin. "For that alone I owe you a great debt. I would not much like to live through that again."

Corin frowned. "Again? What do you mean?"

Oberon shook his head. "Silly farces. Silly farces. What more can you report to me?"

Corin searched his memory. "Most of it you seem to know. That Ephitel collected writs of provender in order to buy guns and powder from the starving dwarves. That he has his regiment already armed. That he intended to collapse the plaza and isolate the palace. And that Kellen and the House of Violets acted as heroes in your name. They deserve a rich reward."

"They do. I won't deny it."

"Oh! And there are heroes too among the dwarves. Even those who served the prince showed honor when it didn't serve them. I beg some clemency on their behalf."

Oberon spread his arms. "They will not suffer by my hand. You have my word. I will spend what energy I can to protect them from Ephitel, but I must protect the city first."

Corin felt some tension ease within his breast. "You have some plan for the city, then?"

"Of course, but it is complicated. It will take a mighty effort on my part, and I do not have much to spare."

"Can I help? Corin asked.

"Or I?" asked Delaen.

"Or…or I?" Maurelle asked, her eyes wide.

Oberon gave a weary chuckle. "You all will help, in time."

Corin frowned. "How much time is there?"

"If I remember right, we have four hours yet before Ephitel is ready to move. Nearly five. It will be a close thing, but that is time enough."

Corin nodded, feeling even better. "Hours till you need me. Good. Then I will find something to eat and grab a nap."

"A well-earned reward! Go to the Midnight Grotto and choose your bed. I will send servants with a feast to please your belly. You must be strong and rested when Ephitel finally moves against the city."

Corin took his leave, with Maurelle right behind him. They turned their backs on the king and headed up the long path toward the exit, but they had barely gone a dozen paces when a new figure darted onto the landing ahead of them. Corin recognized the druid Jeff.

Short of breath and pale of face, he sprinted down the aisle toward the king, shouting as he came. "It's Ephitel, Your Majesty! He's armed his regiment with rifles. Even now, he moves against the city!"

(32)

Corin shouted, full of righteous rage. "Gods' blood and sinners' stains! I'd give this kingdom for a sandwich!"

Behind him, Delaen called an admonishing, "Corin!"

Oberon said, "Calm yourself. I'll see that something's brought for you." But his voice was shaky.

Corin sighed and turned back to the throne. "Never mind. I'll eat when this is through. How can I help?"

"Just bring me the sword."

Corin blinked. "I don't have it."

"But you wrestled it from Ephitel."

"Aye, and lost it in the dark. The dwarves have it. Avery stayed to bring it to me."

"Oh." Oberon's eyes went distant, and then he said more quietly, "Oh."

Corin sighed. "I can go and try to talk them back around—"

"No. I may need you here. We can count on Avery."

Corin frowned. Something in the king's tone seemed strange, but Corin couldn't place it.

Before Corin had time to ask, the breathless Jeff reached the throne and launched into his report. "Six hundred men. With horse. One musket each. One pistol. And a bayonet. We saw no powder horns or kegs, or even bags of shot, but they had hard leather cases of a strange design. We don't know what's in them."

"I do," Corin said. He described the paper packets filled with shot and powder.

Jeff gave a low whistle. "That will help with loading speed considerably. We may have a problem."

Oberon nodded. "Close the gate."

Jeff looked doubtful. "That won't slow him long."

"I need whatever I can get. Go. Kellen will...no. Not this time. Jeff, I appoint you lord protector—"

Corin interrupted. "What about Kellen?"

Oberon sighed. "As you said, rewards are due. For the valor he has shown this day, I name Kellen, son of Kellen Strong, as the lord protector. But until he joins us, Jeff, it falls on you. Will you be my lieutenant?"

"Of course, Your Majesty."

"Good. Then close the gates, and muster whatever loyal troops you can find within the city."

Delaen cleared her throat. "Should we send word to the regiments?"

"No. That hasn't changed. Bringing them would only start hostilities sooner. And we will need the regiments intact, afterward, to put things back together."

Delaen now watched the king with the same skepticism Corin felt.

Oberon could not have missed it in her expression, but he clearly had no wish to explain himself. "Maurelle of House Violet, for the aid you've given me today, I appoint you hostess to the royal court."

Maurelle squealed and clapped her hands. She threw her arms around Corin in a strong embrace and planted a great kiss upon his cheek, then darted over to kneel before the king. "Oh, thank you! Thank you! You're so gracious. I wish Avery were here to see this. *Such* an honor! Really!" She paused to catch her breath, then cocked her head. "What's a hostess to the court?"

"You will keep track of all our houses and the channels of command. You will coordinate our social efforts and maintain situational awareness and response."

Maurelle blinked. "I'll what?"

"You'll gossip," Corin said. "And listen to gossip. And filter gossip and keep track of who gives the best gossip." He closed his eyes, reviewing all the things that Oberon had said. "Oh. And sometimes you'll throw parties."

She grinned at Corin, then turned to the king. "Is that really it?"

"In essence, yes."

"Yay!"

"But for now, this is what I need of you: spread the word within the city that trouble's coming. Raise the fire brigades. And evacuate everyone within a mile of the city's southern gate or anywhere at all on Moneylender's Lane."

Delaen started forward. "She can't do all that! Even I couldn't do all that."

Maurelle looked crushed at Delaen's words. Corin said, "No. She can't. But I suspect she could name the ten people who among them could accomplish it. She could likely even tell us where to find them."

"Oh, I could!" Maurelle cried, triumphant. "It won't even take ten. Give me half an hour and I'll have it done."

"Then go," Oberon said. "But before you do, hear this proclamation. For the service he has given on this day, I name Avery of House Violet as mayor of Gesoelig. I'll entrust to him the smooth running of this city. As soon as he reports for duty, I will place him at your service for the evacuations."

"Oh, he'll like that," Maurelle said. "He does love making plans and setting them in motion." She grinned, imagining, then snapped back to herself a moment later. She threw a hasty curtsy, whispered, "Majesty," then darted from the hall about her errands.

"And your reward will have to wait, I fear," the king told Corin. "I would not send you home without the sword."

"Would not, or could not?" Corin asked.

Oberon shrugged. "It matters little to a king and less to a creator."

"And less to me, I suppose," Corin said. "For I would not leave anyway until this mess is done."

"That might be too much to hope for. This mess will not be over for an age. Still, you shall see the shape of things, and that should satisfy."

"Perhaps," Corin said, doubtful, but Oberon clapped his hands.

"I will settle for perhaps. Now go and eat and wait for Avery. I must discuss my plans with Delaen."

Corin looked longingly toward the Midnight Grotto, but then he gave a groan and tore his gaze away. "No. I think I'll stay. I've seen too much to walk away at this late hour."

"You've earned your rest."

"I've earned a place upon your council," Corin snapped. "I may know other things of value, like the paper bullets. I beg the chance to contribute to your plan."

The king hesitated, clearly on the verge of saying no. Then he threw his hands up and sighed. "Very well. If you insist. But at least hold your tongue while I sketch out the shape of things."

Corin nodded his assent and sank down cross-legged on the soft grass before the throne. He fought a weary yawn while he stared up at Oberon.

The king spoke mainly to his druid. "Ephitel means to break my power. That is all he needs. He would prefer to have me dead. He would prefer to take the throne by force and wear this crown upon his brow, but none of that is necessary. If he can show the city that I bleed, if he can *start* a war, then he will win it."

Corin nodded in silent agreement, but Delaen seemed surprised. "No. Surely there are those loyal to your name."

"Not enough," Oberon said. "Not near enough. Because even if I conquer Ephitel, I will have shown the world that I'm assailable. There will be others sure that they can succeed where Ephitel failed."

"And you will crush them, too. Right?"

Oberon shook his head slowly. "There was a time when I would have. There was a time when I rode out to war against monstrosities and myths."

Delaen licked her lips. "And what has changed? Surely you don't grow old!"

"Not I," the king replied. "But the kingdom. This world grows heavy beneath the weight of all the stories it has spawned, and it takes everything within my power to keep tomorrows following on the heels of yesterdays."

The druid took an involuntary step toward the throne. "Your Majesty! You never told us. We might have helped."

"You do, daily, just by being you. But already I've invested more of myself than I ever should have risked. There is just enough left of me to do what must come next."

Delaen stifled a sob, but Corin could not guess what Oberon intended. Despite his promise, he couldn't stop himself. He leaned toward the king and whispered, "What? What comes next?"

Oberon turned heavy eyes on him. "We abandon Gesoelig. We give the world to Ephitel."

"That is no answer at all!"

"It isn't meant to be the end. It is just a start."

"But I have seen the end! Ephitel becomes a god over a wretched world where tyrants treat honest men like their possessions."

"And yet you want to return…"

"Aye! To save someone from just that fate."

"Your love?" Oberon asked. "This Iryana?"

"She is not my love," Corin said. "I barely know her."

"But still you care so much?"

"Aye! Because she's my responsibility. I placed her life in Blake's hands, so it falls to me to rescue her."

Oberon bowed his head. "Gesoelig is no different. More than a million noble lives, and all of them at risk if Ephitel reaches the city. You saw what he had planned at the Piazza Autunno."

"So you'll evacuate?"

"Something like it, yes. We'll disappear, regroup somewhere safe, and come back in force to answer his treachery."

"Disappear," Corin said, a growing fear in his belly. "How?"

Oberon spread his hands. "I shall move the very city. I'll whisk it out from under his advance and hide it in a mountain. Ephitel will march against an empty field."

Corin only nodded, but his heart felt empty. He remembered the ancient, empty city he had found. For the first time since the fires took him, he remembered the ghostly voices that had so frightened his crew.

This plan never worked. The world forgot Gesoelig and its elf king, and Ephitel built kingdoms on the backs of slaves.

Remember us, the ghosts had begged. *Avenge us.*

Corin sighed and shook his head. "It isn't going to work."

(**33**)

Oberon arched an eyebrow. "I did ask you to forebear—"

"I know," Corin said. "But I have seen where this all leads. If you believe any part of my story, you must believe that. I have *seen* the cavern where the city ends, and it was not a thriving new home."

"It isn't meant to be," Delaen said. "We *have* discussed these things before. We'll make our haven on the Isle of Mists where Ephitel's magic will not let him see. But *first* we'll jump away to the Endless Desert to throw him off the scent."

Corin blinked. "Oh. Well. I see. That is not a terrible plan."

The druid loomed closer. "I *would* like to know how that turns out. What do you know of the Isle of Mists in your own time?"

"Nothing," Corin said. "No one ventures there, neither men nor gods. For all I know, there could be a bustling metropolis beneath the fog, but…"

"Yes?"

Corin looked away. "It is said the isle is home to none but restless ghosts and ancient sorrow."

Delaen's bright-eyed hope faded. Oberon rose and clapped her on the back. "Take heart. That is just the sort of rumor we would spread."

Corin frowned up at the king, still anxious for a straightforward answer. "Would spread? Or will?"

"Hmm?"

"Binding though you claim they are, you've changed your story more than once. These rumors about your final home—are they a plan you're looking forward to, or a memory you're looking back on?"

"You would not much like an honest answer."

Corin snorted. "I have not liked much at all since I came to this place."

"Then on those terms I'll tell you plain: it's neither memory nor expectation, but a dream within a dream."

"That is no answer at all!"

"But it is the only honest one."

Delaen raised her voice "Gentlemen, we don't have time for this."

Corin was prepared to agree. Anxious as he was for answers, he was beginning to suspect he'd never understand them anyway. Oberon did at last seem prepared to talk, but every answer only raised more questions. And for all the rage Corin had expressed, he'd admitted twice now that he would war with Ephitel as a puppet or as a free man. There would be time enough to understand the things that had been done to him after Ephitel was dead.

He opened his mouth to say as much, but the king spoke first. "As it happens, Delaen, there is nothing more important, here and now, than this conversation."

"But the preparations—"

"Are entirely inside my head," Oberon said. "For my part, anyway. I am hard at work, shifting history, and it will cost me nothing to spare some attention for the man who will have saved a hundred thousand lives on Piazza Autunno."

The druid twisted her hands together, anxious, and Corin understood her frustration. Everything hung in the balance, and there was nothing she could do to tip it. Talking hardly satisfied.

Oberon seemed at last to sense her angst. He caught his breath and nodded. "That is for me," he said. "I only have to move the city, but you will have to deal with the aftermath. Go. Find Maurelle and see how you can help prepare the people."

Delaen swept a graceful curtsy. "Yes, Your Majesty." She went two paces, then turned back. "Fortune favor, and statistics all be damned."

It had a ritual sound to it, and Oberon grinned in answer. "And you as well. Evermore and evermore and evermore, amen."

The king and Corin watched her go. Neither spoke until she'd left the landing, and then Corin realized that he was left alone in that vast chamber with the king.

The world was ending, but for just a moment, there was nothing more important than a conversation. The maker-king himself had said so. But for all the maddening things he'd seen, with Delaen's parting words still hanging in the air, Corin could only think of one question. He turned toward the king. "What are proofs and postulates?"

Oberon smiled. "Filthy words."

"And…scientist?"

Oberon gasped. "Who in all Hurope would speak that name?"

"Kellen. He said it to Ephitel."

"Ah. If ever any black soul deserved such slander, it is Ephitel." Oberon thought for a moment. "No. It is fitting. A scientist is one who would trade all the magic, all the majesty of this world for a little bit of power. It can be done with ways of thinking, or by remembering forbidden lore, or through certain artifice…"

"Guns," Corin said. "And cannons. Ogden said you feared the dwarves."

"Not the dwarves themselves," Oberon said. "No more than I would fear my precious druids, though they carry living science in their strange little hearts. No, I fear what other men would do with their secrets."

Corin nodded, very nearly understanding. "Tell me the story, then. What is yesterworld?"

Oberon heaved a weary sigh. "It is math and science. Schools and jobs. Reason unrestrained, taming all the fascinating mystery into one broad and pale monotony, as far as the eye can see. Politics and forms. Taxes. Statistical significance." He sniffed and dabbed fresh tears from his eyes. "I watched a world of wild fancy reduced to tedium by the postulates and proofs, and then I dreamed a dream. I dared to make a new world untarnished by such things. I formed Hurope and welcomed certain of my brothers and cousins to enjoy the taste of *magic* once again. I even brought some selected few from among the mortals of that world—"

"Your druids."

"Even so. Because…no matter how I hated reason, a world must have *some* to work at all. I chose representatives as devoted to the dream as I, and they brought with them just enough of rationality to keep the sunrise running smoothly."

"I thought…" Corin started, but he trailed off, considering his words. He nodded. "I thought perhaps you were drifting, there. Perhaps you were telling tales to avoid thinking of the matter at hand."

"No."

Corin shook his head. "No. I think Ephitel is threatening your dream, in a very real way."

"Just so. For the sake of power, he will undo the world he wants to rule."

"I have seen the world that he rules," Corin said. "It is not as bad as you predict."

"Are there schools?"

"Aye, in the larger cities. Rikkeborh has a famed university, but it is lovely. It is useful. Ephitel's true villainy lies in his abuse of honest men."

Oberon waved that away. "Honest men will always be abused. It is their nature. In a fairy world or yesterworld, honest men will suffer. But we could have a world with *mystery*—"

"There is magic in my world," Corin said. "There is mystery enough to drive a storm."

"Heroes?" Oberon asked. "True heroes?"

Corin hesitated. "There are stories."

"Old or new?"

Corin shrugged. "We know Aeraculanon. Tcilleas and the Hivernan War. Disis. The heathen Alleshim and his companion. And…well, there are those who know of Avery of Jesalich."

"So. Age after age has passed, and these are the names you know? Avery who made his name on this very day. Aeraculanon who is ten years dead. Tcilleas lived to see the fall of Old Maedred, and Disis might still be enjoying himself on his little island kingdom. I remember Alleshim, and a hundred other heroes you've forgotten. But you cannot name me one I haven't met. What does that suggest to you?"

"That there is greatness in your land—"

"No. It tells you greatness *died* at some age long past. It began to die when Ephitel attacked the city. In my time—in this time—there were heroes ever rising, falling, but in your time they are just a memory."

"And you blame Ephitel?"

"I blame order. I blame reason. I blame schools and science. The traitor Ephitel will open those floodgates just to fill his cup, and everything I've made will wash away."

"Does it have to be so grim as that?"

Oberon sighed. "I had a dream. But now this world, like every world, awakes to sad reality."

"Because of Ephitel! We can stop Ephitel."

"I wish that were enough."

"That *is* enough. If the thing you fear is guns, we can take away his guns. If the thing you fear is challenge, we can answer his challenge. Swiftly and absolutely. Even if some of your soldiers die, is it not worth that sacrifice to save a world?"

"Would you sacrifice the members of your crew to save your ship?"

"Aye. I *have*. I could name you half a dozen worthy men who gave their lives to the roaring waves. That is the nature of the game we play."

"And nothing in that answer surprises me. But would you sacrifice Iryana for the sake of your ship?"

Corin hesitated, jaw hanging open. "I…"

"That is what you're suggesting. I would fight my brothers to save this land. I would lead soldiers into battle for a greater good. But how many of my children, how many of my loyal subjects can I risk just to protect my dream?"

"Stop calling it a dream!" Corin said. "Even if that's where it began—"

"It is a dream."

"It is my world," Corin said. "This is reality to me. I have never known a yesterworld. This—" He waved around him. "This is my real life."

"Not *this*," Oberon said. "Surely you don't mean your time here in Gesoelig."

"I do. I mean my other life, too—the fate of Iryana and my crew burns bright and real inside my heart—but since I've come here, I have met real people. I have come to know Maurelle and Kellen, Avery and Ephitel. All of this is real, and I would fight for it!"

Oberon smiled despite his tears. "You soothe my aching spirit, Corin Hugh. But it serves you not to think of this as real. As I said before, this time is neither past nor future. It is a dream within a dream."

"What does that mean?"

"It isn't real. It's even less real than the life you left behind. It is just a sliver of my memory, trapped in time and saved to share with you—"

"With me? A pirate out of Aepoli? I scarce believe it."

Oberon hesitated. Corin watched while the king considered sticking to the flattering lie, but Oberon shrugged and answered, "No. Not so specifically. It was preserved for anyone who might come later. This, just as the Isle of Mists, has long been part of my plan."

"So you remember what comes next? You remember how these things will go?"

"Not...entirely. There already have been changes. Your presence shifts the narrative, and every little act has ripples."

"Ripples?"

"Who will die and who will live. You've saved a normal city's worth of souls by discovering Ephitel's plans for the piazza. You've changed the fates of all my regiments who might have been rescuing the fallen in the hours to come. I cannot predict how much will shift from that—"

"But I have changed the future? Or...the past? I have changed how the story goes? If I can save a hundred thousand lives, then I can finish one."

"Do not spend your energy on that. Killing Ephitel would gain you nothing."

"Why are you so determined to give up? Killing Ephitel would save the world."

Oberon shook his head. "That would do no good."

"It would make him dead."

"Please, Corin, that is not how this story goes. There are more profitable ways to spend our time."

"More profitable than saving your kingdom?"

"From *this* threat, in *this* dream, yes."

"How? How can that possibly be true?"

"Because it's all become too much. When the world was yet young, I had no trouble keeping it alive. But the years weigh heavy on me now. Even without Ephitel, I would be weak. Even without the threat of gunpowder and blood, my time would be limited."

Corin shrugged. "We all grow old. That is no reason to despair. You may find a better successor than Ephitel. Delaen or Aemilia. Or...oh." He swallowed hard. "Is that why you've chosen me? Is that why you brought me here?"

"A pirate out of Aepoli?" He chuckled. "I could do worse. But no. There is no succession for me. For who but I could dream my dreams? When I die, the dream dies with me."

Corin gaped. "The...the dream? The *world*?"

"The world and everything in it."

Corin forced a smile. "Then I suppose we should be glad this is a memory. We should be glad to know that you survived—"

"I didn't."

Corin shook his head. "You did. You must have."

"I didn't. I didn't know, last time, but I remember now. It took everything I had to move the city."

"Then don't—"

"I have no choice. This is my memory, and I remember how it happened. Those who survived the fire slipped off to the Isle of Mists, but I was trapped within the city. I never left this throne again. I died with Gesoelig beneath the mountain."

(**34**)

How?" Corin asked. "If you died, how are you here to answer me? You see? It is impossible."

Oberon smiled sadly. "Aeraculanon died, but his memory lives on, even in your age. Is it so strange that my memory does the same? I am the world's creator, after all."

"But…how? Aeraculanon's shade has never spoken with me."

"As I said, I am the world's creator. I play by other rules. Perhaps the universe gave me some extra reach from a sense of self-preservation."

"Or perhaps I have gone mad. Likely sometime long ago."

Oberon tapped his temple and gave Corin a wink. "I have thought the same. Quite often, really. But I ever reached the same conclusion."

"Yes?"

"If I am mad, no choice I make can matter in the least. If I am not, then it is the world that's mad, and I must address that madness with whatever resources I have."

"But I'm so *tired*."

"I have thought this also," the king said.

"Yes?"

"Yes. And it only gets worse."

Corin groaned.

"Please," the king said softly. "We come at last to the point of everything. Give me ten minutes more, and all will be made clear."

"All?"

"As much as I can grant."

Corin sighed. "Very well. Go on."

Oberon nodded. "As I said before, all Hurope is my dream, and if I die—"

"The dream ends."

"Indeed. And in the end, in the days after *this* day, even as my spirit faded, I saw that more than I feared the nothing, I grieved the billion pretty little lives that I had created. I ached to know that everything I'd made would be undone—"

"Then let me ease your heart. It was not. The world without you is no paradise, but it is not undone."

"That is the story I brought you here to tell. You see, as I lingered, waning, in Gesoelig's magnificent tomb—"

"It *was* magnificent."

He smiled. "Thank you. Before I slipped away completely, I devised a plan to keep the dream alive. There was one, among all my subjects, who would not leave me for the Isle of Mists. I demanded it of her, for her own sake. I begged it of her. But she would not leave my side."

"Delaen?"

Tears shone in the king's eyes. "A well-thought guess, but no. My druids' craft in trade is logic, and though it broke her heart, sweet Delaen saw reason and went off with the others to keep the kingdom of my refugees in order."

"Then who?"

"Maurelle. The loveliest of Violets. She blossomed while Gesoelig burned and coordinated our response, but when the survivors left to found New Soelig, she stayed with me. And when my memory began to fade, when I felt my fire burning out, she spent a thousand years in darkness, in silence, imprisoned on a wild, foolish errand to preserve the dream."

Corin swallowed hard and told a lie. "I don't know what you mean."

"She wrote it down. She caught my dream and pinned it to a page. She wrote down the fifteen million lives that made Gesoelig. She captured everything I could recall of these last days."

Corin said, "The books." And in his heart, he thought, *Please, fortune, no.*

But Oberon nodded. "The books. They are my legacy. They are my memory writ down, the dream preserved."

For a while, Corin marveled at the immensity of it. Then he frowned. "But...where'd she find the paper? Or is that the wrong sort of question?"

Oberon laughed. "It is. You have an unromantic soul. But there was paper in the city. You have seen Aemilia's shop. Even Gesoelig had its documents and forms. She used those at first."

"At first?"

"She filled them up—every empty page within the cave, though it did not tell half the memory. Still, I begged her once again to leave, to take her memory and return to the world of living men. She would not leave me. She devised instead a way to scrape the pages of old books, erasing what was there to record my dream."

"Cunning."

"Indeed. When she had filled all the books, she tore bits of linen to write lives upon. She sought other fabrics, but the refugees had stripped the city bare to supply their journey. In the end...but no. You would not be grateful for that news."

Corin rolled his eyes. "Do you imagine I enjoy any of it?"

"No, but this—"

"Tell the tale."

Still the king hesitated for a heartbeat, but he relented with a sigh. "Very well. In the end, using books and sheets of linen and all manner of other things, she caught those other lives and most of the chronicle of what happened on this day. I thought at last her task was done. We said a sad good-bye—though I was more a shadow than a man by then—and she was to the city gate before she stopped. When she came back to the throne, I pretended I was not there. I spoke no word, but she felt my presence. She was crying. She sobbed her apologies."

"For what?"

"In all the years she had toiled, we had both forgotten the one life that most needed recording."

"Yours."

"Mine. And there were no more books. No more paper in all the cavern. We brought lore of paper with us from yesterworld, but that world also knew an older means of making pages."

"Vellum?" Corin asked, with a gruesome sense where this was headed.

"You know of it?"

Corin swallowed hard. "There are places in the world where it is used. A lamb's skin or a deer's, scraped smooth and flat, then dried…"

"Indeed," the king said, grim.

"But there were no lambs or deer within the cavern," Corin said.

"Indeed. There was only Maurelle."

The silence stretched out for far too long. At last, the king cleared his throat. "She wove threads of her lovely hair to tie the binding. She made ink of her blood. She spent her life to write the sad story of mine, and we died together there beside this throne."

"Why didn't she just leave? Surely she could have purchased paper in the Khera markets."

"She feared that if she left, she might lead someone to the cave."

"Why fear that? Surely she was writing these books for someone to read."

"In a last resort," Oberon said. "But no. It was our hope that the books would be enough—that the written story would be enough to preserve the dream—and discovery seemed more likely to destroy the memory than to preserve it."

Corin swallowed hard. "You were right in that."

"How so?"

"The fire," Corin said. "I told you earlier. Ethan Blake burned the city. That is how I came here."

"No…" Oberon said slowly. "That was part of your parable. That stood for Ephitel's attack against the city."

Corin shook his head. "That really happened."

Oberon sprang forward to shake Corin's shoulders. "It can't have! Without those books…without those books…"

"Yes?"

"The world should be undone."

"You keep saying that. Perhaps it takes some time. Or…perhaps the books aren't necessary at all. Perhaps the world can live on—"

"Can a dream continue after you wake up?"

"You are perhaps beginning to stretch the metaphor too thin."

Oberon narrowed his eyes. "There is no metaphor."

"Your dream," Corin said. "You mean it like an idea, a grand plan. You dreamed about someday building this world, and then you did it. Perhaps you built it well enough to go on without you."

Oberon shook his head. "You do not understand the ways of fairy. I build this world *within* a dream. *My* dream."

"All the world's a dream?"

"And everything in it."

"Impossible. I know how dreams work. If this were a dream, I would not have had to spend hours slogging back and forth across your city! I could have just turned around and been somewhere else."

Oberon shrugged. "Have you tried?"

"No! Because I know reality from dream! If this world was your dream, why were there ever heathen gods? Why would anyone have died at Old Maedred? Why have your *enemies* in your own dreams?"

"You've never had a nightmare?"

"Aye, but—"

"The dream is real for you. That's why I brought the druids. They have some power, though they may not know it. They tame the dreaminess somewhat, but with that rationality comes consequences, cause and effect. We found a careful balance for a while, but now it's gone."

"It's not! We are still here."

"I have guessed an explanation," Oberon said. "The books are gone, but you somehow stepped into the memory itself. The books are gone, but now the dream lives on in you."

Corin shook his head. "I do not want that burden."

"Nonetheless, it falls to you—"

"I won't accept it!"

"It is not a choice," Oberon said. "You alone in all the world now hold the dream within your head."

"Not I alone! There is still you!"

Oberon patted Corin's shoulder. "My time is nearly done. We know that much already."

"But…but that was in another dream. In this one, you're still alive."

"And I still must move the city. The consequence will be the same."

"Then don't move it! Now you know the cost, so make a better choice."

"And watch how many of my people slain? No. I cannot bear that."

"Perhaps they won't be slain. Perhaps they'll win!"

"Against Ephitel's guns? Against an immortal god?"

"He *can* be hurt. Ogden's pistol slowed him for a while. And if we recover Aeraculanon's sword…that can kill him, right?"

"It should. It should. I suspect he's bathed himself in the waters at Aubrocia, just as the heathen Memnon did. Aeraculanon quenched his sword in those same waters, and so slew Memnon."

"And so will I slay Ephitel!"

"It doesn't matter! Nothing really changes. This is just a memory."

"I don't know what that means!"

"It is…a brief time. Limited. Delaen would call it a parallel time stream, or something of the like. The things you do in this world will not carry through to yours. You do not change your past, only the things that I remember."

"Be that as it may, you say my past was just a dream. And this is just a memory. I see no difference between the two! Let that one burn, and save this one instead. You have a chance."

Oberon considered Corin for a while. "Let that one burn? A whole universe would die. *Your* reality. Are you prepared for that?"

"If I could kill Ephitel?"

"Even if you could, is that worth losing Iryana?"

"I don't…" Corin couldn't finish the sentence. "What are my other options?"

"Leave this place. Go back to your world, rescue your pretty slave girl, and remember me. Remember the dream and keep it alive. You alone, in all the world, will have that power."

"But if I choose this world?"

"You cannot choose this world. That is not an option."

"But—"

"I know how much it aches, but there is the difference between memory and dream: I cannot change what really happened."

"Things here have changed. You said yourself—"

"You changed them. You were not here before, so you are not bound by history. But I must act out my own doom."

"But things *can* change." Corin sprang to his feet. "I can change them. I can kill Ephitel and *then* go home."

"He would remain unscathed within your world. Nothing in this dream will change the future as you know it. The friends you've made here will not know you, even if you find them—"

"But I could change *your* future," Corin said. "Even if it's just a memory, I could change it. I could leave you a world with no fear of Ephitel's guns. Maurelle would not have to give her life in darkness. Avery and Kellen…what became of them?"

"As you heard, Kellen became my new lord protector. He trained the resistance to fight and to survive. And Avery was mayor of New Soelig, though I believe he left the post when Maurelle never arrived. He wasted years in an attempt to find the cave again, but it was well hidden."

"It *was* well hidden," Corin said. "I suppose that was when he brought the Nimble Fingers to the lands of men, while he was wandering in search of you."

Corin shook his head. "There. That is another tragedy I could avert. Avery could have his sister, and she could live her life. Kellen wouldn't have to raise some secret army. You give me every reason to see Ephitel dead before I go."

"It is a senseless risk. I cannot guess how long this memory might last, but it will not be a thousand years—"

Corin snorted. "I would gladly trade another hour here to buy some peace for those good souls for a thousand years. I would trade an hour for an hour, if it meant the chance to murder Ephitel. Even if it's just a dream."

"That would be a foolish risk indeed!"

"*What risk?*"

"The risk of dying in the attempt."

"But...I thought this was a dream!"

"Reality's a dream, and you are in it. Death is death, and more for you than most. If you die—in this dream or any other— you die for real. And all the world dies with you."

(35)

Corin sank down on the grass again and wrapped his arms
around his knees. "I...I do not want this burden."

"I never meant to lay it on you," Oberon said. "Nevertheless,
you have it. And with it, all my sympathy."

"I don't know what to do."

"And I can't tell you," Oberon said. "Although I know this
much: don't bury yourself in an early grave. It profits you nothing and costs you everything."

"But isn't that what you're about to do?"

"My hands are tied by history. Yours are not. Live free."

Corin nodded, numb. "Very well. Send me home."

"It isn't such an easy thing as that," Oberon said. "Not with
the feeble power I have left, to cast you safely over so much time
and space."

"Then what do you intend?"

"I'll move the city first, and then we'll have a sympathy. Once
we reach the cavern, I will send you home."

"And until then?"

"Get some rest," Oberon said. "Find sustenance. And enjoy
one last reunion with an old friend."

"What friend?" Corin asked.

Oberon nodded past the pirate's shoulder. "You will leave this memory behind, undone, but here and now you are close friends with a hero you've admired since you were a child. I take pride in that. It was the one kind thing I did for you in this whole dream."

Corin craned around in time to see Avery step out onto the landing. The gentleman thief looked weary and bedraggled, but even so, Corin was surprised how slowly he approached down the path toward the king.

"I enjoyed meeting Kellen," Corin said while they awaited Avery. "Where is Kellen?"

Oberon did not meet Corin's eyes. His gaze was fixed on Avery. "We will ask the Violet."

Corin nodded. "And then there was Maurelle. And Ogden Strunk. And you. I have learned so much from you."

"And I from you," Oberon said. "Every child of this world brings me some joy, some sense of pride, but it has been an honor seeing you in action. Now, here is Avery, and I see he brings a gift."

The sword was unconcealed. Avery carried it in an ill-fitting scabbard. The ruby burned bloodred in the strange light beneath the throne room's canopy, and that same fire seemed to burn in Avery's eyes.

"Welcome," Corin said. "I'd begun to fear for Kellen's health in spite of things I'd heard." He flashed a smile over to Oberon, but the king kept his eyes still on Avery. Corin's smile slipped. "Ahem. I…anyway, the king has news for you."

"Avery of House Violet," the king intoned, "for the service you have given on this day, I name you mayor of Gesoelig."

Avery nodded, eyes downcast. "You are kind, Your Majesty."

Corin cleared his throat. "What ails you? Where…where is Kellen? You have the sword. Ogden said he wouldn't release it unless Kellen gave his word."

Avery nodded again. "It wasn't long after you left. Kellen woke enough to hear what had come to pass. He swore unequivocally that we were good and honorable men."

Corin smiled. "He doesn't know us very well."

Avery didn't look up. He didn't smile. "Having said those words, Kellen died. We buried him beneath the earth, and I brought you your sword."

He raised his head, eyes flashing with tears, and shoved the bundled weapon violently into Corin's arms. Corin took it with a grunt, then turned to Oberon. "You said he lived. You said he trained the refugees—"

"That is how I remember history."

"But you said *this* is your memory! You said your hands were bound and you could not make changes."

"You changed things," Oberon said, solemn.

"He might have been the only honest man I've ever met! They called him coward, but he fought for *you*. He was a true hero!"

"And it was a villain who gunned him down," Oberon answered. "The three of you interrupted a plot that would have seen a hundred thousand dead. I suspect the noble yeoman would have paid his life to save so many."

"But *you* paid his life!" Corin said. "You knew this was happening, and you did nothing."

Oberon sighed. "There is so little I can do. Everything within my power I spent on bringing you to this place, to this understanding, so you can now take it home."

"Do not lay Kellen's death on me!" Corin snapped.

"I don't. I lay it on Ephitel. He is the one responsible, and he will pay in time."

"He won't! I have seen it. He gains power and glory without end. A thousand years or more he'll rule. You call that justice?"

"The world is mad, at times. Even this one of my making. I can only do as much as my resources will allow. I'll do what little good I can, and you must do the same."

"You said the things I do here don't matter—it's just a dying dream—but I *knew him*. He was a good man."

Oberon hung his head, but he offered no apology. "Good men die every day. Take Avery and raise a toast to the noble yeoman. I have my work to do."

"Your work is wasted. You kill yourself to preserve a twisted dream."

"I kill myself to save some handful of those lives you hold so dear. And I will spend my last breath returning you to a world that dies without you."

Corin drew a deep breath and let it out slowly. His gaze sank down to the bundle in his arms. It was Kellen's scabbard, part of his uniform, and far too small for the legendary sword. Corin sniffed. "You may keep that breath."

"What?"

"I have no intention of going back. Not until I've dealt with this."

"I've already warned you of the risks."

"I cannot bring myself to care. I know the traitor will never have to pay in the world I know, but I can make him pay in this one." He tore the scabbard free and held the naked blade before him.

"Please, refrain from this," the king said. "No good can come of it. I need you here, alive."

"Any authority I might have granted you died with Kellen." Corin turned to Avery. "What say you? Will you serve your glorious king, or will you help me kill the monster?"

Avery showed his teeth. "I would like nothing more."

"Then come. We will make plans on the way."

"Stop!" Oberon called behind them. His voice was weak and worn, his brow creased with the strains he bore. Corin raised his eyebrows, waiting for some compelling argument.

"Stay," Oberon said. "Stay here, with me, or I may not be able to send you home at all."

"I like that world little better than this one."

"But it will die without you! Come. You needn't wait. Come before my throne, and I will send you now!"

Corin shook his head. "You need that power to move the city."

"What is one city compared to a world? I will…" His voice cracked, but he shook his head and pressed on. "I will sacrifice them all for you."

Corin spat. "You are a wretched king. I thank sweet fortune that you are not my liege."

He turned and left the throne room, Avery at his heels, while behind them the elf king wept upon his throne.

They were past the Midnight Grotto before Avery found his voice again. "What are we about? Corin, I saw the soldiers rushing through the city. I heard a call for the fire brigades. What is happening?"

"Ephitel is on the march. He has a regiment all armed with guns, and he means to contest Oberon for the throne."

"He will win."

"The king won't even fight him."

Avery shook his head. "Why should he? What could stand against such power?"

Corin gripped the sword *Godslayer* until his hand ached. "I will stand."

"You said before that this was not your war."

"Ephitel made it so when he murdered Kellen. You said before that you would follow me to battle. Will you still? For Kellen? For Maurelle?"

"Maurelle? Has he—"

"No. The king gave her a pretty title, just like yours, and she is hard at work preparing our retreat."

"Retreat." The word sounded bitter on Avery's tongue.

Corin nodded. "Aye. The court and all the pretty lords and ladies will run away and hide, while Ephitel and his followers divvy up the land of men."

"This is Oberon's plan?"

"Aye."

"But you think we should challenge Ephitel."

"I think we should plant him in the ground."

Avery rolled his shoulders, loosening up for a fight. "I like your plan better."

"I thought you might."

"But it will take us half a day to cross the city on foot. Even longer if a panic's growing in the streets."

Corin stopped. He glanced back over his shoulder, toward the distant throne room, then he gave a shrug. "Close your eyes."

"What?"

"Close your eyes and come with me."

Corin fixed his mind upon the task at hand. He thought about the city gates near Moneylender's Lane, where he had first met Aemilia and Ephitel. He fixed his mind on that place and the fight he meant to take to the lord protector. Then he turned around, opened his eyes, and gasped.

Moneylender's Lane was empty, almost as he remembered it from another life. But here, a noonday sun burned hot and bright above, and it was a graceful gate of iron that surrounded the city, rather than ten paces of solid stone.

Avery shouted when he opened his eyes. "Age of reason! Where'd you learn to do that?"

"From the king," Corin said, a little numb.

"Why haven't you been doing that all along?"

Corin barked a laugh. "I didn't know I could. I never tried."

"But how—"

"There isn't time for that," Corin said, raising his arm to point. "Ephitel approaches."

From their place near the gate, Corin could see Ephitel's battle lines. There might have been a thousand men, mostly mounted and all wielding the flintlock rifles Jeff had mentioned. They had their attendants, too, and as Corin looked closer, he frowned.

"Are those catapults?"

"Mangonels, by the looks of them. Is that so strange?"

"For a man who has access to cannons? Yes."

"Perhaps he had no time to have them built. Or he lacked the resources."

"He equipped a thousand men with rifles and pistols," Corin growled. "He could have made a pair of cannons."

"You seem to suspect a reason. Say it. Why would Ephitel bring catapults?"

Corin bowed his head, remembering so many things the king had said. He sighed. "Why would Oberon raise the fire brigades?"

A quarter mile out, among Ephitel's lines, someone gave a short, sharp trumpet blast, and Corin turned to Avery. "Take cover. Here, inside this shop!"

He grabbed the gentleman's sleeve and dragged him off the street just as the two catapults slammed into violent motion. They hurled their ammunition high into the air, overshooting the walls by at least a hundred paces. Avery chuckled. "That won't get them in."

"That was not the goal," Corin said. "They weren't stones or darts. They were wooden barrels."

One of the barrels lost itself somewhere behind the building Corin and Avery had used for refuge, but the other smashed down two blocks over, among the shops and houses, and as it landed, it shot a pillar of fire ten paces above the rooftops. It boomed, and an answering explosion rang out to the west.

"He meant to start a fire," Corin said. "He meant to kill the townsfolk. That man needs to die."

(36)

Avery screamed. "What was that?"

"A powder keg with a long fuse."

"He fired on *the city*?"

Corin heaved a weary sigh. "We locked the gates and he wants in. Perhaps he hopes in the panic, some of our people will open the gates. Or...gods' blood, he might have done it for fun. He wants to break Oberon's dominion, and killing off a lot of people should accomplish just that."

The explosions' thunder was long since gone, but a new roar was rising. It came with the wall of thick black smoke and the heat haze heavy in the air.

"It's working," Avery said. "Age of reason, the fire will take the whole city soon."

"No," Corin said. "Oberon already raised the fire brigades. Maurelle's coordinating them."

"Even so, they aren't *here* yet, and there are people in those buildings."

Avery darted for the street, but Corin caught his shoulder and spun him back around. "Where are you going?"

Avery frowned, looking confused. "There are people in those buildings."

"Let someone else see to them. We have a higher calling."

"Killing Ephitel? There will be time enough for that later."

Corin licked his lips. "Maybe not. There is not much time at all."

"Then I would spend it on my friends before my foes."

"This is *for* your friends. This is for Kellen."

Avery sucked a deep breath, then met Corin's eyes. "Kellen's dead. These people aren't."

"You're not a hero. You're a *thief.*"

"I am a hero. Oberon himself said so. But that is not what matters. The important thing is that I am not a monster."

He tried to leave, but Corin would not let go. "Those people do not matter!"

Avery's eyes went cold. Corin tried to stammer an explanation, but the gentleman thief—the mayor of Gesoelig—shrugged out of Corin's grip and turned away. He called back over his shoulder, "I am sorry, Corin, but this is what I must do."

Corin nodded, watching him go. Of course. His hands were bound by history. Corin took a deep breath and released it as a string of curses.

Oberon was right. This was a memory, a temporary shard. Corin had proved it with his step across the city. Nothing done here *really* mattered. He would have been much better served to grab a warm meal and a cool beer and wait to be sent home. He might have shared a pleasant hour with his hero instead of leaving him on such unhappy terms.

Leaving Oberon had not been any better. The king seemed critically weak. From ten paces distant he'd asked Corin to come closer to the throne, to be sent home. What chance that he could accomplish that from across the city? Corin had been a fool to leave.

What chance had he alone to cut down Ephitel, even if he had the sword? He could have chosen to go home. He *should* have chosen that, with the fate of all reality trapped inside his head.

He shuddered at the thought. Reality deserved a better keeper. It hardly mattered if he came back from the dream. He couldn't live a century. Truth be told, he'd be lucky to live a decade, and then the world was over.

The only difference it could make was for Iryana. Ah, he'd used her poorly in every way. For her, he should have stayed with Oberon. For her, he should have taken the sword and run. For her, he should have been more cautious of Ethan Blake. At every step he'd failed her, and now he'd sacrificed his only chance of making it right in this mad-hearted attempt at impossible revenge. And an ephemeral revenge at that! He'd sacrificed the world for the idle daydream of a hollow victory.

Even as he cursed himself, he felt that hungry fire in his heart. Ephitel was not an idle threat. He was a monster that needed slaying. His crimes rang out in Corin's heart, not least the fires raging now to the east and west of Moneylender's Lane. Corin *hated* Ephitel. But revenge would gain him nothing. He clenched his empty hand into a fist and repeated those words in his head. *Revenge would gain him nothing. Revenge, however sweet, would gain him nothing.*

So he would not fight Ephitel. It was the choice he should have made all along. As much as he longed to kill the beast, he closed his eyes and strove to put the bastard from his mind. He fixed his thoughts on Oberon's grand throne room. He would leave this dream to its sad fate and take its tragic memory to a world where Ephitel was god. He focused on the king and turned away, shifting himself within the dream. And when he looked again, he'd left Moneylender's Lane behind.

But not far enough behind.

He stood upon the battlefield, just at the edge, beneath the great arch of the closed gates. And Ephitel was there. Alone. His regiment still stood arrayed a quarter mile distant, but Ephitel stood ten paces out with a sword in one hand and a pistol in the other.

Anger flaring in his eyes, the wicked prince leveled his gun at Corin and said, "I believe you have my sword."

Corin met his eyes and growled. He had tried to use the dream to return to Oberon, but as Oberon had warned, every dream could become nightmare. Dreams were unpredictable creatures. Corin had tried to do the right thing, the noble thing, the *practical* thing, but the dream had not cooperated. So here and now, he decided, staring into Ephitel's dark eyes, it was time to kill a rabid god.

If the world hung in the balance...well, it could hang.

He swung the legendary sword, rolling it in a long arc, and grinned up at the prince. "Come and get it."

Ephitel fired his pistol, but Corin was already diving aside. He hit the ground and rolled and came up four paces closer to the prince. There was no fancy revolver this time, so Ephitel threw his gun aside and raised his sword.

Corin stalked toward him.

"This is a clever trick," Ephitel called. "How did you bring me here against my will?"

"The sheer power of my hatred bent reality."

"You bear such hate for me? But I don't even know you."

Corin didn't answer. He closed and lunged a feint, then slashed down hard toward the prince's neck. Ephitel tried to riposte the feint and had to stumble back from the true strike.

Corin pressed after him, a slash, a stab, a lunge, and then he nicked the prince's wrist even as Ephitel brought his guard around. Ephitel cried out, in surprise as much as pain, and Corin flashed a shark's cold grin.

"You are Ephitel of the High Moor, but I will make you bleed."

The prince shrank away, but Corin stomped after him. "You were a lord of war and prince of all Hurope," he screamed while raining blows upon the prince's frantic defenses. "But I will make you a memory, a stain on history. You will mar my world no more!"

As Corin screamed this last, the prince attempted a stand. Ephitel braced himself and raised his sword two-handed in an overhand block. Corin might have undercut him—he saw the opportunity—but burning as he was with rage, he brought the ancient longsword smashing down on Ephitel's light rapier. *Godslayer* smashed the prince's sword to pieces and carved a long, deep gash down his lovely face, from eye socket to jaw.

Ephitel threw away his ruined weapon and turned to run. His regiment was waiting some way off, in evident disorder at the sudden disappearance of their commander. The prince sprinted for them now, but Corin dragged Ogden's pistol from beneath his cloak, took aim, and fired his final shot through the prince's back.

Ephitel went sprawling. Corin stalked up after him. The hatred in his heart was now a bonfire, and it warmed him to the bone. Corin jabbed *Godslayer* through the prince's right shoulder, and the legendary blade parted flesh and bone like water. Corin crippled the other shoulder, too, but he saved the killing stroke. He locked one hand around the prince's ankle and dragged him backward through the dirt toward the city gate. The fires were raging now, the townsfolk caught in panic. Corin knotted a fist in the back of Ephitel's shirt and heaved him to his feet.

He hurled the prince against the city gates and pressed his face into the bars. Skin sizzled on the fire-scorched steel. Corin held him in place and shouted, "Look what you have wrought! This is your villainy."

Then Corin heaved him back, flinging Ephitel to the ground beneath the gates. The pirate stepped over the fallen prince and flourished the legendary blade. "And I am your punishment. For Kellen. For Maurelle and Avery. For Oberon." He raised the blade to strike. "For Iryana."

And then the sun went out.

A midnight darkness swallowed Corin in a gulp. With an animal scream, he brought the sword slamming down, and he drove six inches of sharpened steel into the earth, but Ephitel was gone.

He gasped against the shock of darkness, blinking frantically, but he had clearly not gone blind. There was still light enough to see, red and flickering and hot. But the sky above was dark.

No. Not sky, but solid stone. And beneath Corin, by the fire's light, the floor was empty. Oberon had moved the city and Corin with it, but he'd somehow left the wretched prince behind.

Corin howled his rage into the ringing cavern, but it was lost with the roaring of the flames. The fire blazed quite close at hand, and Corin swam within its suffocating heat. The city's gates had been left behind as well. They were no more than sketches on the outer cliffs now. Corin didn't even try to leave the cavern. He threw his cloak over his head and ducked down low, then sprinted past the flames down Moneylender's Lane. He needed to find the fire brigade, or someone organizing the evacuation. Avery or Maurelle would be best, but anyone at all could point him in their direction.

But as his streaming eyes sought desperately down each side street he passed, he saw no sign of rescuers. *They must have worked fast*, he thought, because he saw no one else at all. He hadn't seen these streets so empty since he'd stepped through time into a memory.

At worst, he could head for the river. Not an easy jog, but with the streets cleared, he might beat suffocation to the nearest banks. Better to reach the palace, Oberon's great throne room—

Even as he thought it, he remembered his new trick. He closed his eyes and focused on the throne, then dove forward, looking, hoping he had moved.

And he knew instantly he had, for the scorching heat was gone. His searching eyes showed him, dimly in the darkness, that he had found the throne. He knelt before it, a throne too tall for any man, carved into the foundation of a giant living tree.

But the throne was empty, and the tree lived no more. It yet towered over him, but it was hard and gray and dry with time. Its bare branches reached toward the cavern's ceiling and out toward the distant fire like skeletal fingers, and even now their farthest tips began to burn. Half a mile off or more, but once it caught, the whole tree would go like tinder.

Corin turned back to the empty throne. "You managed it at last. You robbed me of my killing stroke, and gave me the only favor I ever asked of you." He heaved a weary sigh. "You sent me home. Or…back to my own dream, anyway."

As the fire's light began to brighten the artificial cavern— Ethan Blake's fire now, not Ephitel's—Corin frowned. "A dream."

Panic bubbled behind his breastbone. Was it all a dream, borne of pain and fear? Had he ever left this cavern? This time?

He held the answer in his right hand. The sword *Godslayer* glowed with reflected firelight, cold despite the cavern's heat.

Corin gripped it tight, clinging to it for his sanity, and then his eyes touched something on the empty throne. It was a single book on vellum, its ink a cracking crimson. Even with the flames racing toward him, Corin had to stare.

He reached out with a trembling hand and flipped back the cover. It opened to an inner page marked with a softened strip of bark, where a new chapter started with his name, "Corin Hugh," written in an ancient elven script. He had seen the like at Rikkeborh, in long-forgotten texts, but he had not known its meaning. Now he read it easily in the fire's rising light.

> *Now you have heard the story of my king, who lived and died within this darkness. But one final task he asked of me, and this one greater than all the rest. He bade me tell a story of a life that's yet to be lived—a dream he had, a fantasy about a man-ling outside time. This is not my memory, but it is Oberon's, and I set it down as he related it to me.*
>
> *Corin was a peasant, born in Aepoli beneath the reign of Cosimo Vestossi, and in his time the name of Oberon was not known. In his time, Ephitel was thought a god among the man-ling nations. Corin Hugh was not a righteous man, but for the sake of Oberon, he was good...*

Corin shook his head in disbelief. He flipped forward through the brittle pages, spotting references to the Nimble Fingers, his brief apprenticeship to the wizard Jonderel, his first encounter with Old Grim the pirate, and then his years upon the seas. How much life he had lived in two short decades!

And there was more. He turned page after page, and still it spoke of him. Of heroic acts and legendary wars. Of battles with the gods and a new kingdom for men, but these were things he hadn't done. Yet.

He swallowed hard and wiped the sweat from his brow. Was this his future? Was this his whole life, borrowed from the dreams of a dying god? He wiped his brow again and realized the sweat was from more than just his fear. The air was cooking now, all around him, the fire crawling along the branches overhead. Soot and embers rained around him, until he feared the book might catch a spark and burn.

He nearly snapped it shut, but one last curiosity stayed his hand. He flipped forward to the end, to the last pages, and read what was written there. In a shaky hand and blotted ink, he read of Oberon's end.

> *This was the last memory shared with me by my dying king. Oberon is no more. His body is destroyed, his kingdom stolen, his people driven into hiding. Oberon was maker of this land and good king to his people, but all that now remains to this world are his dreams of a world that could have been, his enemies victorious, and an unending hunger for vengeance.*
>
> *I share these things. If ever manling reads this book, if anyone can comprehend, my final wish is my king's final wish: destroy the traitor Ephitel.*

Corin raised his head. He touched the winter-cold steel of the stolen sword while fire rained around him, and nodded once within the vast silence of the eerie tomb. "I swear upon the blood of gods," he said. "I will grant you vengeance."

Then he closed his eyes and stepped out into the world.

THE END

About the Author

 Aaron Pogue is a husband and a father of two who lives in Oklahoma City, Oklahoma. He started writing at the age of ten, and has written novels, short stories, scripts, and videogame storylines. His first novels were high fantasy set in the rich world of the FirstKing, including the bestselling fantasy novel *Taming Fire*, but he has explored mainstream thrillers, urban fantasy, and several kinds of science fiction, including a long-running sci-fi cop drama series focused on the Ghost Targets task force.

Aaron has been a Technical Writer with the Federal Aviation Administration and a writing professor at the university level. He holds a Master of Professional Writing degree from the University of Oklahoma. He also serves as the user experience consultant for Draft2Digital.com, a digital publishing service.

Aaron maintains a personal website for his friends and fans at AaronPogue.com, and he runs a writing advice blog at UnstressedSyllables.com.